Erased

OTHER BOOKS BY
MATTHEW DUNN

Day One

The Dummy Sign

The Good Silver

Bingo Bango Bongo

Visit Matthew at:
www.matthewdunn.net

Erased

By

Matthew Dunn

ONONDAGA HILL PUBLISHING

This book is a work of fiction. The characters, incidents, and dialogue are drawn from the author's imagination and are not to be construed as real. Any resemblance to actual events or persons, living or dead, is purely coincidental.

Copyright © 2007 by Matthew Dunn

All rights reserved. No part of this book may be used or reproduced by any means, graphic, electronic or mechanical, including photocopying, recording, taping or by any information storage retrieval system without the written permission of the publisher except in the case of brief quotations embodied in critical articles and reviews.

Published by Onondaga Hill Publishing

ISBN-13: 978-0-9794908-4-2
ISBN-10: 0-9794908-4-7

Printed in the United States of America

Acknowledgements

This, my fifth novel, could not have happened without the tireless faith of my wife, Judy, the support of my family and friends, along with the hard work and candid advice of my friend, Matt Hotham.

1

Sparkling Stars

Sunny had a funny feeling about this gig. Having just stepped away from a taxi, she stood frozen at the curb gazing up at the towering New Yorker Hotel. Actually, it was short by Manhattan standards—only about fifty stories high—but every building in New York City looked tall to the twenty year-old from Maine, even after six months.

A pyramid, Sunny thought. *It's shaped like an Egyptian pyramid.* She took a few steps back to get a better perspective, looking like an awestruck tourist. *A little skinnier, but a really cool pyramid.* She'd never seen a pyramid in person, only pictures in the book she kept next to her bed depicting the Seven Wonders of the World.

The sidewalk before her was jammed with anxious people, a bustling parade seemingly bent on separating her from the hotel entrance, as if to remind her to stay on her side of the tracks. But that was in *her* mind, not theirs. Tonight, she looked every bit a big city woman. A little young—she couldn't hide that—but sexy and sophisticated none the less. Tonight, men would rush to open doors for her, crawl over each other to buy her drinks, thump on their chests and empty their pockets to capture her eye. *A movie starlet,* passersby were guessing, or perhaps the heiress to an overseas fortune. Sunny understood the mirage, but inside was the tomboy who grew up in a little town along the Appalachian Trail.

What am I doing here? She asked herself for the second time since pulling up in the cab.

"It's an easy spin, one hour, tops," Marko had assured her some weeks ago when he first approached her with the opportunity. She had believed him then, but her flip-flopping stomach wasn't so sure now.

Sunny's intuition was rarely wrong. Her premonitions had saved her skin at least a dozen times but yet here she was shaking her head at the realization that she was about to put herself in yet another ticklish situation. And for what, a short stack of one hundred dollar bills? It didn't seem like so much money now that she was standing in front of the hotel with the clock ticking down. But the truth was, a grand *was* a lot of money, ten times what she could make these days dancing in the laps of drunken stock brokers and horny, traveling salesmen. Business had been slow at the club for months and Sunny's ten year plan to save enough getaway cash to buy a horse farm upstate was falling behind schedule. She had promised herself she would retire before she was thirty and that was only going to happen if she softened her rules of engagement. *I'll do the job, Marko,* she resolved, *but you better appreciate it more than this damn watch.*

Holding out her wrist, she wondered how much she could get for the newly acquired adornment, a slim, gold Gucci with Roman numerals that half the girls at the club couldn't read. *Marko probably stole it from Macy's,* she reasoned. *I could buy a good riding mare with a saddle thrown in if I returned it for a refund.* Tilting the band toward the glimmering hotel lights, Sunny checked the time. It was 9:45 p.m. and after searching up and down the block, Marko was no where in sight.

"Whatever happened to punctuality?" Sunny mumbled to herself.

Tidying up the full-length, black leather trench coat she'd borrowed from one of the girls to keep the night's intentions hidden from what Marko had called the "tight-assed hotel management," she took a deep breath and walked toward the golden double doors.

"You'd look a lot classier walking in on my arm, babe," Marko said as he reached for the door. A tall, slender man in his late twenties with tightly cropped hair and a perpetual five-o'clock shadow, Marko looked older in the crisply-tailored Armani suit he only wore on special occasions. He was also short of breath, having just darted across Eighth Avenue where he narrowly escaped an angry deluge of horn-blaring cabs and limousines. Smiling, he apologized for being late and then escorted his willing companion inside.

Marko was what *he* called an "independent businessman" and the sponsor of tonight's "outing," as he referred to the freelance work he routinely proposed to the girls at the Sin City Lounge, one of the many topless clubs located in and around Manhattan. As far as anyone knew, he had no last name and no known address, but he never cheated a girl a dime and, more importantly, never hit on them. With Marko, it was strictly business and regardless of the nature of the deals he arranged, he had a reputation for always playing it straight up. It was the one reason Sunny committed to the gig in the first place—her first with Marko.

"Not a bad joint to pop your cherry, hey Sunny?" Marko said, nodding his head in admiration of the three-storied, grey-marbled lobby.

"I'm not having sex with anyone," Sunny replied. "I was very clear about that." She then gazed up at the biggest crystal chandelier she had ever seen. *This is a ritzy place*, she thought. *Maybe it's just nerves that are kicking my anxiety into overdrive.*

"A figure of speech, babe," Marko said. "This *is* your first outing."

"With you," Sunny replied with a wry grin. It *was* her first outing, but she didn't want him to know that. She was younger than most of the other girls at the club—they called her *Baby-*

cakes—and she hated that they treated her like some naïve little sister. "I've been around the block a few times," she would argue to disbelieving eyes. She never elaborated, and they never asked. Like Marko, the dancers at the club lived and breathed anonymity, competing shamelessly for the almighty dollar with every wink and wiggle they had. And like wolves, only the strong were allowed to run with the pack where loyalty vanished as soon as the prey bellied up to the stage. Sunny knew in her heart she could never be like them —a wolf—but tonight she wanted Marko to believe he had one on his arm.

Feigning disappointment, Marko said, "And here I am all excited, thinking that you were a virgin."

"In your dreams," Sunny said.

"Yeah, with you and Diamond and Barbie."

"I didn't know you were into the group thing."

"Hey, the more the merrier," Marko chuckled, attempting to keep the mood light. He could tell that Sunny was nervous and he knew from experience she might trip the deal he'd worked very hard to set up if she didn't loosen up. Tonight, he was looking at a five figure payoff—the biggest of his back-alley career—and he wasn't about to kiss it goodbye because *Baby-cake's* stilettoed feet were getting cold.

"So," Sunny said. "What room are we in?"

"You in a hurry?"

Sunny didn't answer. The truth was, she *was* anxious to get it over with. Giving a customer a private dance in the safety of the backroom at the club with a bouncer and ten other dancers a single scream away was one thing, but to do it in some guy's hotel room was something different altogether—something a little more…ticklish. And there was that funny feeling again, scratching at the back of her mind like the stray cat she'd found at her apartment doorstep the week before. It was the cutest thing she had seen in the months since moving to New York City, a matted clump of orange and white fur. When Sunny opened the door, it just sat there shaking, begging for a meal and a home with its big brown, lonesome eyes. Without another thought, Sunny picked it up and took it in. Now, hearing the sudden ting of the elevator, a rush of dread washed over her. *Don't go up there,* her inner voice warned. *Go home and curl up with Garfield.*

Thinking a short detour might salve her growing apprehension, Marko asked if she would like to have a drink at the bar first. "But only one," he added abruptly. "You need to bring your A-game tonight."

Sunny didn't know it, but Marko was counting on far more from the young beauty than her best bump and grind. He didn't know exactly what that was; only that it was making *him* twitch for a shot of Jack Daniels.

Is it my imagination or is Marko a little tense? Sunny thought. It wasn't like him, but then she hadn't been on an outing with him before. She had only seen him at the club where he was Mr. Calm, Cool & Collected, the self-proclaimed title he did a helluva job living up to. *Am I being paranoid?* Knowing she needed to get a grip if she was going to pull this off, she calculated what her bank account would total tomorrow after she presented the teller with the one thousand dollar deposit slip. *Don't listen to the voice, girl. Get back on schedule.*

"I don't drink, Marko," Sunny said. "I thought you knew that."

"Well, I thought, maybe under the circumstances," he replied. He knew more than he was telling but being the crafty chameleon that he was, he quickly changed colors. "Did I tell you how gorgeous you look tonight? Black leather really suits you, Sunny. I mean, *wow!*"

"Thanks, Marko. Diamond let me wear it."

"Are you wrapped in that red-laced number I suggested?"

With a giggle, Sunny flipped open her coat lapel, flashing the single crimson spaghetti strap snaking over her bronzed shoulder. Enjoying the moment, she continued her tease right down to her

Sapphire pierced belly button. As heads turned and whispers stirred, a wave of goose bumps washed across her soft skin, excited by the in-rushing cool lobby air and suddenly spellbound eyes.

Marko took a step back and then, looking more like a farmer inspecting his tomatoes than a voyeuristic playboy, studied her glitter-peppered cleavage levied tightly by a glimmering satin bra. He nodded in approval.

"Perfect," he said as he pulled the coat back up to her chin. "Johnny's gonna go ga-ga over you."

Any uncertainty Marko may have had vanished. Sunny was *exactly* what Johnny wanted. She was young and had that elusive girl-next-door appeal—strikingly attractive but with a wholesome, seemingly untouched grace. But more importantly, she had the key ingredient that had cemented the deal. Sunny Dai had fire in her eyes.

"I don't want a bimbo who'll drop to her knees at the snap of my fingers," the man had told Marko several months ago in the alleyway behind a Brooklyn bar. "I want a fighter who'll spit in my face when I grab her and force her hand down my pants. Give me that and I'll happily hand you ten grand."

That night Marko sat in the bar sipping a beer wondering why someone would pay that kind of money for a lap dance and a blow job (if they were lucky) when they could get it for a hundred bucks at any club in town. He knew there had to be more to the deal than the guy was saying, but Marko had ten thousand reasons not to ask. Eager to make the score as soon as he could, he visited every strip joint in town that night looking for a match, finding his girl at the very last stop of the night at the Sin City Lounge.

"Put *any* appendage in the wrong place with her, honey, and I guarantee you'll lose it," Diamond laughed after Marko had made a wise crack about the "high school virgin" stepping onto the stage. Five minutes and one black-eyed patron later, Marko knew

Sunny was the one who could triple the wad of cash hidden in his mattress. All he had to do was earn her trust, Marko's only natural talent.

"Is that the guy's name?" Sunny asked. "Johnny?"

"It might be, I don't know. I don't ask. They don't tell. So, they're all Johnny as far as I'm concerned."

"That keeps it simple."

"That's the name of the game, babe. KISS—keep it simple, stupid. You ready to start the show?"

It's now or never, Sunny thought. "Lead the way," she said, thinking only of horses and rides into the sunset. She then hooked Marko's arm once again and they sauntered off toward the elevators.

"Here," Marko said as he handed Sunny an old, banged up cell phone while the evaluator hummed its way to the 21st floor. "Clip it where you can get at it in case you run into trouble. Press 1 and it'll speed dial me down in the lobby."

Sunny took the phone and snickered. "It's kind of big, don't you think."

"It's the only extra one I had," Marko replied. He then pulled open her leather coat and gave her the once-over. "Stick in your garter," he said.

She scrunched her nose and shook her head.

"You're right, that might kill the mood." He took the phone back and then tried to stuff it into her bra.

"Hey," she growled, slapping his hand away. "I'm jammed into this thing as it is."

"All right, all right," he said backing off. Frustrated, he then stuck it her coat pocket.

"What makes you think I might run in to trouble," Sunny asked. Her intuition was nagging again and if Marko had called the whole thing off right then and there she wouldn't have argued.

But Marko had no intention of missing this payday. "This one's a walk in the park," he said, though his gut was churning a different tune. "Walk in, give him that gorgeous smile of yours and cowgirl him until he wet his pants."

"You sure that's all he's looking for?"

"That's the deal, signed and sealed."

"And it's just the one guy, right?"

"I've seen you in action, Sunny. You could handle ten guys."

The elevator jerked to a halt as Sunny punched the emergency stop button. She jutted her index finger into Marko's face. "One, Marko. One and only one," she said.

Marko retreated, instinctively covering his crotch with one hand and his wallet with the other. "It's cool, babe, its cool. There's only one guy waiting for us. I'll walk in with you to be sure if it'll make you feel better."

"Yes, you will," Sunny said. Feeling empowered, she lowered her menacing finger and pressed button twenty-one to resume their ascent.

As he had promised, Marko escorted Sunny into the predetermined rendezvous, a small, single bedroom tucked away in the corner of the west wing of the hotel. It certainly wasn't the nicest room in the place—Marko had been to The New Yorker many times before—but he didn't give it much thought as he made the introductions and scanned the room for a reason to cancel. Other than the fact that Johnny wasn't the Johnny he'd talked to in the alleyway, everything looked normal. The guy was an average, harmless looking dude in a business suit and there were no gang-bangers hiding under the bed or in the bathroom. Satisfied, he helped Sunny off with her coat—slowly unveiling her—and set it on the chair next to the bed.

Johnny watched but exhibited no emotion. It was the one tiny clue that could have saved Marko's life.

"You kids have fun now," Marko said heading toward the door. He gave Sunny a wink and left, his voice trailing off as he walked down the hallway. "I'll be back in an hour with your pumpkin carriage."

The moment the door clicked shut Sunny felt a chill scurry up her back. The room felt cold—icy cold—and not just because she was nearly naked. She spotted the heating and cooling unit tucked into the bottom half of one of the windows and walked over to it. The glow of light beyond caught her eye. Glancing outside, she saw that the room was situated in a tiny u-shaped alcove, a line of illuminated windows stacked along the façade like pantry shelf cans. *Cape Cod Bay*, Sunny thought. She'd been there only once a long time ago but still remembered sitting on the beach at night, marveling at the "sparkling stars" on the distant shoreline. They seemed close enough to touch, and tonight they were, the opposing wall of rooms being only about twenty feet away. Cape Cod was one of her good memories and as she considered pulling down the shades she decided to leave them open and fill her head with "sparkling stars" for the next hour.

Johnny abruptly cleared his throat. It was time for Sunny Dai to take the stage.

"You don't mind if I…warm things up a bit, do you stud?" she asked as she bent over to examine the controls.

The man Marko had introduced as Johnny just looked at her blankly and said nothing.

The strong silent type, Sunny thought as she fiddled with the temperature knob. Turning it to high, she then peered back at him and wiggled her round, smooth, g-stringed ass. "You hear that bell ringing, baby? That means it's time to find your seat. Class is about start."

Robotically, the man sat down on the end of the bed. He then glanced out the window, locking his stoic eyes on something unseen. Sunny didn't notice. She was dancing on a quiet beach somewhere, squishing the frothy sand between her toes, happy she had found a momentary refuge.

Down in the hotel bar, Marko ordered a second shot of whiskey. As the bartender set it in front of him, he asked for the time. "Two minutes later than the last time you asked," he answered.

After returning to the lobby, Marko had gotten a call from Diamond, Sunny's co-worker at the Sin City Lounge. There was a guy at the club running his mouth about some Spielberg wannabe he knew who had just gone online with a freaky-sex website specializing in movies staring unsuspecting dancers. He was encouraging other customers to check it out. Diamond said he called it "Manhattan Uncut," a Candid Camera kind of thing with some really "wild shit."

"What kind of wild shit?" Marko asked. He was thinking of Sunny and the ten thousand reasons he'd been given to keep his mouth shut.

Diamond said she didn't know.

Wrestling with thoughts of aborting the outing, Marko decided not just yet, reasoning there were hundreds—maybe thousands—of lap dances going on in New York City that night. What were the chances of Sunny's date being the perv? He didn't look like a perv. Marko needed more details.

"Well, go stick your tits in his face and find out!" he snarled into the phone.

An old woman walking past threw him a disgusted scowl.

"Who am I, James Bond?" Diamond replied. The two exchanged obscenities before she finally agreed and abruptly hung up. It was then that Marko spotted the hotel lounge, went inside and ordered his first drink. The next hour was going to be a very long one, even longer without a full glass for company.

"You got a girl?" Sunny asked. She was sitting in Johnny's lap, facing him, rolling to the ocean waves in her imagination as he sat stiff-backed like an old wooden chair. Her arms were draped over his shoulders, her heavily scented breasts inches from his nose.

She was ten minutes into her routine and he hadn't touched her yet. Not anywhere. In fact, his hands hadn't left the mattress where they sat flaccidly like two spent condoms. *Timid*, Sunny thought as she quickened her pace. *Or a homo trying to convert.*

During Sunny's first week at Sin City, Diamond had explained that sometimes the "limp" customers were actually gay men desperate to go straight. "They come to the club searching for the North Pole," Diamond told her with a snicker, "inspiration of sorts, if you know what I mean."

If he was gay, Sunny didn't care. If he wasn't, that didn't matter either. They weren't going to have sex, not if she had anything to say about it. And if he wanted to play possum for the next hour that was fine with Sunny, she could slow dance on a mannequin all night. At a few minutes past ten that evening, she began to think that Marko had been right, that this gig *was* going to be a walk in the park and all her worries had just been first time jitters. Her horse farm wasn't going to be just a dream after all. She was getting back on schedule. As Sunny closed her eyes and swayed in the silence, she didn't see the red, blinking light in the darkened window directly across the alcove from theirs. Or the shadowy figure that stood beside it, peering back at her, smiling a devilish smile. She was on the beach, rolling with the waves, thinking she would call her first horse Pilgrim after the monument she'd seen in Cape Cod. *Pilgrim, that's a good name...*

Suddenly, Sunny was underwater. She couldn't breath and for a split second, her daydream was pulling her out to sea, hooked by the ocean's undertow. *I'm drowning!* Her mind screamed. Panic raced through her veins. Opening her eyes she instantly remembered where she was—the hotel room, the lap dance, the man Marko kept calling Johnny. She wasn't drowning. She was being choked. Johnny was on top of her and his no-longer-flaccid hands were wrapped around her neck, squeezing with inhuman strength. Her arms flailed, punching helplessly into the air. But his arms were too long and she couldn't reach any vulnerable flesh. Her eyes began to water and just that quickly his electrified face began to fade into a darkening blur. She was blacking out. Then, with her consciousness hanging by a thread, she felt a terrifying poke between her legs. Sunny knew all to well what it was.

This wasn't the first time Sunny had been pinned down on a bed. Her stepfather had tried and his brother too one night when her mother had gone to the casino with several of her drinking partners. She was all of fifteen at the time but still chased the two from her room, hunched over and wailing. She had her mother's temper and some of her natural father's brute strength. And both were beginning to swell up insider her now. *Damn, if this son-of-a-bitch is going to rape me!*

As Sunny gathered up her resolve for one determined assault, the vision of the first pony she'd ever ridden flash across her mind. It was a feisty, tan and white pinto named Arson (named for the fire in his eyes) which had bucked her over the fence five straight times before realizing Sunny wasn't going to quit and gave up, the horse that is. Arson had taught her one thing that day; a well-placed kick hurts like hell.

Knowing she would only get one good shot at it, Sunny jerked her hips upward with everything she had, catching Johnny square in the balls with her pelvic bone. Stunned, he released the grip from her throat, wobbled for a moment and then looked down at her in agony before falling off her and onto the floor. Cupping his crotch with both hands, he curled into the fetus position and began kicking at nothing.

Sunny gasped for air. The room was spinning and she tried to sit up but that only made it worse. Fighting back her fear, she laid there for a minute, taking deep breaths until finally the ceiling came back into focus. *You're all right*, she whispered. *You're all right. Take a minute and then get the hell out of here!*

Above the fallen man's pathetic groans Sunny thought she heard the sound of a cell phone ringing. It was Beethoven's Fifth Symphony…da da da *dah*…da da da *dah*. Turning her ear toward the sound, it was coming from her coat pocket. *Marko!*

Staggering to her feet, she stepped over Johnny and picked up the coat. She glanced at the door, thinking she should take it and leave, but it was whirling like everything else around her. *You'll never make it. Get Marko up here!* She frantically searched the pockets as Beethoven played, finding it in time to read the screen; "Missed Call—Caller Unknown!" She groaned in frustration.

Focusing her still watery eyes on the tiny display, Sunny scrolled to the address book and scanned through the names. Angel, Aurora, Bambi, Blossom...nothing but exotic dancers. Then she remembered Marko telling her to speed dial him. But which button did he say? Frantic, she started pressing them all, which only froze the old phone's obsolete computer chip.

"Shit!" Sunny exclaimed. She shoved the phone back into the coat pocket and took a deep breath. *Calm down, girl. Calm down.*

"That wasn't very nice," a voice said. "Kicking me in the balls like that."

It was Johnny. It had to be, uttering his first words of the night. Sunny turned and looked down at the floor. It was empty. Then, out of the corner of her eye, she spotted him standing between her and her way out. His shirt was off, his pants were around his ankles and his erection looked no worse for the damage she had inflicted. Damn if he wasn't a muscular son-of-a-bitch. The suit hadn't done him justice.

"When somebody tries to rape and kill me, I fight back," Sunny said defiantly. "I'm funny that way."

"I wasn't going to kill you," the man said flatly.

"Ok, for arguments sake we'll just call it rape then," Sunny replied. She was buying time while her hands rummaged through every pocket in Diamond's coat, desperately hunting for the bottle of mace Diamond swore she never left home without. But all she was finding were stray mints and condoms, lots and lots of condoms.

The funny thing was Johnny appeared indifferent to her frenetic search. In fact, it was almost as if he wasn't aware of her actions at all. As Sunny examine his detached gaze, she realized he was looking right through her and out the window. *He's hypnotized by the "sparkling stars?"* She turned and scanned the row of windows lining the alcove. All were lit but oddly empty. All except one. It sat directly across from theirs and it was dark, a black hole in a galaxy of stars. A shadow moved; a tiny red glow flickered. *A cigarette?* Sunny thought. *Someone's watching us.*

Before she could reason it out any further, Johnny was yanking the coat from her hands. "We need to finish this," he said. "He wants a pop shot."

"A pop shot?" Sunny asked, involuntarily. Her mind felt paralyzed, her limbs like icicles. She stared back at the murky shape draped in the darkness. *He?*

From behind, Johnny grabbed her arms and forced her down onto the table, bending her like pretzel while he forced her legs apart with his knees. Then, using his weight to hold her down, he slid one hand around her throat while the other tore at her thick blond hair, pulling her head back and her terrified face toward the invisible peeping tom. She rocked and squirmed, praying the table would tip over and give her a chance to break free. But it didn't budge. It was bolted to the floor.

"Hold still," Johnny demanded. He was panting now and frustrated that he still hadn't penetrated his prey. "I don't want to have to hurt you."

No, you just want to kill me! Sunny's frantic mind screamed. *And rape me!*

At least now she could breath—his one hand wasn't nearly as effective as two—and that was helping her think clearer. But bent over the table as she was, she couldn't get any leverage to buck him off again. And even though her hands were free she couldn't reach his testicles or twist her shoulders enough to go at his face. Knowing she had no other option, Sunny closed her eyes and lay still, relaxing her hips in hopes that it might save her life. But before she did, she took one last look at the darkened window across the alcove. A face was visible now, illuminated by the New York City neon as it pressed closer to the glass to watch her suffer. And it seemed to brighten when it saw that *she* could see. It was an ugly face, an evil face, a face Sunny knew she would never forget.

The shivering came swiftly as she felt the bulbous head of his penis forcing its way into the depths of her soul, stealing the virginity she had never told the girls at the club she still possessed; fought against her stepfather to keep; hid from the mother who wouldn't understand. In the next few horrifying seconds it would be gone...forever gone. As Sunny lay helpless, praying to God for intervention, she wanted to cry but couldn't. Even though her mind had all but surrendered, her body had not. Transforming itself into a desert wind, it was revolting against its attacker who now, in a momentary retreat, had removed his hand from her throat and was spitting into the palm for lubrication.

"Damn, you're a dry bitch," he grumbled, "and tight, too." He was working saliva onto his sluggish erection now, eagerly stroking it back to life. The struggle had taken a toll on Johnny as well, and as his focus *and* weight shifted off Sunny, he unwittingly presented her with an unintentional offer she couldn't refuse.

With a quick and sudden spin of her upper torso, Sunny turned on the man, catching him in the jaw with her elbow. There was a loud crack and a flash of fire. It was blood, Johnny's blood, shooting from his mouth like a primal ejaculation. Not exactly the pop shot he'd wanted but he was in no position to complain as he fell backward from the blow, tripped over a chair, careened off the edge of the bed before smacking his head down hard against the thinly carpeted floor.

Lifting herself off the table, Sunny could tell he wasn't out, but he didn't appear in any hurry to get up either. *Get out! Get out now!*

Sunny took two urgent steps toward the door and fell to her knees. The battle and sudden rise to her feet had made her dizzy again and short of breath. And she was cold, so very cold. *Crawl if you have to, damn it!* Her inner voice screamed. *But get out of here!*

Minutes passed. Minutes that, to Sunny's frazzled mind, seemed like only seconds.

I just need a few seconds, that's all, Sunny convinced herself. But then, Johnny was sitting up, wiping the blood from his chin and mumbling obscenities that told Sunny ready or not, here he comes. Using the bed as a crutch, she struggled to her feet, took one step and stopped dead. The room was spinning wildly and she knew if she took one more step she'd land face first on the floor. Recognizing that she would never make it to the door, she clenched her fists, preparing to fight for her life.

"Sunny!" Marko said. "Are you all right?" He was standing in the doorway like a hazy vision of Christ in an Armani suit. *Mr. Cool, Calm and Collected to the rescue.* But before Sunny could utter a word, a shot rang out and then a second and she watched in horror as her savior fell to the ground. The last remaining drop of adrenaline raced into Sunny's veins and without thinking she pulled the sheet from the bed, knelt over Marko and desperately tried to dam the blood pouring from his chest. Pressing down with all her strength, she then turned toward Johnny, expecting to see his enraged face coming toward her. But he wasn't there. *Could he have run past me?*

She looked out the door held open by Marko's sputtering body and searched the hallway. It was empty. *Where did he go?*

Marko's blood was filling the sheet in a fury, puddling in the folds and running down onto the carpet like a waterfall. Sunny didn't have time to think about Johnny, she needed to stop Marko's bleeding. Hurriedly, she gathered in the clean corners of the sheet and pressed harder, using both hands and all of her one hundred and ten pounds, but within seconds her fingers began to glisten red. She knew she needed help or she would lose him. She peered down the hallway again. Still empty. *Didn't anyone hear the shots?*

Then, a groan drifted into the air from the dark side of the bed. Cautiously, she turned just in time to watch the gun fall from Johnny's lifeless hand. She couldn't see the rest of him sprawled out on the floor, or the life spewing from his heart.

"Did I get him?" Marko said in a low, raspy voice.

"Yeah, Marko," Sunny replied. "You got him." It was then that Sunny noticed the gun in Marko's hand.

"Good," Marko said. He winced in pain. "Some Lone Ranger I turned out to be."

Sunny tried to smile, but she couldn't. Marko was dying and there wasn't a thing she could do about it. She slid up against the door and gingerly put his head in her lap.

"How did you know?" she asked quietly.

"Diamond called," he said. "She tripped over something at the club. Thought it might involve your outing tonight. That girl is always looking out for you."

My big sister, Diamond, Sunny thought. And the tears came, slow and deep.

Marko was squeezing her hand now and if she had been able to feel anything it would have hurt terribly, but she was numb. *Why is this happening? Why is Marko lying in my arms bleeding to death?* Her thoughts jumped to the shadowy figure in the window.

"I'm sorry, Sunny," Marko whispered. "I should have sniffed it out. The price was too good to be true…"

"Shhh," Sunny said. "Just lie still and hold on." She tried to quiet him but he kept on.

"When Johnny didn't notice you as I took your coat off, I should have seen it was a ruse." He coughed and winced again. He was slipping away but he wasn't going to go until Sunny knew the truth.

"They always gasp and swallow hard. You girls are so damn hot, how could any man not?" Even as the world was fading, Marko still wanted Sunny to know how beautiful she was. "But Johnny wasn't here for you," he said, half choking on his own blood. "He was just doing a job."

Puzzled, Sunny gave him a look that begged him to stop. She didn't want to hear anymore. But Marko knew he had to keep going if he had any chance of completing the rescue. It would take his dying breath.

"A snuff scene, Sunny, that's why Johnny was here; to play the role of your lover and murderer."

Sunny couldn't believe her ears. *My murderer?* The whole thing had been a setup, a pre-scripted play with her as the lead actress and a final act that would climax with her death.

"But why?" she asked. "Why me?"

Marko shook his head. "Not you, babe. Just any pretty young thing who would fight back. And you sure did, didn't you?"

Finally, Sunny smiled a tiny smile. *Yes, I did.*

Marko was staring up at her now, his eyes as serious as she had ever seen them.

"You've got to run, Sunny," he said. "Get out of Manhattan—get out of this whole fucking city. And don't tell a soul about this. Don't go back to the club and whatever you do, don't go to the cops. Hide, Sunny. Hide somewhere where he'll never find you."

"Who?" Sunny asked, thinking only of the shadow in the window. "So who won't find me?"

"Caesar," he said. And then Marko was gone. Seconds later, so was Sunny.

2

I Believe, therefore, I am

If all the world's a stage, it would appear that my part has been written out. I am no longer a player—my entrance forgotten, my exit seemingly absolute—and the final curtain now stands poised, eager to drop with nothing more than my own sanity to prevent its release.

Let me say right now that this is not amnesia. I have memory, full and clear. The road taken; the journey made; my footprints still hollowed in the sand. Clear images that even now as I recall them are slowly being swept away by an invisible surf. *Am I really who I think I am?*

Am I really?

"Yes!" With every ounce of strength I shout, "Yes!" But for how much longer? How much longer can I hover above my own identity, worn and wondering? How much longer can my fractured thoughts and beliefs stand alone while my splintered, probing fingers reach out into the emptiness?

I must make a choice: reclamation or transformation. In the alluring eyes of the former, I see hope and vindication; in the dark gaze of the latter, isolation and potential madness.

What if I am not who I think I am?

What if...I am not?

"I believe my name is Daniel Rayne," I said to the young

woman standing before me.

"You believe?" she asked, her face twisting with tickled bewilderment. She nodded as though she understood and sat down at the table across from me, a bowl of hot bean soup erecting a wall of steam between us. She didn't know it, but I had been watching her since I'd walked into the place, fluttering like an exotic butterfly from table to table, salting each man's meal with a smile and a chat. She was too young to be in this place, too beautiful, I thought, but then I didn't think that I belonged there either. Not in a homeless shelter that reeked of rotting pride and overcooked bean soup.

"Just call me Rayny," I said. "Everyone else does." *At least, they used to...I think.*

"That'll be easy," she replied, "because that happens to be my name too. My first name, that is. Although I'll bet I spell it differently than you do. R—A—E—N—I, Raeni. You know, like *I love a rainy night.*" She sang the last part, sounding a little like Bonnie Raitt—gritty, but sexy—as she swayed back and forth in her chair.

As Raeni hummed a few more bars, I couldn't help but smile, my first in the past several days—several very long days. Her inquisitive brown eyes were like soft leather and she didn't wear a spot of make-up, not that I could tell anyway. Her hair was so short I couldn't tell if it was brown or black. The rest of her, well, I was having trouble getting past her eyes. "You got a last name, Ms. Rainy Night?" I asked.

"Not officially," she said. "Not here, anyway," she added with a wink.

Looking around at the sorry souls scattered about the dining hall like discarded beer bottles, I couldn't help wonder if she was this direct with everyone. When she announced with unflinching confidence that she was going to call me Daniel, and not Rayny like *everyone else*, I actually allowed myself to fantasize that she had picked me out of the crowd, that she was sharing secrets with me and only me.

"Daniel is such a strong, earthy name," she said. "It suits you much better than *Rayny*."

"Well, you know," I said, eager to cement our bond, "since we're on the subject, Raeni doesn't exactly suit you either. You should be a Star or a Daisy, something that compliments the way you sparkle."

Raeni blushed and giggled modestly. She was obviously uncomfortable and I could only guess that flattery didn't sober up long enough to pay her many visits here.

"No, I have a better name," I continued. "I'm going to call you Sunny. I'll let you call me Daniel, if I can call you Sunny."

And just that quickly, the warmth drained from her face as she abruptly stood up and combed a suddenly shaky hand through her hair. "You're always welcome to come back again if you ever need a hot meal," she said with a vacant gaze. And then she fluttered away, taking with her the only connection I'd made with the rest of the world in the past three days. Watching her settle at another table, I began to wonder if she had really been sitting with me at all. *Was she just a mirage?*

I *believe* my name is Daniel Rayne. And either I have gone mad or I am *my own* mirage.

3

Fenway Park Tickets

They gave me a cot to sleep on in a back room with a dozen other men of various degrees of smell and sanity, promising me a more private bed if one became available. I'd like to say it was more comfortable than the back seat of my Camaro where I'd slept the last two nights—better equipped for sleep at least—but I can't. The thin canvas "mattress" was still fermenting from its previous occupant and two out of its six legs were shorter than the rest. The damn thing pitched like a lifeboat in a storm every time I attempted to find a comfortable position. And if that wasn't enough to keep me awake, half of my bunk mates wanted the lights left on and half of us—me included—wanted them off, resulting in a debate that last several hours until the night janitor blew a fuse starting up a floor polisher. With a good excuse to take the rest of the night off, he disappeared out the back door after lamenting that they didn't trust him enough to issue him a key to the utility room. To me, it was a small, but long-overdue victory nonetheless. (For some reason, odors aren't as pungent when the source is hidden by darkness.)

"For now all we can offer is a cot in the Roosevelt Room," the man behind the desk had said. His nametag read Vincent, but he looked like a Vinny to me—short and stocky, with tufts of coarse, dark hair peeking out from his shirt collar. "But I'll let you know the moment something better opens up. Are you planning on being with us for a while?" He'd been nodding politely and scribbling down condensed versions of every question I answered, but when I said that I planned to have things straightened out within a few days and be on my way, his knowing smirk was inescapable.

"If it turns out you need to stay longer than expected, just let me know," Vinny reassured me as he plopped my bedroll onto the cot, an extremely-off-white pillow, matching sheet and red, Salvation Army logo-emblazoned blanket. He then scurried off in response to a distant shout, his head twitching like a squirrel's, exasperated by the shrill of his name being taken in vain. It seemed he had left the walk-in cooler unlocked again and someone had made off with tomorrow's entrée, a carrot, corn and green bean meatloaf. As far as I was concerned, whoever took it deserved a medal.

Now, it was a few minutes past three in the morning and I was lying on my back, staring into the darkness, wide awake with nothing but the occasional horn of digesting bean soup to remind me where I was—rocking in a thick fog of uncertainty.

One month ago to the day I had just left Greenville, a western suburb of Providence and my home for the past three years, to come here—to Boston—with a new job in my pocket, a spring in my step and a sweet little one bedroom sublet with a view of the harbor waiting with open arms and a satellite dish. The miles went by in a blink that day and yet somehow, in what seems like another blink, I found myself watching the moths outside the window kamikaze into a pale yellow lamp instead of rainbow spinnakers frolicking in the wind. How could everything have changed so fast? *How*?

With my heart flapping wildly to the winged beat of death, my minded raced through the past thirty days. There had to be an answer somewhere, or a clue pointing me in a new direction. There simply had to be. I had taken a wrong turn somewhere, gotten off at the wrong exit. That's all this was, a wrong turn. That would explain everything.

But what if it wasn't? What if I am *not* Daniel Rayne, the man every memory in my dazed and confused brain pronounces me to be? What if it is all a lie, a hoax, an alcohol and drug induced hallucination? *Look around you, Daniel, you wouldn't be the first.* I decided right then and there that if it was, I might as well open the window and join the bugs. I wasn't ready to do that. Not yet, anyway.

I rolled onto my side, missing the firmness of the mattress in the condo I no longer lived in.

"That's some view, isn't it?" the man had said, a portly and balding retiree (I assumed) who, according to him, was filling in for the regular welcoming committee, the condo owner who was vacationing in the Caribbean. He had already conveyed the owner's apologies for not conducting the grand tour himself, several times in fact, and was now detailing the finer points of what he called the "living *slash* dining *slash* party room."

"It's incredible," I replied, thinking that it was even better than I had imagined during the sixty mile, three hour plus, bumper-to-bumper drive from Rhode Island I had just survived. Stretching my limbs in front of the generous windows, I sucked in the full expanse of Boston Harbor, feeling a tickle of delight over the dumb luck that had brought us together—my new bachelor pad and me. I'd just been offered the job of my young dreams—Assistant Controller for a big and growing internet service company—and was exiting Exchange Place, the sleekest glass skyscraper I'd ever seen and home to my newly acquired corner office, when a gorgeous red-head freight-trained me on her hurried way into the building. Gloria—she introduced herself after helping me back to my feet—was a real estate broker who, after an overly affectionate apology and some rather personal small talk about how much she enjoyed *bumping* into me, said she knew a guy who might be willing to sublet a furnished place for a song.

"He's rich and married and was using the cozy hideaway for his extracurricular activities, if you know what I mean," she added, offhandedly. "But his wife got wind of it and now she thinks he's selling it. But he's not. He's going to hold onto it until the storm blows over, which, knowing his wife as I do, might be a few years."

We exchanged numbers and the next thing I knew I was being handed two sets of keys from the Mr. Roper look-alike.

"Enjoy," he said as he left, his hand clutching my check for a third of what I estimated my new neighbors were paying. That was a Friday and it was the last I saw of him until a few days ago.

I had spent the first weekend at my "cozy hideaway" gathering supplies—food, cleansers, toiletries, entertainment beverages, etc.—and getting familiar with the local terrain. The waterfront was only a block away and I exhausted the better part of Sunday afternoon sitting on a bench, filling my lungs with the crisp sea air while my eyes leap-frogged from one jogger to another. Mostly, I looked forward to Monday morning and my first real opportunity to show the world what I could do. I had been a small town, boy-in-the-bubble up until then, but feeling the ocean breeze splash against my face that day, I absolutely knew that Boston was the place to be. Toe-to-toe and elbow-to-elbow with the best and brightest the MTV Generation had to offer. Ironically, wallowing in self-pity as I was now in one of Beantown's many homeless shelters, the only elbows rubbing mine were covered with dirt and week-old vomit. Still, I couldn't help but smile thinking about the first step into my cherry corner office on the first day of my new job.

"Sweet," was all I said, again and again as I strolled around the walnut desk, running my fingers along the mammoth credenza as I paced like a caged tiger in front of the double windows, gazing out into the heart of Boston. It was a dream—better than a dream actually, because I was wide awake. (I pinched myself a dozen times just to be sure.) And when my secretary knocked on my open door—a beautiful young woman who could have been Sandra Bullock's twin—I nearly fell to my knees to thank God for letting me know that he really, really liked me. Her name was Irene—Irene Doolittle—and she wanted to know if I wanted some coffee.

"No thanks," I replied. "I never got into coffee. But you could *do a little* something for me later, when you've got a minute." I chuckled at my lame play on words and so did she. Irene had a sense of humor to go along with her stunning good looks. Could it get any better? Much to my surprise that first day on the job, it did.

After Irene delivered all the office supplies I'd asked for—pens, paperclips, folders, etc.—she escorted me down the hall to meet with my boss, introducing me to a variety of clerks and other secretaries along the way. Everyone smiled and congratulated me, but quickly went back to what they were doing as if thirty seconds was the prescribed policy for social interaction. It was a glimpse into the future that my starry eyes didn't notice at the time.

"Daniel!" Henry Stallworth said as I entered his office, a mirror image of my own, except twice as big. "I was beginning to wonder about you." He leapt out from behind his desk (all one hundred and thirty pounds I guessed, buried beneath an expensive looking, gray pinstriped suit,) exhaled a ferocious laugh that didn't fit his slight frame and then nearly dislocated my shoulder shaking my hand as if I were a candy machine who'd stolen his last quarter.

"I've been here since seven," I said, eager to earn points from the get-go. "Irene's been introducing me around." I turned toward the door thinking she had followed me in and that I should include her in the conversation, but she was gone.

"Well then, it sounds like you're ready to slap on a helmet and hit the track," he said. I had learned during my interview that Henry used metaphors with the same zeal that some folks slathered barbeque sauce. And he liked it when others did too.

Most importantly, he preferred to be called Hank.

"That I am, Hank; ready as a razorback in a mudhole." I had done a little research before I had left Rhode Island and learned that Hank's Alma Matta—the University of Arkansas—used the wild pig as a mascot. *One can never earn enough brownie points.*

He gave me a firm slap on the back and said, "I knew you were a go-getter the moment I laid eyes on you. Come on; let's go meet your staff."

As we walked down the corridor, I tried to recall him saying anything during our interview about me having a staff. But nothing came to mind. If he had, I certainly would have remembered it; I had never supervised anyone before. It was a big career rung to climb and as we stepped onto the elevator and headed downward, I began to wonder how many they were that they required a separate floor from Hank and I. One, two, twenty, fifty? The excitement I'd felt all weekend kicked up a notch, if that was possible. Before I would allow myself to skip up and down the hallways singing Halleluiah, I decided I had better inquire.

"My staff?" I asked.

"Yeah, your staff," was all Hank said just before the elevator doors opened and I caught myself in a Bennie Hill double-take.

A tiny city, that's what it looked like. A tiny city abuzz with people bustling about, phones ringing, dogs barking—yes, dogs— and even a robotic cart that Hank explained was delivering the mail. Instead of office buildings and apartment high risers, there were cubicles, dozens and dozens of cubicles of every shape and color. Some were painted to look like real red brick, complete with pretend windows, while others had ivy crawling up simulated stucco. I felt like I had landed in Oz, just without the munchkins.

"Welcome to Accountantville, *Mr. Mayor,*" Hank said.

I had never seen anything like it and…did he just call me *Mr. Mayor*? Before that question could rise to my lips, Hank grabbed my arm and led me down Main Street.

"Acquisitions," Hank said, his tone turning serious. "Right

now, we're all about acquisitions. Interactive online communication networks, web browsers, video sharing services, music downloading, anything with a hub and USB port is fair game. We're growing, Daniel, faster than a Great Dane pup. You ever have a dog?"

I shook my head no.

"I did once, when the wife and I first got married. It was a fawn-coat Dane, tan with a little white mixed in. Cutest thing when he was first born; fit right into the palm of my hand. We took him home a month later, called him Beowulf after that old English poem. Ever read it?"

I shook my head no again, but I don't think he noticed. He was busy monitoring the activities that now had us surrounded.

"Well, let me tell you *little* Beowulf grew into a monster before I had a chance to hang our wedding pictures. I'm talking huge." He held his hand up past his nose. "Damn thing out-weighed me by twenty pounds, at least."

"I noticed a few dogs in here," I said.

"According to the latest study it supposedly improves staff morale and productivity," Hank replied, apathetically. "Employee camaraderie and all that happy horseshit."

"Does it?"

"The boss thinks so," he said, grinning. "And that's what counts. You just have to watch where you're stepping." He belted out another big laugh, which curiously didn't turn a single, ledger-engrossed head. I reasoned they had all gotten used to it, like cows at the sound of a passing train.

"Anyway," Hank said, "the financing structure for these acquisitions can get pretty complex, requiring a steady volley of creative brain power. Like marines storming the beach at Normandy, you know what I mean?"

I nodded that I did, sneaking it in as he took a breath.

"We'll dig into the details of some of that later, after you've had time to get your feet wet. In the meantime, I've scheduled a handful of one-on-ones for you and your direct reports. That'll give you a chance to digest who's doing what before you go at it with your own knife and fork. Where'd you park this morning?"

Remembering the misery I had experienced searching for a slot for my Camaro in downtown Boston, I downplayed a ten-block hike into a two-block stroll. "I got lucky and found a broken meter with one hour remaining," I said, lying to sidestep the complaining, non-team player label. Glancing at my watch, I realized that at that very moment the real meter I'd parked at was expiring and my vintage '67 convertible was on it's own in the wild.

"Today, luck be a lady who only has eyes for you," Hank said. "Because it just so happens I was able to finagle a spot for you in the garage under the building. A stone's throw from the elevator, two slots down from mine."

Amazingly, the day was getting better and better with each tick of the clock. I hadn't done a lick of work yet and already I was in love with my secretary, had been granted full charge over a horde of willing accountants, and handed a primo slice of the parking garage. As I stood there exposing my pearly whites, I seriously thought about letting it ride with one final roll of the dice. Hank beat me too it.

"Did I mention the change in your title," he said, tilting his head in thought. "I don't believe I did. Anyway, while you were off packing your toothbrush and buying new underwear, we made a few personnel changes and, to make a long story short, your official title is now Acquisitions Controller, AC for short. Cool, huh?" He laughed and poked me in ribs. "Get it? AC? Cool? They really love my sense of humor around here."

I didn't find it that funny, but I laughed anyway, envisioning a scene from a Jim Carrey movie to aid my political correctness.

"Of course, we knew you wouldn't take if we didn't sweeten it with a salary raise. Thirty grand more a year sound ok?"

He said it so matter-of-factly I didn't fully comprehend how much money it was until I got back to my office and calculated out its monthly impact on my finely tuned budget. In a few years, I would be rich, well, rich relative to where I was coming from. Between the raise, the free parking and the paltry condo rent, I could wipe my nose all day with ten dollar bills and still have a wad in my pocket as big as John Holmes. As I stood at my corner office window, the warmth of the late morning sun caressing my blissful face, my wildest fantasy began to materialize. *Fenway Park season tickets!*

Looking back, I guess you could say it was the Red Sox that blinded me. Sure, the cash had quickly filled one of my sails, I won't deny it, but the thought of camping out eighty-one afternoons a summer atop the Green Monster was more than any Red Sox fan could handle with sound judgment. It was greed, that's what it was, one of the seven deadly sins. Or should I file it under gluttony, one of the other seven? Either way, now the best I could hope for was a special day at Fenway that let homeless people in free. If there was such a thing, it wouldn't be a game against the Yankees. I knew that much for sure.

4

Two Nickels

The next morning I woke up spooning in my cot with a little, five-year-old girl. It's not what you think…don't judge me!

It seems that sometime in the pre-dawn hours, after I had finally fallen asleep, a destitute woman and her two daughters staggered into the fuse-challenged shelter and, through some crazy mix up, ended up in the Roosevelt Room with me and the rest of the snoring boy's choir. Then, according to three-year-old Brittany, her older sister Jessica had gotten up to go to "wee-wee" and never came back. Fortunately for me, Jessica corroborated my story, explaining that when she couldn't find her mother and her sister again after her bathroom adventure, she went searching for an empty cot. I was sitting before the shelter's impromptu interrogation committee as Jessica told her tale, a four person jury comprised of Vincent, Raeni, a short Latino name-tagged Bubba and a calm man in a neatly pressed suit who'd introduced himself as the Executive Director, Charles Woodland. Looking at me with watery eyes and trembling lips, Jessica told them all that I smelt just like her daddy before confirming, after some extensive cross examination from Raeni, that I hadn't touched her anywhere "ticklish." I left the office several hours later a free man, but with a suspicion I was on double-secret probation.

"She just misses her father," Raeni said as we sat in the dining hall, our pushed-aside lunches sitting half eaten on the table.

"Did he skip out on them or something?" I asked. I wasn't sure how much I really cared; after all, the little cot-hopper had nearly added a pint of vinegar to the pickle I was already in. But still, she was cute and helpless and she pulled at my heart in a way I hadn't felt lately. It was an urge to help.

"I wish he would," Raeni said. "That would be a blessing in disguise." The sigh that followed was heavy. "No, he sticks around and beats on Jessica's mother every month or two." Raeni then glanced across the room to where Jessica sat eating with her sister while her mother chatted with one of the counselors. I watched Raeni looking at them, noticing a sad rinse wash all the color from her face, before turning to follow her gaze. The two little girls were playing with their macaroni, stuffing tiny elbows in their noses, giggling as if they were away from home on vacation, instead of hiding from their father.

"They've been in here before," Raeni said, "the three of them. I don't know if the girls have ever seen it happening, but they've seen the results, their mother's bruises. We all have."

"Why don't they arrest the guy?" I asked.

"We've tried that, but she won't press charges. It's an old story that I'm afraid will keep getting told long after you and I are dead and gone."

Her words hung in the air like one of those helium-filled birthday balloons cut loose from the pack, lost to the sky without any hope of ever getting it back, words that were full of hopelessness. Surprisingly, they made me...angry. Angry at my own situation. For the second time that day, I had an urge to help. But help, how? And with what? Raeni was the employed counselor, the one with her shit together. I was the hapless homeless man who just happened to smell better than the rest of the inmates. It was *her* job to help *me*. But as I contemplated finishing the rest of my limburger cheese sandwich, which, even though I hadn't showered in a few days, I also smelled better than,

I couldn't help sense that maybe our relationship was meant to be the other way around.

"So," Raeni said as she turned her attention back to me. "How did you end up here? I don't think I ever asked you that yesterday."

Aside from the fact that I hadn't figure it out yet myself, the thing that struck me about her inquiry was that she appeared sincerely interested. She wasn't just another apathetic, fast-food clerk mindlessly soliciting my unconscious desire for fries or a baked potato to go along with my chicken nuggets. I sensed she wasn't just doing her job. She really wanted to hear my story. Thinking I had nothing left to lose, I decided to leap before I looked, before the mirage disappeared.

"That was some first day you had," Raeni said, her bright smile filling the room. I had just told her about my first day at work, touching upon everything I thought about the night before, before I had finally fallen asleep.

"They don't get any better than that," I said. "A promotion; a raise; a free parking spot right in the building. Yeah, it was some day all right."

"What was the name of the company again?" she asked.

"Earth Nexus," I replied. "Catchy, isn't it? Nexus means link or chain, which reminds me, my secretary told me—I had a secretary—they were pursuing a deal with Fleetwood Mac—the rock group—to use their song *The Chain* as a company theme song. You know, *never break the chain*."

"Nexus is also used to mean core or center and *The Chain* is actually a song about betrayal," Raeni said. "You know, love and lies? I love that song. I used to dance to it all the time."

"Like in hip hop clubs, you mean?"

"Yeah," she said. Her eyes trailed away, leaving me to wonder if there were more to the dance.

Before I could pursue it further, she asked what happened at work after my first day. "After the honeymoon was over, and the two of you got to see each other just after you'd crawled out of bed."

"It's kind of a long story," I said. "Are you sure you want to hear it? You probably have things you need to attend to around here, responsibilities and what not."

She reached out and put her hand on top of mine. "I've got all afternoon, so take your time."

"What about your boss, Chucky?"

Raeni laughed. "Oh, you mean the Executive Director? Don't worry, he lets me do my own thing. And besides, I'm off the clock. My shift officially ended an hour ago."

So, you sat down and had lunch with me on your own time? I thought. I didn't know what to say, so I didn't. I just sat there staring into her caring eyes, wishing I'd met her a month ago when I was still somebody, a freshly shaven somebody in clean clothes with more than two dollars in loose change in his pocket. A six foot tall, brown haired and brown eyed, some-would-say handsome and athletic looking man who might stand a chance of getting to know her better; a chance at taking her out on the town; a chance of kissing her goodnight. Suddenly, images of the two of us together flashed in my mind. We were walking along the harbor front, hand in hand. She was smiling, laughing, beautiful and alluring. I was smiling too, and dirty and smelly with a brown paper bag in my other hand and bed-head. I shook the image from my mind as a new one took its place.

"Are you all right?" she asked.

"Yeah, I'm fine. I just remembered that I left my car in a tow-away zone behind the shelter. The city has probably taken it away by now."

"I doubt it. They don't worry too much about the availability of parking around here. It's not like we get a lot of visitors or site-seers. There's an employee parking lot around the block you can move it to if you want; just to be on the safe side."

"If it's still there I will. Is that where you park?"

"I'll bet it is and no, I take the bus. I don't own a car."

"How much?" I asked.

"How much what?" she replied.

"How much do you want to bet that my car is still there?" The way my luck had been going, I was sure it was gone and a bet with Raeni seemed like easy money. Hell, if I could get her to bet me a dollar I could double my current net worth if I won.

"Everything in my pocket," she said. A glimmer of mischief flickered in her eyes.

I hesitated. She had something up her sleeve. "You're trying to trick me," I said, grinning. "You keep your money in your purse, right?"

"I don't carry a purse."

"I thought all women carried a purse?"

"I don't. It's an old work habit. I used to have a job that didn't allow for a purse."

"Ok, then. Let's see every penny in your pocket on the table. It's time to put up or shut up." I was a bit nervous, knowing that I barely had two nickels to rub together but I didn't care. We were flirting and it was the closet thing to feeling alive that I had felt in days.

One by one, she proceeded to empty the pockets of her jeans, the clang of coins echoing off the walls and ceiling like raindrops on a tin roof. Then, she tallied them up, pushing each dime, nickel and penny toward me with her finger.

"What? No quarters?" I asked, interrupting her count.

"I used them for the bus."

"That makes sense."

She did the pennies last, looking up at me proudly when she had finished. "One dollar and eighty six cents."

I nodded appreciatively. I then pulled the change from my pockets before mimicking her adorable, but rather rudimentary accounting. "A buck fifty seven."

"Well, mister," she said. "It looks like I've got a bit more cents than you."

I laughed. "It sure looks that way. How about we make the bet a dime and go see who won. It doesn't look like either one of us could afford to lose any more than that."

She agreed and we went off to find my Camaro.

As we stood before the four-wheeled, sky blue convertible that was the last remnant of my vanishing life, she bit the dime I'd just handed her with her teeth just to be sure it was real. "You never can be to too careful." She winked as she slid it into her pocket. "Is it a '67?"

"It is. You've got a good eye."

"My stepfather had one just like this, only his didn't run." She ran her hand along the fender, admiring the way it reflected the sun. "It just sat in the yard along side the septic tank, rusting away." She paused a moment, lost in a memory I assumed, before blooming once again in a way I was growing very fond of. "I love the color. Blue is my favorite." At that moment, she looked up at me—a sparkling star that held me mesmerized. I wondered if she knew how unbelievingly captivating she was.

"I painted it about a year ago," I said. "Right after I finished rebuilding the engine."

"You did all this by yourself?"

"Most of it. I had the body work done at a shop."

"Take me for a ride," she blurted out. She was beaming now—the North Star, the brightest in the sky. Every man on the planet would have answered in a heart beat "hop in," but not me. I had one small, but significant obstacle between me and the heaven in front of me. It took every ounce of courage I could muster to spit it out.

"I can't. I don't have a driver's license."

She tilted her head, puzzled.

"I did," I added quickly. "Up until a few days ago, anyway. The cops have it now. It's another long story."

Then, she surprised me. She opened the passenger door and

got in, motioning for me to join her as she did. "I've got nothing else to do today, do you?" she asked.

No, I certainly didn't. I was a homeless man with one dollar and forty-seven cents in his pocket and a wallet recently relieved of its credit cards—a garbage hand, by poker standards. But I did have a set of keys to a classic Camaro convertible, which just happened to have a gorgeous young woman sitting in it, begging to take a spin. Without another word, I got behind the wheel, started the engine and headed toward Boston Harbor.

As if the afternoon was destined to be ours, the traffic was light and we easily made our way out of the city and onto a road hugging the coastline. Traveling south, we flew past signs for Old Harbor, Dorchester Bay and Quincy Bay, enjoying the warm ocean breeze and the freedom of the open air. After twenty miles not a word had been spoken, only contented smiles exchanged, until I popped the question that had been gnawing at me since we had left.

"Are you this nice to all the bums and losers that stumble into the shelter?" I asked.

"I've never seen a bum or a loser walk through those doors," she answered. "Quite a few people down on their luck yes, but no losers."

Good answer, I thought. "Is that how you see me? Just another poor guy down on his luck?"

"You," she said thoughtfully. "You don't fit. I don't know how to explain it, but when I first saw you sitting in the dining hall amongst all the other homeless people, it was like I was looking at a river stone in a rock quarry. Do you know what I mean?"

My scrunching face told her I didn't.

"A river stone is smooth, polished by time and the steady flow of water. Quarry rocks are rough with sharp edges. The first day I worked at the shelter it reminded me of a quarry back home, full of rocks that had fallen from the walls and ledges. And when I saw you I said to myself, he's a river stone, he doesn't belong here." She looked at me and laughed softly. "Crazy, huh?"

"Still want to hear about how I ended up at the shelter?" I asked.

"Absolutely," Raeni replied.

5

Seduction 101

Just as Hank had promised, there was an open space with my name on it in the parking garage underneath the building. It was only my second day at work—my fifth day in Boston—but after I tucked my Camaro into bed and walked confidently toward the elevators that would carry me up to my walnut-embroidered, thirty-eighth floor office, I felt as though I had just arrived. I was walking on air, ready to wrestle a grizzly bear. *Look out world, here I come!*

Irene was standing at the door waiting for me with a chilled glass of freshly squeezed orange juice.

"Good morning," she said with a Hollywood smile as she handed me the ceramic mug with my name on it. The dawn was still yawning but she looked bright and chipper dressed in a clingy, short black skirt and bodacious red top that had me to tripping on the invisible jump rope I had been skipping since I had opened my eyes and leapt out of bed. Her soft, auburn curls fell barely over her semi-bare shoulders and when she turned to greet me, her dazzling, hazel eyes jimmied the lock to my judgment and nearly emptied the vault. But I knew perusing my lust would make for a very precarious situation. I was her boss, for Christ's sake, who only had one day under his belt, not to mention a plate so overloaded with work I could have feed a small African nation had it been lentils instead of journal entries. As I caught myself imagining her crimson v-neck sweater falling to the floor, I decided that if I were to maintain my balance on the corporate ladder, I would have to make it a personal policy to work with my door closed. *Out of sight, out of mind...* I hoped.

Still, it did give me one more reason to tighten my tie in the morning, not that the exulted corner office, amorous parking spot, first day promotion and life-style altering raise hadn't.

"Good morning," I replied. I sipped the orange juice, pleasantly startled by the tartness having never had freshly squeezed before. "This is great. Where'd you get it?"

Coyly, she just grinned and returned to her desk. "A girl shouldn't tell all her secrets, should she?"

Recalling my new policy, I went straight into my office, noticing the unobstructed view of the steam rising from her warm cocoa legs as I closed my door. *Journal entries, remember the journal entries...*

By noon, I had digested only the first of a dozen spreadsheets I found waiting in my company email inbox. According to the time stamp, they had been sent between one and four that morning, each with a separate note from Hank Stallworth, my boss, explaining the importance of completion by the end of the day. He had said something about a backlog of work the day before and as I sat at my desk, my LCD monitor-soaked vision blurry, my stomach grumbling obscenities about lunch, I realized that my good-humored boss had not been joking. Fortunately, a knock at my door pulled me from the accounting abyss.

"Come in," I said.

The door opened and Irene waltzed in with an orange plastic tray in her hands. She set in down in front of me.

"Turkey on a hard roll," she said pointing at a paper-wrapped bundle the size of a softball. "Mayo, swiss and little bit of lettuce." Altering her aim, she then called out the rest of my tray like a seasoned auctioneer. "Barbeque chips, white chocolate and macadamia nut cookie, and a diet Mountain Dew."

Dumbfounded, I couldn't stop staring at it. She had just delivered the exact lunch I had been eating four out of five days a week my entire adult life. Finally, I looked up at her and asked, "How did you know?"

She didn't answer. Instead, she just winked, turned on her heel and left.

"I know, a girl and her secrets," I said as she closed my door.

At the time, I hadn't given it another thought. A month later, I was wishing I had pressed my curvaceous secretary—former secretary—a little harder about it.

"How could she have possibly known that?" Raeni asked.

After I had decided to share all the sorted details surrounding my descent into homeless shelter hell, I had pulled the Camaro over into a parking area that provided a spectacular view of Boston Harbor, the Massachusetts Bay and the Atlantic Ocean beyond. It was a warm summer day and the great panoramic was the perfect excuse to stop. (That and the fact that I only had a quarter tank of gas left and enough money to buy maybe another half gallon.) I had a very strong need to retrace my steps and having found an attentive, if not now overwhelmed, audience, it would have taken a bullet to the brain to shut me up.

"I don't know," I replied. "Maybe it was a lucky guess?"

"She doesn't sound like the kind of woman who would take that chance," Raeni said.

"What do you mean?"

"Well, from what you've described, it sounds to me like she was dangling her carrot in front of you the moment you arrived; leading you exactly where she wanted without you even knowing it."

"Leading me…where?"

"To the foot of her bed, where else. Where she'd tease and promise to please for as long as she wanted while you knelt down before her, rubbing your crotch and praying she'd invite you between the sheets one day. But she never did. Did she?"

"No," I said, meekly. As I had discovered back at the shelter while facing the circumstantial child molestation charges, Raeni had an inescapable directness about her. She didn't mince words, and even though I didn't think she truly meant to, her extremely sharp pointedness was slicing an artery of my already battered ego.

"She was seducing you," Raeni added. "But for what, that's the question."

"That's a pretty quick deduction, Sherlock," I said, testily. I didn't like the idea that Irene Doolittle had done a little number on my judgment, enough to blind me while she laced me up with marionette strings. My brain had never migrated below my belt buckle before, at least not that I could remember. Although, there was a scorching waitress at a Sizzler once that had temporarily put the South Pole in charge. But that was different; I was a twenty-one year old kid back then. I was almost thirty now and in far better control of my privates than even the wiliest drill sergeant. No, I wasn't buying that my secretary had seduced me. Swayed me a little, yes, but seduced, no way. "How do you know she didn't have a real thing for me and was just afraid of getting fired if she pursued it? Or, that I might reject *her*."

"I know how women like her work. She was just playing with you, like a kitten with a ball of yarn."

"No way, I'd have sniffed it out."

"Ok, if you say so," Raeni conceded. Seemingly content to let the topic fade, she began to stretch out in her seat; her head tilting back as she closed her eyes, a warm glow blossoming on her face. The white cami she was wearing, held in place only by invisibly thin straps, clutched at her slender torso, pulled erotically taunt as she tacked toward the ocean breeze, a splash of cleavage hitting my face as she finally settled down. Then, with her short shorts growing ever shorter from the tug of the leather bucket seat, her fingers began to slowly skate up and down the length of her bare thigh, stroking her silken skin that I swear was budding a golden luster right before my eyes. Finally, she sighed softly, seemingly in rapture.

Spellbound, I sat there like a Greek statue, twitching uncomfortably in my seat and tugging at my jeans to ventilate.

"Let's go to the Cape," she cooed.

"Ok," I replied without thinking. I started the car but just as I shifted it into reverse to back out onto the road, Raeni grabbed my hand and stopped me.

"Got enough gas?" she asked.

She knew I didn't, that was the main reason we had only driven as far as we had. "I'll buy some more on the way," I said, without thinking.

"How far do you think we'll get on a buck and a half?"

It was then that the light bulb went on, mind-numbingly bright. "You were messing with me, weren't you? To prove your point."

She straightened up in her seat and smiled. "Yes, I was. And I promise you, Daniel. I'll never mess with you like that again. Now, what do you say we pool our resources and split a hot dog and a soda? I think you could use an energy boost to finish your story."

I nodded in agreement before shutting of the engine. I had a few years—maybe more—on this woman but I certainly hadn't acted like it a moment ago. She played me like Charlie Daniels plays the fiddle and I didn't even know it until she turned off the volume. After we exited the car and began to walk toward a gathering of sidewalk vendors, two thoughts nudged their way to the front, pushing aside my feelings of stupidity for being so easily manipulated. First, what was Irene's motive for catching and holding my apparently obtuse eye? And second, where did Raeni learn to do that? Whip a man's brain into mush without lifting a finger, I mean. As the sweet smell of burning animal fat lead us onward, I vowed to find the answer to both.

6

Follow the Yellow Brick Road

I have to admit that half a foot-long is better than no foot-long at all. That was Raeni's philosophy and like so many of the viewpoints she offered that day, I found myself agreeing.

Following Raeni's lead, the two of us managed to coerce an amiable and plump mobile restaurateur (victim of his own cholesterol laden wares, no doubt) to sell us a jumbo hotdog for half price, citing the almost non-existent, post lunch-hour crowd as reason for the inventory thinning discount. "If you don't sell it to us, you'll probably just end up throwing it away," Raeni said. "And there's no profit in that." She did all the talking while I flashed our pooled-together cash—all three dollars and forty-three cents of it. I could tell the man didn't really want to burden his pocket with all our coins, but in the end Raeni wore him down. He even threw in an extra soda, just to watch her smile, I think. Damn, if it wasn't the best dog I ever ate.

The sun was peaking in the cloudless afternoon sky as I picked up my story again, the part of my journey where I began to wonder where the folks at Earth Nexus learned their accounting; or if they had ever learned the proper methods at all. Analyzing that first spreadsheet made me feel like Dorothy in the Wizard of Oz, like a stranger in a strange land. And Hank Stallworth, my boss and creator of said spreadsheet, was the Scarecrow, the jovial cornfield guardian without a brain. His entries were all wrong. Some of them were backwards, most just plain mystifying. That was my first impression anyway, until a cockroach of self-doubt crept in. Had *I* learned it the wrong way? Was it me that had it all backward in my head? After all, this was a multi-billion dollar corporation of which Hank was the Acquisitions Division CFO. How could I be right and he be wrong? It hadn't made sense then, and it still didn't now. So, how was I going to explain it to Raeni? Sensing that somehow this young woman could help me sort through it, I took a deep breath and headed down the yellow brick road.

"For the next several weeks," I told Raeni, "I was holed up in my office grinding through spreadsheets, compiling acquisition summaries and struggling to comprehend the accounting they'd created for several deals so bewildering I ended up at the MIT library each weekend for assistance. I spent days there, digging through accounting text books, business journals, and magazine and newspaper articles. During that month, I'll bet I logged more hours in that place than the whole freshman class. But, I'm glad I did because the stuff I found only reinforced my suspicion."

"Your suspicion?" Raeni asked.

"My suspicion that Earth Nexus was cooking their books, creating a grand illusion of steadily increasing profits to keep the investing public salivating and coming back for more. The thing is, for a company like them to grow they need cash. To get cash, they need investors. To attract investors, their financial outlook needs to be promising. And to get the big money—to draw in the really big fish—their profits must be exceptional if they want the major players to bite, investors with millions. Fresh investment capital means new cash for new acquisitions and new growth; and new acquisitions means new complex financing structures and make-believe profits to enter into the cooked books; and new profits means new investors come knocking. And with their pockets laced with fresh investor money they go looking for more companies to buy. And bada-bing bada-boom, they start the cycle all over again."

"You lost me at hello," Raeni said.

"I was lost too, the first week or so," I said. "But then I bumped into an MIT professor at the library who was generous enough to share her thoughts over lunch."

"*Her* thoughts?" Raeni asked with a grin. "You sure it was just a lunch?"

"Please, she was old enough to be my mother."

"A Mrs. Robinson type perhaps?"

Perhaps, I thought. I was blushing now, embarrassed knowing that I *had* given the woman a look of interest as a tiny, but deceitful bribe to join me in the cafeteria so I might glean her intellect. She taught accounting and finance and, as I learned during dessert, human sexuality. Actually, she was an attractive woman for her age who had a profoundly provocative way of eating her whipped cream-topped jello. If another professor hadn't come by our table and whisked her away to an emergency board meeting, I might have found myself groping her in the dark, just as Dustin Hoffman had with the fictional Mrs. Robinson.

"Let's not get sidetracked," I said.

Raeni giggled a laugh that reminded me how young she was, spirited and childlike. She radiated youth, but held herself with more certainty and confidence than the girls I remembered when I was her age. I was guessing that she had been born only nineteen or twenty years ago but for reasons I couldn't explain, had lived a lot longer. Both things made me want to tell her more.

"I'll start over," I said. "And I'll try to put it in simple terms."

She threw me a good-humored scowl.

"Accounting terms, I mean."

"That's better."

Not knowing how savvy she was to the world of stock investment, I decided I best begin at the beginning. "Have you ever bought a share of stock?"

"Of course, I have a portfolio with a local investment firm. Mutual funds mostly, with a 60-40 split between stocks and bonds. The rest is in T-bills. I'm saving for something."

"Wow, that's great. I wish I'd started when I was your age."

"Which is?"

"Nineteen?" I said. *Always guess low.*

"Aren't you sweet? I'm twenty."

"What are you saving for?"

Raeni hesitated.

"Oh, come on. Here I am spilling my homeless guts to you. At least you can tell me what those T-bills are going to buy you someday."

"A horse farm," she said cautiously, as if she expected me to laugh.

"Really," I said, smiling. I could see her raising horses. Riding them up and down the coastline, turning every dazzled head like a movie starlet or an heiress to a fortune. She had that look about her.

"Hopefully, by the time I'm thirty."

The accountant in me reared up and posed a personal question. "I didn't know homeless shelters paid that well?"

"They don't, but I moonlight now and then," she replied. "Telemarketing from the comfort of my own apartment. It's boring work, but it pays well if you're good at it."

I have no doubt that you're good at it, I thought. So why work at the shelter? My logical mind asked. Wanting to explain what I'd found at Earth Nexus, I decided that was a question for another time.

"Ok, now that I know you're a savvy investor chick," I said. "I can skip the basic Wall Street lesson. Let's consider your portfolio. It's filled with a handful of stocks and bonds out of the thousands available to investors. So, how does one narrow down the list to the ones that will make you the most money?"

"Simple. You pick the companies that are making the most

money for themselves."

"Exactly; the more profits they generate, the more cash they have to pay dividends. Every investor loves to get dividends. It becomes their mad money to buy a new car and get a tummy tuck."

"Or buy a horse farm," Raeni interjected.

"Or a horse farm," I smiled. "Now, if your portfolio manager gives you a call and says he's got a stock that pays great dividends, you're going to invest, right?"

"As long as it's not a ploy by some loser to entice me to board their already sinking ship," she replied.

"What difference does that make, as long as you're receiving a healthy dividend check?" I was goading her now, a little payback for the lesson on seduction. I should have known better.

"Because, while they're greasing my palm with a couple of Benjamin's, my original investment of ten times that amount is either getting chewed up by their bankruptcy lawyers or being spent on lifeboats."

I had to give her credit; she was smart and unwavering. I looked at her approvingly, noticing the fire in her eyes as she contemplated losing her life savings. At that moment, I could tell that her dream—her horse farm—would have to be pried from her cold, dead hands before anyone could take it away. She was a fighter and as I sat next to her on a picnic table overlooking the harbor, sucking the life from the bottom of an ice cube filled plastic cup, a little bit of her resolve was spilling over to me.

"So, the trick is," I said. "To look like a mighty sailing ship, your sails full, a steady wind at your back and a bright red sky on the horizon."

"Red sky at night, sailor's delight," Raeni added.

"Precisely. Nothing but tranquil waters and full steam ahead. Eager investors swarm all over companies like that, fast movers with rising stock prices that double your original investment while churning out juicy dividend checks along the way. You'd jump on that ship, wouldn't you?"

"In a heartbeat. Horses aren't cheap, you know."

"No," I chuckled. "I don't imagine they are."

"So, this Earth Nexus company, they're a big fancy yacht that's really just a mirage?"

"I think so," I replied.

"You *think* so?"

"Well, I don't exactly have any evidence. I got shit-canned before I could gather any."

"They fired you? After only a month?"

I fell silent. This was the part of my story that got weird and I had been dreading trying to explain it ever since Raeni had asked about my arrival at the shelter. It had been a Monday and I had arrived at Exchange Place at around seven like I had every other morning for the past four weeks. It was a beautiful, sunny day; the traffic was light and my Camaro was humming like a top. Everything was normal and I was still riding high on that first day wave. By noon that same day, I was sitting in my car questioning my own sanity. It was the first day I began to wonder if I truly was Daniel Rayne. How do you explain that to someone?

"Daniel?"

"It's…not a simple answer."

"Well, either your boss said 'Daniel, you're fired,' or he didn't."

"He didn't say that."

"What did he say?"

I didn't answer. I couldn't answer. I just stared out at the harbor, scratching nervously at my three-day-old beard that was beginning to itch; fearful this would be the fork in our road together.

Raeni was the first person to call me Daniel in three days, the first person to acknowledge that I was who I said I was. Everything she had done, everything she had said up to now told me she would listen to my story. But it was just too…weird. There was no way she was going to believe me; no way anyone was ever going to believe me. Christ, I didn't believe it myself.

7

The Moon

On the way back to the shelter, I offered to drive Raeni home. I wasn't looking to make a move on her or anything macho and stupid like that, I just didn't want to say goodbye, even if it would only be for the day. She was the only friend I had, the only person I knew in Boston—correction—the only person in Boston who knew me, Daniel Rayne. With what had happened in the past three days, it seemed like a bad idea to let her out of my sight.

"Thanks, Daniel," Raeni said. "But I need to go back to the shelter. I remembered that Charlies—Chucky—asked me to sort through a box of files this evening. I'm going to take them home and bring them back in the morning."

"Sounds like an awful heavy load to be lugging on the bus," I said. "We could throw it in the back." *Chivalry, that's the ticket.*

She looked at me, her head tilting in contemplation. Was she assessing my trustworthiness? *No doubt.* My potential as a conman, rapist, or ax murder? *Possibly.* And could I be one of those dreadful things? *Sweet Jesus, I hope not.* Might it be that I am afflicted with some strange, self-induced amnesia; my subconscious altering my memory to hide all the horrible crimes I had committed? Could Daniel Rayne be the Dr. Jekyll to my real identity of Mr. Hyde? *God damn, my head hurts.*

"Daniel?" Raeni said. "Did you hear me? I said ok. You can

drive me home."

With the hideous image of the Mr. Hyde looming before my eyes, I remained silent, keeping my focus on the road ahead while seriously reconsidering my offer. This woman was my whole life. I'd only known her for twenty-four hours and yet she was exactly that—my whole life. Could I take the chance of harming her? A blaring horn pulled me from my nightmare.

"Whoa," I said as I jerked the Camaro back into our lane.

"Are you ok?" Raeni asked.

I took a deep breath before telling her that I was. But inside I knew I was losing it—losing my grip on reality. *Mr. Hyde? Come on Daniel, get your head out of your ass!* I wasn't a rapist or a murderer, my skull wasn't in that deep yet, but as we headed back into the city, I had a sense that it *was* wedged in fairly tight and that it would take a concerted effort to yank it free. And, that I was definitely going to need Raeni to help pull.

"How about I wait out front while you get your stuff?" I offered.

"You mean you're not going to carry the box out for me?" she replied. "A big, strong guy like you?" She squeezed my modest bicep for affect, giggling as she watched me blush.

"Sure, I can do that." I said, knowing I should have thought of it in the first place. *Some gallant knight I am.*

"I was kidding. I can handle it myself, it's not that big. And besides, doesn't it use more gas to start a car than to let it sit idling?"

"That depends on how long you keep me idling."

"I'll be in and out before you can recite the Pledge of Allegiance."

She had a way of making me smile, a way of lightening the load that had come crashing down on me like a tornado tossed house. She was sunshine and that was when I remembered suggesting to call her Sunny. She had reacted oddly, ruffled. I didn't know why, but I wanted to and decided that an apology would be the best way to start.

"I think I owe you an apology for the other day," I said.

"For what?" she asked.

"I called you Sunny. I don't think you liked it."

Just that quickly, her expression went blank as it had the day before. I'd tripped on something—something very prickly—and I couldn't imagine what it was. Was I being an insensitive, chauvinistic jerk and didn't realize it? It was possible. I'd innocently stumbled a few times before in today's thin-skinned, politically correct world but what was wrong with calling an effervescent woman Sunny? My personal moral codebook didn't suggest an answer. One thing was for certain, I was walking on ice with absolutely no idea of how thin it might be.

Several long, quiet minutes passed as Raeni gazed out at Boston Harbor. We were zipping along at fifty miles an hour, utility poles and exit signs flashing by, while the harbor remained solid and stationary like the moon on a cloudless night, offering its constant, comforting presence to us, no questions asked. Maybe, for now, that's all Raeni was meant to be to me.

"I promise I won't call you that again," I said.

She turned and gave me a muted smile. "Ok," was all she said.

8

First Day of Kindergarten

"With liberty and justice for all," I said, as Raeni dropped a big, dusty box full of paper-filled folders into the back seat of my Camaro.

"See, I told you I'd be quick," she said. "It was heavier than I expected." She stepped back onto the curb and groaned. There were red lines on her arms where her cargo had exerted its weight and a bead of perspiration leaking from her brow. *It was the heat*, I thought as I watched her brush the box residue off her taut, pleasingly muscular legs. The temperature had to be in the nineties and even I, who hadn't lifted a thing, was sweating. As I caught myself ogling, I tried to imagine what she did to keep her figure, aside from being twenty years old. *A runner, perhaps? A ballet dancer? Maybe both?* Whatever it was, she had great legs.

It was at that very moment, while I was studying her calves that my car engine decided to die.

"Shit!" I said. I turned the key off and then on again, but all I got from it was a half-hearted grumble. Reaching into the dashboard, I tapped on the gas gauge glass. Sure enough, my jostling startled it back to life long enough to confirm my fear. The thing had stuck a few times before, but only in the winter when the thermometer dipped below freezing. Moisture had gotten inside and after many aggravating hours with a hair dryer I thought I had had it licked. Now it was licking back.

"Out of gas?" Raeni asked.

Afraid to look her in the eye, I slumped down in my seat and nodded affirmatively. *You're supposed to run out of gas while you're driving her home from a dinner date, numb nuts! Not parked out in front of the homeless shelter.*

Up until now, I had hope. I still had my wheels—my freedom and machismo. I know it sounds crazy, but that car was a part of me, a big part of who I was. With nothing else to link me to my past—my Daniel Rayne past—it had become more essential to my sanity than I could have ever imagined. This wasn't just a boy and his toy; this was a man and his verifiable existence. And now, it too was teetering on the edge. If it hadn't been for Raeni, I'm sure I would have run screaming into the shelter kitchen and drowned myself in a vat of bean soup.

"Come on," she said. "I've got enough money for both of us to take the bus. I'll buy if you carry the box."

At that moment, only God knew how badly I ached to call her Sunny.

Resigned to mass transit, I got out of the car and lifted the box from the back seat. I then followed Raeni to the corner and set it down with a thud, thinking the whole time that it *was* heavy and wondering how she had lugged it all the way out to the car. This young woman was surprising me at every turn and the day was still young.

"The bus should be by any minute," she said, shading her eyes as she gazed down the empty street. "This is one of its regular stops."

"How far is it to your place?" I asked.

"Only a few miles, but it takes a while because there are a lot of stops along the way." She was on her tiptoes now, stretching her line of sight as far as she could. She didn't belong here, working at a shelter in a beaten-down part of town. She belonged in front of an audience, tripping laughter and drawing tears, not to mention a long line of suitors. Suddenly uncomfortable in my three-day-worn clothes and polluted skin, I wanted to turn back the clock a month and then recreate this very moment so that I could tell her how beautiful she was—how magical—without the shame of what I was now, a dirty and no doubt, smelly homeless man who didn't even have a quarter for the bus. But when she turned and smiled at me, her eyes sparkling like stars, there was nothing there that said my circumstances mattered.

A wave of questions flooded my mind. How long had she lived at the apartment at the end of this bus ride? Had she always lived in Boston? Did she have family here? Did she have a roommate in said apartment and, if so, was it male or female? I realized these were trivial issues, except for maybe the last one, and as I contemplated my opening query, I remembered something my mother once told me: *the shortest distance between two hearts is a straight line.*

Summoning the courage to ask, I inquired about her living situation. My stomach felt like a cave of restless bats and it took every ounce of willpower I could muster to look her in the eye as I awaited her answer.

"Yes," she replied. "But I think you'll like him."

They were vampire bats now, circling in a death spiral, ravenous and blood thirsty. I thought I might lose my half of the hotdog we had eaten for lunch.

"But he's so lazy. Just lies on my bed all day, waiting for me to come home."

Some guys have all the luck, I thought.

"I'm not sure how old he is, though. Seven or eight, I think. And he loves to have his belly scratched."

Seven or eight? Belly scratched? Who is this guy?

"He showed up on my doorstep a few months ago when I lived in New…at my old apartment. We've been best buds ever since. Do you like cats?"

Her roommate was a cat, a male house cat, and here I was

conjuring images of an unemployed and scruffy-faced pretty boy sprawled out on her mattress in nothing but tidy whities. *Damn, I really do need to get my head out of my ass.*

Apparently she noticed my puzzled expression.

"You're not allergic, are you?" Raeni asked.

"No," I replied. "I just thought you were talking about...nevermind. What's your cat's name?"

"Garfield. I know; it's not very original. But he's orange and white and he likes to get into mischief."

"Sounds like a Garfield to me."

"That's what I thought," she said, visibly pleased that I agreed with her logic.

The drone of a distant automobile engine stole our attention away. Turning our heads, we saw not the expected bus, but a long white limousine headed our way. *It's Richard Gere*, my weary mind said. *He's come to rescue Raeni from her penurious plight. Rich and handsome and decked out in a* clean, five thousand dollar tuxedo. I stepped in front of her without even realizing it, my subconscious directing me to defend and protect.

It was one of those converted Hummer limos—huge—with five doors on each side. As I prepared for battle with the former sexiest man alive, the space-shuttle-on-wheels turned the corner and rolled right past us before pulling up in front of the shelter, effectively boxing in my comparatively pocket-sized Camaro.

I watched like an expectant father as the husky limo driver exited and circled around the front before opening the last door on the curbside. Two feet emerged, adorned in glimmering black shoes, followed by the attached body of a tall, athletic looking man with a clean-shaven head and a confident, bordering on arrogant, manner. He surveyed the street, assessing its worthiness it seemed, and then with a nod to his driver, proceeded to walk into the shelter with a determined gate that told me he'd come with a purpose.

"Who was that?" I asked Raeni.

"I've never seen…him…before…." she said. Her words trailed off like my mother's voice on the first day of kindergarten, after the bus driver had slammed the door shut and was slowly rolling away from her. Something in Raeni's tone reminded me of how scared I was that day, leaving my mother's side for the first time, frightened of what lay ahead—the unknown.

I stood there for a moment, studying the limo driver as he swiped perspiration from his steroidal forehead. He looked more like a bodyguard than a wheelman the way his protruding muscles lumped beneath his dark suit. When he leaned down to fleck a spot of dirt off his shoe, I could swear I saw a holstered gun nestled against his chest.

"Whoever that guy is, he's important enough to require protection," I said. "Did you see that revolver tucked under his arm?"

But Raeni didn't answer because she never heard the question. When I turned to where she had been standing, the young woman who had become the only person on the planet that I thought I could trust was gone.

9

Beware of Greeks Bearing Gifts

I'm not sure how long I stood at the corner waiting for Raeni to reappear, an hour, maybe two? But she never did. At first, I had thought about running to the end of the block and checking the intersecting streets, but in which direction? Besides leading back to the shelter entrance, the road continued north in the opposite direction, all the way to Canada as far as I knew. The perpendicular street seemed no better, stretching endlessly into the summer haze like the world's longest garden hose. And each of them was empty; void of pedestrian traffic. *How could she have slipped out of sight so fast? And why?* After the first few precious minutes had ticked by, I realized my uncertainty had rendered the option of pursuit futile. That's when Plan B kicked in—waiting for her to come back.

With my burning skin voicing its discomfort, it finally dawned on me that she might have gone back into the shelter through another entryway, one to which I was not privy. After all, I had only been there a day and Raeni had been working there how long? Feeling modestly optimistic and particularly stupid for standing there so long, I picked up the box of folders, plodded past my fallen Camaro and the metallic monster beside it and went inside my new home.

I dropped the box off in the business office where I was told no one had seen Raeni since that morning. It appeared she hadn't fled the hot street for the cooling comfort of the shelter as I'd hoped, leading my paranoia to conclude it was something I had said. *Or had the whole afternoon been another mirage?* Dispirited and heat weary, I was heading to the Roosevelt Room for a army cot catnap when I noticed the shelter's Executive Director, Charles Woodland, sitting in the dining hall with the knight from the shining Hummer. There was something about this stranger, something drawing me in, like a mouse to a baited trap, and even though my gut was protesting heavily, my nose was winning the battle. *Who are you? Why do I think I know you?* Noticing that Chucky didn't look very happy in their conversation, I decided to forgo the forty winks and eavesdrop.

Lunch was nearing its end and even though I wasn't very hungry, I snagged a bowl of soup to blend in with everyone else.

Wanting to see and study the man's face, I pulled out a chair at the adjacent table and sat down next to Dexter, one of my bunk buddies. Dexter hadn't uttered a word since I arrived the day before, sipping his soup quietly from sunup to sundown. After sitting down, I slid my soup in front of him. He silently, but happily, accepted it and dove right in, providing me perfect camouflage for a little espionage. *Don't mind us; we're just two homeless men sharing a bowl of soup.*

"It's not that we don't appreciate your extremely generous donations, Mr. Vinson," Charles said. His voice held a hint of uncertainty, a tremor of cautiousness.

"Please, call me Louis," the knight said, attaching a faint smile to the offer.

"Mr. Vinson—Louis—the people who stay here have the same rights to personal privacy as you and I. Just because they're homeless and the taxpayers pick up the tab doesn't mean their files should be open to anyone who wants to see them. They're not stray dogs and cats. They're human beings and their identities must be protected."

The knight's glistening armor suddenly turned dark. "I," he said, stressing the word heavily, "paid for all of this, not John Q jerk off. If it wasn't for *my* money, the city would have leveled this place years ago and put in a parking garage. Do you remember that Charles? Do you remember not having a pot to piss in? I bought the pot and everything else in this place and here you are now, pissing on my brand new shoes."

"I'm sorry you see it that way, Louis," Charles replied. "It's nothing personal, it's the law. And our policy is to follow the law."

I watched Louis Vinson's skinny lips expand into a twisted, evil grin. *Laws were made to be broken*, they said. You didn't forget a look like that and it was then I knew for certain that I'd seen this guy before. *But where?*

"Surely, you can make an exception," he suggested.

"Surely, I can't," Charles said, his jaw tightening. "I have a responsibility to these people and I intend to live up to it. As I said, we truly appreciate all that you've done."

Vinson cut him off. "Spare me the sentiment," he growled. "The next board meeting is in two weeks. I'd polish up my resume, if I were you."

"Is that a threat?" Charles asked. To his credit, he wasn't wilting and as Vinson stood to leave, Charles held his steely gaze.

"I could say *it's not a threat, it's a promise*, use that tired old line," Vinson said. "But we both know better."

As Vinson was angrily straightening his suit coat and tie, his face reddening into a flame, I noticed him looking at me from the corner of his eye. And then, as if dosed with a bucket of water, he calmed. In fact, he suddenly became quite jovial.

"All things aside," he said, I assumed to Charles though he was staring right at me. "I'm glad I put the money into this place." He strolled around the table, once again looking as arrogant as when he had exited the Hummer, before breezing past Dexter and me. "It's still a source of satisfaction," he said as he slapped me on the back on his way by. "*Great* satisfaction."

I watched him saunter out as if I had just seen Elvis, Charles following a few steps behind like a nightclub bouncer ensuring his exit. Vinson got clipped by one of my down-and-out-club members before reaching the door, his sudden groan turning every head in the place. "Watch where you're going, miscreant," he snarled. Even Dexter's bloodshot eyes flashed a spark of curiosity, momentarily lifting from the comfort of his soup. "Prick," he mumbled as he trawled the bowl bottom for a fresh spoonful of beans. Later, I would learn that Mr. Louis Vinson didn't find satisfaction in helping humanity, only in the predicament of some of its less fortunate members.

"Who parked the hotrod smack-dab in front of the entrance?" Charles shouted. I'm sure his dictatorial scented question was aimed at his staff, but I absorbed his irritation nonetheless as a raised my hand and announced the car was mine.

"Oh," he said. Seeing it was one of his clients, as he referred to us, his demeanor softened. "Could you please move it? Our vans pickup and drop-off in that very spot; where the sidewalk is tapered for wheelchair access."

I hurried over saying I would be happy to move it, explaining that I would just need to put some gas in it first.

"Come on," Charles said, his mood elevating. "There's a gas station a few blocks from here. I'll drive you over."

"I don't have any money," I said. Surprisingly, it was getting easier to say that.

"I'll take care of it," he replied, smiling genuinely.

Faced with the opportunity to help me, he eagerly pushed aside his unpleasant exchange with Vinson and immediately focused on the needy, asking me about myself and my plans for the future. He never asked a single question about how I had ended up at his shelter, only what I was hoping to get out of my stay there and how he might help.

"We're not about where you've been, Daniel," he said earnestly. "We're all about where you're going from here."

10

The Walls Come Tumbling Down

My second night in the shelter was a mirror image of the first—long and restless. I'd at least solved the cot rocking problem by wedging a dirty sock under one of the legs—a smelly gift left on my pillow by an admirer, I assumed—but if I was ever going to get some sleep, I needed a dozen more to squelch the chorus of sawing logs filling the room like lovelorn crickets. Somehow the group had managed a consensus on dousing the lights but as I lay there in the dark, wide awake and lonely, feeling trapped inside a bar-less prison, Chucky's words kept coming back again and again. *Where* am *I going from here?*

And I thought about Raeni. Should I have told her how I had landed at the shelter? The whole, unbelievably strange story? *Tomorrow*, I thought. *I will definitely tell her tomorrow when she comes back—if she comes back. She can help me figure out where to go from here. If she truly exists, that is. Stop it! She exists, just as you do.*

I really couldn't imagine how Raeni could help or why I felt so strongly that she could, but what I did know was that when I was with her I felt stronger, like a man ready to stand and fight back. Maybe it was just a macho thing, my testosterone bubbling over whenever her scent swirled around me. Whatever it was, I liked it. It made me want to be Daniel Rayne again, the real Daniel Rayne, the one who had left everything he knew a month ago to come to

Boston in pursuant of his dream—a dream that hadn't died as my identity seemingly had.

But if Raeni was to help me, I needed to be able to help myself. I needed to understand what had happened since arriving in Boston. I needed to believe that it actually did happen the way my memory kept replaying it. But how does one do that? How do you convince yourself that you're right when everything around you says you're wrong? How do you stop the madness from creeping in when you feel its grip tightening? *My name IS Daniel Rayne and I AM NOT going insane!*

It was that last day at Earth Nexus, that's when the walls of my life—the walls of my sanity—came tumbling down. That's what I needed to focus on. If I could sort all that out, sift through the ruins and make some sense of it, I might have a chance at explaining it to Raeni. And if she could get her lovely arms around it, I was willing to bet she could break it down into something simple. Hell, she'd ferreted out my secretary, Irene Doolittle in a blink. Hopefully, the events of that day would be a snap to decipher, provided I didn't describe them like a three year old telling Santa what he wanted for Christmas. *I wanna…um…a…um…a red…um…no, a green…um….*

"Where do you think you're going, buddy?" The lobby guard had said. His name was Bruce and I had been saying hello to him everyday for the past four weeks. He was a single guy who lived at home with his folks and drove a black Mustang Fastback originally built the same year as my Camaro. I had asked him about it my first day at Earth Nexus when I had noticed the picture he kept of it at his guard post. We were both muscle car buffs and quickly become casually friends, at least until that Monday when he grabbed me by the collar as I attempted to piggyback off the person ahead of me at the keycard gate.

"Sorry, Bruce," I said, thinking he was just adhering to policy to protect his job.

I backed up, pulled my identification card from my pocket

and swiped it through the electronic reader. To my surprise, the authorization light remained red as an annoying buzzer erupted, seemingly from every direction. I tried it a second time and then a third. No green light; only more annoying buzzing. By this time there was a line behind me of eager, if not mildly agitated, fellow employees with plastic cups of steaming caffeine, wondering what my problem was. After my forth attempt, Bruce asked me to step over to his desk. Flustered, I did so to sarcastic applause.

"It's probably just scratched," I said as I handed him my ID card.

He looked at the picture on the card and then looked up at me. He nodded, though a little more grimly than I expected.

"It's me," I said, pointing at my picture. "Camaro-man?" That's what he'd been calling me after I'd introduced him to my machine. The look he returned made my mouth go dry. He picked up the phone. I tried to smile as he punched the buttons but all I could muster was a perplexed grin. I then nervously retreated from his gaze, scanning the desk behind him as he whispered inaudibly into the receiver. The desk was empty. No clock, no papers, no picture of a '67 Mustang. My eyes hastily jumped to his nametag. George, the nametag read George. *What the hell?*

Bruce—George—whatever his name was, was off the phone now and looking none-to-happy about the conversation he had just had.

"Where'd you get this?" he asked.

"From you," I said. "You gave it to me on my first day, four weeks ago. Hank Stallworth's new Acquisitions Controller? Although, I know it says Assistant Controller. I got a promotion." I tried to show him on the card where it specified my title, but he pulled it away, apparently suspicious I might try to take it back. "He came down here and got me."

"I gave this to you?" he asked. It didn't seem like a question he really wanted answered. "A month ago?"

"Yeah," I said. His skepticism was obvious and I decided to

try a different tact.

"If you just call Hank Stallworth, I'm sure he'll come down and vouch for me. He runs the accounting department where I work."

"I know that's what the card says," the man I had known as Bruce said. "But I just called up there and they've never heard of you; said no one named Daniel Rayne works here."

"What do you mean?" I said, startled by the panic in my own voice. "I've been working here for a month; said hello to you every day. You drive a black Mustang, same year as my Camaro." I reached for my wallet, anxious to solidify my claim with a picture.

"I drive a Nissan, chump," he replied "Ford's are shit; never owned one, never will."

He then swung around the reception desk, hooked my elbow with a powerful grip and escorted me toward the door, all while I was still digging for the hotrod photo, the bond I thought the two of us shared.

"Now, I don't know how you forged that ID buddy, and I don't really care," he said as he shoved me out. "But if you show up again with another one, I'll put it somewhere a surgeon wouldn't even be able to dig it out. Get my drift?"

Yeah, I got his drift all right. I'd just been laid off, let go, released. No farewell party, no severance package, and by the looks of it, no final paycheck. I was now un-gainfully unemployed, that was the drift. Scratching my head, I walked back to my car, which coincidently, was parked along the street after my now confiscated ID card had failed at the parking garage entrance. *Is this how they cut the cord in the big city? Yes, Virginia, that's how we do it here in Bean Town.*

I drove back to my apartment somewhat numb, my rattled brain already calculating how long I could pay my rent without a job. Not long, it said. As it turns out, it was a moot point.

"Come on, you bastard," I snarled.

When my apartment key slide into the lock without a hitch I

could feel the knot in my head loosen ever so slightly. In another ten minutes, I would feel better. I would go in, grab a beer and an aspirin and regroup, browse through the help-wanted ads in the newspaper I had snagged on the way home. Boston was a huge city with thousands of businesses. There had to be lots of accounting jobs around. I had already decided that I would grab the first one I could to secure the income before looking for something better a few months later. *They knocked you down, Daniel, but they didn't knock you out.*

As I said, my head had begun to clear, that is, until the key refused to turn. After one month of use and over a hundred flawless openings, the damn thing wouldn't budge. Not a pinch of an inch. I jiggled it, wiggled it, pushed it, pulled it, spit on it and wiped it clean with my shirtsleeve and still it wouldn't turn.

"Son of a bitch!" I exhaled. My frustration echoed up and down the hallway, which only heaped embarrassment atop my already fallen ego. *What is going on?*

Unwilling to concede, I kept at it until my wrist tired. I switched hands and as I prepared to attack it southpaw, I heard someone coming down the hall. It was the old guy who'd given me the tour of the place—Mr. Roper, my brain said though I didn't think that was right—along with an elderly woman in a bad wig and a housecoat. *Mrs. Roper?* Maybe, maybe not, but she certainly looked the part.

"Can I help you?" the man asked. There wasn't the slightest hint of recognition on his face. Even though I'd only met him once—it had only been a month ago—he clearly didn't know me. If fact, he was looking at me exactly the way Bruce *slash* George had, uncomprehendingly. *Talk about some bad Déjà vu...*

"Huh, my key doesn't seem to work," I said as I slid it in again and demonstrated that it indeed would not turn.

"Well, it could be that you're standing in front of the wrong apartment."

"I don't think so," I said. I checked the number on the door just to be sure. It read the same 3C as my memory. "I've been living in 3C for the past four weeks and this is 3C." The two of them were staring now, studying me like some carnival sideshow freak.

"Are you high?" Mrs. Roper finally asked.

"No," I replied indignantly. "What makes you think I'm high?"

"Because my husband and I have been living here—in 3C—for the past eight years," Mrs. Roper replied. "And so by the process of elimination, you must be high if you really think *you* live here."

"Or maybe just loony-toon," Mr. Roper added.

I didn't know how to respond, so I didn't. I just stood there, my mouth agape, looking up and down the hallway for something—anything—that would tell me I was in the wrong place. But like a completed Rubik's cube—every color, every door, every strip of molding lined up perfectly with my mind's eye. I had climbed the same stairs, walked the same hallway and stood before this very door a hundred times in the past month. I was sure of it. The only thing different this time was the damn key didn't work. But still, after what had just transpired in the lobby at Earth Nexus, there was a tiny voice whispering in my ear, confirming Mr. Roper's assessment. *You're losing it, dude.*

"Mind if I take a look at that key?" Mr. Roper asked. His hand was extended as if to inform me his request wasn't really a request at all. It was a demand.

Reluctantly, I handed him my key.

After pulling a pair of reading glasses from his shirt pocket, he examined the silver, mushroom shaped piece of metal closely, as if he were diagnosing a potentially cancerous mole. "Same brand as our key, but the cuts look fresh. Probably made this morning." He yanked his glasses off angrily and asked me where I had gotten it—the same question Bruce had asked. I had a feeling I knew where this was headed.

"From you," I replied anyway. *I'm not leaving here without a fight, not this time.*

"From me?" he said. "I've never met you before in my life." He must have sensed I was preparing to hold my ground because he then told his wife, who's name was Doris, to call the cops. "And tell them to hurry."

"Hey, I'm not looking to cause any trouble," I said. "I don't think we need the cops getting involved with this."

"I do," he said.

"Look," I said. "How about you open the apartment door with your key and if you're stuff is in there I promise I'll leave without another word. But if my stuff is in there, you make me a new key and all is forgiven." It was a big bet on one final card, but every bone in my body was telling me this was *my* place, that my life was behind that door. I would be damned if I didn't go in and take a look before I walked willingly out of the place. I had only left a few hours ago so whatever was going on here—whatever joke someone was playing on me—they couldn't have had enough time to clean out my stuff and fill it with someone else's. Not and make it looked lived in. As I searched Mr. Roper's eyes for the truth, the only thing to surface was his reluctance to gamble.

"When the cops get here," he said finally.

For the next fifteen minutes, we remained in the hallway, twitching nervously like two boxers awaiting the opening bell until the law enforcement arrived.

"Hey, Horace," the first police officer said. He was a big, red headed Irishman, pale and heavy with a nightstick already in hand. The second cop was a little guy, almost invisible behind the girth of his partner. "What's the trouble?"

Great, they know each other, I thought. The drawn weapon warned me that Doris may have spiced the situation up a bit when she had made her 911 call. *I was in a brand new suit, for Christ's sake; did I really look like a drugged-out thug to her?*

"There's no trouble, officer," I said. "Just a little misunderstanding."

"He claims he lives here, Marty," Horace said. "In my apartment, of all places."

"Our apartment," Doris added.

Horace threw her a scowl.

"I've already suggested that we go inside," I said. "It'll allow me the opportunity to prove I'm not some bozo on crack." I too was frowning at Doris now, lured by her husband's example.

"Sounds reasonable," Officer Marty said. "That ok with you, Horace?"

Horace nodded his approval, begrudgingly.

"And you, Doris?"

"Well," she said sheepishly. "The place is really a mess. I normally clean on Tuesday you see, so...."

Horace cut her off. "No one cares what it looks like, Doris. How many times do we have to go through that?"

I wasn't sure if Horace was more aggravated with his wife or with my insistence at exploring the apartment, but as he turned the key and unlocked the portal to my life, I was confident he was about to swallow his anger, along with his pride.

With a determined sigh, he then led us inside.

Doris had been right. It was a mess. But it was *their* mess, as in, not mine. Everything I remembered—the furniture, the wall hangings, even the paint color on the walls—was different; completely and utterly mind-collapsing different. I couldn't believe my eyes. *Am I really losing it?*

Before any of them could stop me, I dashed into the bedroom. The sheets were rumbled and the pillows looked like soiled, half-empty sacks of potatoes. Clothes littered an adjacent, winged-back chair—boxer shorts and a faded Hawaiian style shirt, a deflated housecoat and a grimy red sweatshirt. These were old person's clothes, Horace and Doris's clothes. *Geez, these two are slobs.*

I whipped open the closet. More housecoats and multi-colored shirts and shoes covered with more dust than the dessert with sand. That's when I lost it; tossed into a walking blackout, I believe the term would be. I can't say how long it lasted, but when I woke up, I was sitting in the passenger seat of my Camaro, my legs hanging out the open door as I handed my license and registration over to a sweaty and seriously pissed-off Officer Marty. I could hear the shrill of Doris' overexcited voice in the background and Horace attempting to calm her down. Peering around the eclipsing police officer, I spotted her looming in the apartment building entrance, waving her fist like a civil rights marcher while her husband held her back.

"They should lock you up and throw away the key," she screamed. "You're a maniac, a lunatic!"

"Marty's taking care of it, dear," Horace told her. "Now, let's go clean up. The sooner we do that, the sooner we can forget all about it."

She was crying now, the fight in her evaporating as Horace led her inside.

"Did you see what he did to our home?" she sobbed. "It looks like a cyclone hit it. And my mother's dishes," she gasped. "Oh my god, my poor mother's dishes."

"Destruction of private property is a serious offense, pal," Officer Marty's partner said while Officer Marty walked to their squad car with my identification. "You're lucky the Forrests are not pressing charges."

Horace and Doris Forrest? This had to be some kind of joke. Completely confused, I just looked at the officer and sighed, too apathetic at this point to check his nametag. Surely, I was on Candid Camera or being punked by Ashton Kutcher. A hapless participant of *Girls Behaving Badly*, perhaps? I scanned the horizon, praying I'd spy a camera crew hidden in the bushes or behind a fence. All I spotted was Officer Marty returning and the seriousness tightening in his jaw. *Why do I already know what he's going to say?*

"This license is a fake," he said, jutting the laminated card into my face. "And so is this registration. You've got some explaining to do, pal. So let's start with something simple. Where'd you get them?"

There was that question again. For the third time in the matter of a few hours, my identity was being questioned. First by a memory-challenged security guard whom I'd talked to at least two dozen times before today; then by a two-faced landlord who'd escorted me into the apartment that he now claimed wasn't mine; and now by Officers Laurel and Hardy, whom I'd never met before but appeared hell-bent on ensuring I wouldn't soon forget them. It was like the whole world had suddenly developed Alzheimer's except me. Mentally exhausted, I answered the officer's question without thinking.

"The DMV, like everybody else," I said.

"Don't get smart with us, mister," the little cop said. He puffed out his chest, mimicking his much larger partner in a lame attempt to intimidate me. I was too bewildered to react, but I did appreciate that he had called me mister.

"That's where I got it, I swear," I shrugged.

Though they clearly weren't buying what I was selling, they didn't appear very sure about what to do with me either. *A moment of reflection*, I thought as Officer Marty mopped the sweat from his brow with a handkerchief pulled from his pocket, contemplating my fate no doubt, as his partner played restlessly with the handcuffs clipped to his belt.

A sudden blast from their car radio interrupted our quiet time. There was a 2-11 in progress, the woman's steady voice was calling for all available backup to proceed immediately to 1824 South Main. Potentially armed and dangerous, I thought I heard her say.

"Seems to be your lucky day, pal," Officer Marty said before hustling back to the squad car. Surprisingly, he moved quickly for a big man and then, just before he ducked in behind the wheel, he waved my papers in the air and offered a friendly piece of advice. "Don't let me catch you with another bogus ID, pal. I'll lock you up so fast it'll make your head swim."

I watched them peel away, the smell of burning rubber adding to the dull ache mounting in my *already* swimming head. *Yeah, right, my lucky day.*

My life as I knew it—as I *thought* I had known it—was slipping from my grasp. Everything I owned was in the apartment building in front of me; my clothes, my laptop, my personal papers—birth certificate, bank statements, the title to my Camaro. It was all in there somewhere, but it may as well have been lying on the bottom of the ocean for all the good it did me. Horace and Doris would have the cops here again in a flash if I so much as stepped near the place. And even if I could get inside, what would I do then? Search every apartment in the whole goddamn building? There had to be fifteen apartments on each of the forty floors, maybe more. I was no cat burglar. Hell, they'd nab me for breaking and entering before I could reach apartment 1B.

I felt tired, beat-up, like I had been through a ten round bout with George Foreman. I needed a breather, a chance to rethink and regroup. With my body pleading for a place to lie down and rest, I slid over into the driver's seat, fired up the engine and drove off in search of a motel. Sure, I'd taken another shot, but I wasn't out yet. Though I could sense my sanity was on the verge of a TKO—the victim of the three knockdown rule—my will still had its legs. I had only tasted the canvas twice and there was no way I was going down a third time. No way in hell!

11

A Helping Hand

It's funny, but merely thinking about riding in a car makes me drowsy when I'm tired, the soothing rhythmic hum of the purring engine and the tires rolling along the pavement. In thought, I was cruising down Route 1, headed back toward Rhode Island and the stretch of motels that I remembered passing during my original move to Boston a month prior. *Cheap hotels*, I hoped. My job was lost, my apartment stolen by a geriatric couple who considered me one of America's Most Wanted, but I still had my wheels and that alone gave me hope. I must have fallen asleep at that moment of recollection, and now, waking with that same feeling of hope in the shadows of the homeless shelter *bunkhouse*, I heard the distant squeak of metal on metal, the echo of filing cabinet drawers being opened and closed. Having worked in an accountant's office for years, I knew the clatter well and it only took me a few seconds in the darkness to determine its source—the business office just down the hall. My first thought was it might be Raeni, returning to gather the files she had left behind. It seemed awfully late for such an undertaking, but then the past few days had been full of unpredictable events so why should tonight be any different? With my mind revving—way beyond any chance of returning to sleep—I got up and went to investigate, anxious to see my one friend again.

As I walked barefoot down the hall, I saw a faint light dancing in the windows of the business office. *A flashlight*, I thought. *Was the power out again?* Suddenly realizing that it might not be Raeni at all, I cautiously approached the door and put my ear to the smoked glass. There was definitely someone in there shuffling through papers. Every accountant knows that leaves-in-the-wind sound, we spend our life preparing forms and organizing reports and I was not different. Uncertain about my next move, I stood listening until the sound stopped and the light went out. *Nice going, Sherlock. They probably heard your flat feet slapping the linoleum all the way up the hall.*

I leaned into the door, pressing my ear harder against the glass, wary that I might break it if I wasn't careful. But just like the Night before Christmas, not a creature was stirring, not even a mouse. Had they gone? Exited through another door perhaps? Was there another door? I straightened up and took a quick glance down either end of the hallway. All was quiet. *Go back to bed, Daniel.*

Then, the doorknob began to turn—very, very slowly.

I shouldn't be here, I thought, but there was no time to run back to my cot and disappear under the blanket. Whoever it was, I was about to introduce myself, whether they liked it or not.

As the door inched open, a slideshow of faces flashed before my imagining eyes. First, it was Raeni, her smile blooming like a dream; then, a disapproving Charles Woodland, followed by an even angrier Louis Vinson. Finally, it was the startled face of the elderly reception lady who filled in for Vincent on occasion and whose name I couldn't remember. None of them would be expecting to see me standing there in shorts and a t-shirt. Recalling their concerns following the lonesome-for-her-father, little-girl-lost fiasco, there would certainly be some hard questions to answer. By the time I concluded that this hadn't been such a good idea, a real face was already emerging from the darkness—a nasty face—the face of Louis Vinson's burly limo driver.

"Bad move, dude," he said. I readily agreed as he grabbed my t-shirt with one hand and pulled me into the office before closing the door. There wasn't much light, but it was still easy to see that neither of us was happy to see the other.

I yanked at his hand, attempting to unhook him, but his determined grip was too tight. He was strong, of that I was certain. But how smart was he?

"You woke up half the place with your racket in here," I said. The rest of my bunkmates were still logging z's, but I was hoping my lie might encourage him to let go and heed a hasty escape. Instead, he calmly set down the folders he held in his other hand before latching onto the other, unwrinkled side of my t-shirt.

"*Really* bad move," he repeated, taking special care to emphasis the first word.

"I walk in my sleep, what can say," I said, trying to breathe some levity into what was shaping up into a life-threatening situation. "What are you looking for, anyway?"

"None of your damn business, you fucking puke," he replied. His knuckles were digging into my throat, cutting back my air supply, just as my wiggling toes achieved separation from the floor. This guy didn't need to be smart, he was *that* strong.

"Well, that's all the answer I need," I said, my words garbled by my nearly crushed larynx. I was looking down at him now, a foot or more off the ground, helpless as a kite in a tree. I jerked and flailed, thinking my weight might wear him down but it only seemed to make him more determined.

"That's it," he whispered devilishly. "I like it when you fight."

I wasn't breathing anymore. It was like my mouth had been stuffed with that dirty sock I'd found on my pillow. There wasn't a speck of air anywhere and that's when the panic hit and I began to kick with both feet. I may have only been half-conscious at that point, but I knew I had nailed him at least once in the crotch. But all he did was laugh. *Why doesn't he go down?*

The dim light was fading into nothingness when I heard a

loud crack followed by a dull thud. I was barely conscious enough to comprehend that the thud had been me hitting the floor, but that was all. It wasn't until I woke up later in my cot, my head bandaged and throbbing, that I learned I wasn't dead.

"Raeni?" I asked as I struggled to clear my vision.

"It's Charles," the shelter's Executive Director replied. "Charles Woodland. You're at the Kingston Street Shelter and you're going to be fine; a little groggy for a day or two, but fine."

The shelter? I thought. Then, unfortunately, my current fate came hurdling back to earth. *Oh, yeah, I'm homeless and living in a shelter.*

I tried to sit up but the room began to spin. And damn, my head hurt. Collapsing back onto my cot, I asked Charles what had happened.

"I'm not sure, exactly," Charles said. "Hillary found you slumped on the floor in the office when she arrived this morning. There was a puddle of blood in the middle of the floor but you didn't have a scratch, only a nasty bump on the head. Frightened her so bad she almost swallowed her false teeth." He chuckled mildly. He was trying to be funny, to loosen the knot in my head, but at the same time, I could tell he wasn't laughing inside. I may have been woozy but I could see in his eyes that Charles Woodland knew more than he was telling.

"If it wasn't my blood," I said, pressing a tentative finger gingerly against my bruise, "then, whose was it?"

"I don't know," Charles replied. "I thought maybe you could tell me that."

The truth was I knew who it was and I didn't know who it was. I mean, I had no doubt it was the limo driver who'd delivered that surly Vinson guy yesterday, but I didn't know his name. And I didn't know who Vinson was either. The night's event seemed clear and I did have a vicious souvenir commemorating my experience. And there was blood. *Don't forget the blood,* Daniel. Chucky had confirmed it. So why then did I hesitate to answer his question? Because in the past four days my memory had been stumbling like a drunken celebrity and I wasn't sure I could trust my recollection any more than a rooster could trust a fox. No, I decided I best keep this one to myself, at least until I found a way to be liberated from the henhouse.

"I have no idea," I said. "I couldn't sleep and had gotten up to stretch my legs when I heard a noise in the business office. The door was unlocked so I went inside to see who it was. I thought it was probably you or Hillary burning the midnight oil. You folks do work too hard around here." This time I chuckled. I was sucking up because I wanted him to buy my story, to believe it was exactly what had happened; to believe me without a doubt until I could truly believe the real story myself.

"Find something you love to do and you'll never work another day in your life," Charles replied with a smile. "I'm lucky. I did."

I believed him, but I wasn't ready to trust him. "All I remember is opening the door and a flash of light. Next thing I knew I was waking up right here with you."

"That came from the whack on the head," Charles said. "The flash of light, I mean. My guess is we had a scavenger, one of the clients foraging for money. Most of them know that Hillary keeps a petty cash box locked in her desk, which, by the way, was still locked when she checked it after calling me about you."

I looked at him, puzzled.

"We allow the clients five dollars a week for miscellaneous needs like candy or batteries for a radio. If we gave them any more than that, they would be out buying liquor. They get it from Hillary, so I suspect they have seen the cash box a time or two. There's not much in there at any one time but still it's a bit of a temptation, now that I think about it."

"It might be a good time to tighten up that internal control," I said, sounding like an auditor. It wasn't lost on Chucky.

"Have you done some accounting work in your travels?" he

asked.

"A little," I said. *At least, my memory says I have.*

"I only ask because we're always short handed in the office. Little non-profits like us can't offer salaries like the private sector so experienced help is hard to come by. I could use a balanced ledger man if you're interested?" He laughed at his play on words before making me an offer I was in no position to refuse. "Just a part-time thing, until you get back on your feet. How does ten to fifteen hours a week at nine dollars an hour sound?"

He certainly was more trusting that I was. Didn't he want a resume or a list of references? Thankfully, it appeared that he didn't, because at the moment I had no way of producing any. As I laid there assessing his motive, I concluded that a man like Charles Woodland didn't have one. He was genuinely trying to help me. Reaching up to shake his hand, I told him I would start working just as soon as I could stand up without falling right back down.

"Which I'm sure will be in no time at all," he said. As he left, I could sense that somehow I had just loosened one of the knots in his head.

I rolled onto my side, trying to get comfortable while wondering if Raeni was working today. I had thought about asking Chucky but reconsidered, wary that mentioning her while we discussed my midnight escapade might lead him down a misguided path. Working in the office would certainly provide me more face time with her and as I lay there relishing the thought I felt something poking me in the ribs. Curious, I reached under the worn towel I used as a bed sheet and discovered two file folders. I pulled them out, carefully concealing them under my blanket while I read the blood splattered labels. *Daniel Rayne* and *Felix Ostrander.*

Who is Felix Ostrander? And who the hell put these files in my cot?

12

Untangling On the Web

It felt good to be working again. Like a man with a future. Even though my past had vanished before my eyes, I hadn't forgotten how to make a journal entry and for that I was grateful. So was the shelter's Executive Director, Charles Woodland. He started me off slow, handing me several bank statements to reconcile while I recuperated from my near death experience that now, a day later, was still an unsolved mystery. No one was talking about it. Not Chucky, not Hillary, not even Vincent, the unofficial shelter bellhop whom I had come to know as quite the chatterbox after he had his mid-morning espresso. Maybe that's the way life was in the shelter. People came and went; events occurred and faded like passing rain showers. As Charles had said, "It's not about where you've been, it's about where you're going." Was it pointless to think about the past, to reconstruct one's steps in search of resolution? For me it wasn't—it was crucial—because the past held the key *to my future*. But here at this shelter, where there were always fresh mouths to feed, there wasn't time for reflection. And for that reason, I concluded, no one had said a word about Raeni's noticeable absence. No one, that is, except me.

"I would be happy to call her for you, Daniel," Hillary offered. "But she didn't leave a home phone number. I double-checked her file and that box is blank."

I was sitting at a desk behind Hillary in the business office, wrestling with yet another snarled bank statement. It was six months old and there was a line behind it a year long awaiting my attention. The shelter had a serious cash flow problem—as in not enough money to pay their employees or their utility bills. As I asked Hillary if she had tried directory assistance, I pondered the possibility that Raeni had quit to focus on her better paying telemarketing career.

"I seem to recall her telling me that she didn't have a phone," Hillary said.

"Not even a cell phone?" I asked

"Nope," she replied.

Then, Vincent appeared in the office needing her assistance. The two left arguing over the best room to place a young mother who had just arrived with her infant son.

No phone? I thought. That would certainly make it difficult to conduct telemarketing calls. Either Raeni had a phone and didn't want Charles or Hillary calling her, or she lied to me about her job outside the shelter. But why would she make up something like that? Was she trying to impress me as a telemarketer? That made no sense. Everyone hates telemarketers, except maybe other telemarketers. No, there had to be another reason. I only wished she would come back to work so I could ask her.

Raeni's sudden disappearance was just another puzzle joining the others, the scatter pieces to which were rapidly overwhelming my brain. Ever since I'd found those two files in my cot—the very ones the unknown man who'd tried to choke the unknown life out of me was trying to steal—the name Felix Ostrander had been haunting my thoughts as well. Who was Felix Ostrander? How were we connected? I had no idea. I had never heard of him before. But evidently, the limo-driver-by-day-murderous-brut-by-night psychopath had. And being that he had driven Louis Vinson to the shelter, would it be a wrong assumption to say that Vinson also knew who Ostrander was? And therefore, that Vinson knew who *I* was?

As a child, I enjoyed assembling puzzles, especially the big ones with a thousand or more parts. I loved sifting through the box full of pieces, searching for the corners and sections of the most colorful object in the picture. It was a fun challenge, one I'm not sure I could have tackled if not for the box cover. It provided a glimpse of the final solution, something I currently didn't have with the puzzle that was now my life. I didn't have anything to show me how the pieces ultimately fit together. But with any difficult jigsaw, the first step is to find a few adjoining pieces and build from there. With Felix Ostrander and Louis Vinson, I finally felt like I had two.

When Hillary returned, I went to work on my first order of business—getting access to a computer and beyond that, the World Wide Web.

"Straightening out these bank statements is proving to be a bigger chore than I thought," I said to Hillary. "There's some great software available that would cut my time in half, if I could get my hands on a copy."

"Oh, we really don't have the money for that sort of thing," she replied.

"It's shareware—free. All I have to do is download it off the internet."

"Really? You can get it for free?" she asked, disbelievingly. "Can you get me something to help organize our client list?"

"Sure," I said eagerly.

"That would be great. Our records are in such a mess. Maybe Charles would even let you help me with it. I'm all thumbs when it comes to computers."

Exactly what I was hoping for, I thought as I smiled and nodded.

As it turns out, I wasn't the only client assisting with shelter operations. My bean-slurping buddy, Dexter, was the strictly unofficial, resident computer maintenance geek in charge of setting up new user accounts on the old, but adequate office network. After Charles had given his approval, Dexter silently set me up with a dusty desktop model he rummaged from a storage closet. It was big and slow, with just enough horsepower to Google, which I spent the rest of the day doing after I had downloaded a free financial software program to toggle in case anyone came spying over my shoulder.

First, I went digging for Felix Ostrander. His file provided me little more than his name—no address, no emergency contact, no former employers—so I was pretty much starting from scratch. After an hour and a dozen alternate spellings, I found myself still scratching my head, finding only two viable Felix Ostrander's; one, a Dutch cross country skier who'd competed in the 1928 Olympics in St. Moritz, Switzerland; and the other, an eight year old boy with a MySpace site dedicated to the musings of Britney Spears. I instantly ruled out the kid, and after calculating that the skier would now be over one hundred years of age, I concluded that he wasn't *my* Felix either. Fortunately, I had a bit more luck with the name Louis Vinson.

As soon as I hit the enter key, my face lit up like a husband who had just caught his wife in bed with another man. There, in the middle of the screen was a picture of the Black Knight himself, looking as bold and arrogant as he had the day he visited the shelter. According to The Wall Street Journal's website, Louis Vinson was the original founder and CEO of the Earth Nexus Corporation, my former employer. That's when I remembered where I'd seen his name before—on my paycheck.

13

David Wants to Be Goliath

The rectangular room was barren grey with no pictures on the walls, no trimmings on the windows. The lights were very bright, almost too bright, and the fact that it had windows at all seemed like a contradiction to the repugnance it inspired. With a tremendous view of Manhattan, and even the distant Central Park on a clear day, it felt more like a dungeon or an underground bunker—uncomfortable chairs as hard as rocks and stifling hot air that reeked of anxious body odor. *Thunderdome*, that's what some called it. *Two men enter. One man leaves.* Only in this particular arena, on this particular day, many men and women had entered, amassing along both sides of an elongated conference table made of reddish-brown mahogany. Several hours in, no one had left bruised, bloodied or otherwise, but it was early yet. Oarsmen— that's how they referred to themselves, the muscle to row the boat. *Don't think, row.* Adaptively interchangeable and categorically replaceable, they spoke when spoken to, bailed when told to bail. That was how they sailed at Earth Nexus under their master commander, Louis Vinson, and mutineers were routinely, and often times ceremoniously, thrown overboard.

"I'd like you all to humor me for a minute or two," Vinson said, his characteristically wide grin emitting an undercurrent of charm and guile. "Everyone stand up and a take a look around the table. Look at the person next to you and the one across from you. Examine them, study them and make a snap judgment and move on to the next. Make it quick, now. It's important that you cover everyone."

Vinson remained seated, observing intently, clearly enjoying the tension he had just injected into the atmosphere of the meeting. His minions, as *he* referred to his immediate staff, did as they were told, hesitantly jumping from face to face—suit to suit—some puzzled by the exercise, others cautiously amused. This was nothing new, nothing surprising, but they sensed perhaps the resulting edict might be.

"I'll give you all a clue," Vinson said after a few long, bristly minutes. "You're looking for skeptics, doubters, the nonbelievers who would sabotage this deal with the mere weakness of their spine." His grin was gone now, replaced by a twisted mask of contempt.

The mood in the room darkened. The master commander was probing for mutineers.

Several more uneasy minutes passed. The room was quiet like the bottom of the sea, murky and breathless.

"Time's up," Vinson said. "Now, everyone who thinks this deal is a brilliant move go to this side of the table." He was pointing to his right—his preferred side—the side of the room that captured a small token of sunlight. "And everyone who thinks it's a mistake, go to that side of the table."

As if they were children playing musical chairs, the entire room hustled to one side of the room, anticipating an abrupt end to the marching song playing in their heads. Everyone that is, except one man—John Oliver, the acting Acquisitions Controller.

"I believe its suicide," Oliver said, frankly. He had sat back down—one against many—conspicuous as he fiddled with a pencil. "This deal would quickly swallow every penny we've got and a few we don't, which would put every other acquisition we're pursuing in the toilet. In my opinion, the price they're asking is way out of our reach. Now, maybe in a year or two, after we've built up sufficient capital..." He stopped there, knowing he had said enough to light Vinson's fuse.

John Oliver had been working at Earth Nexus for over ten years, starting out in the then one room back office as the fledgling company's senior accountant, internal auditor, computer systems analyst, chief cook and bottle washer. A tall, thin man, with short, bristle brush hair and a mustache that he often picked at nervously, Oliver filled in wherever he was needed, currently taking an empty corner office recently vacated by "someone who might cause the ship to take on water," as Vinson had phrased it. Back in the early years the two had been best friends, working long hours side by side to build Earth Nexus into what it was today, a David in the global internet services marketplace hell bent on not only slaying the existing giants, but becoming the world's next Goliath. The two men had survived many trips to *Thunderdome*, along with several more personal and private clashes. Both men had deep battle scars now, Vinson with an even deeper desire to end a resentful relationship that had one too many ghosts hiding below deck to make abandonment easy.

"Suicide?" Vinson asked, mockingly. "A bit strong in the phrasing, don't you think, John?"

"No, I think it's right on the money," Oliver replied. "Yahoo isn't worth two hundred and fifty billion dollars. That price is a chimera, pie in the sky. They know nobody in their right mind is going to fork out a quarter of a trillion for a company with a net book value of ten billion. But with Google venturing into Microsoft's territory with its launch of a spreadsheet application, a partnership with Adobe Systems and the purchase of the video sharing website YouTube, they thought the timing might be ripe to entice Bill Gates to take the hook and pony up some serious dough if he wants to keep pace. But, as we all know, Bill isn't biting. That should tell *us* something."

"Who said anything about meeting their price?" Vinson said,

his returning grin curving mischievously. "Or sitting down with those yahoos anyway?" He then laughed, relishing his wit like a diva in front of a mirror. The crowded side of the table was quick to join him.

John Oliver already knew the answer to his next question, but he felt compelled to ask it anyway. "A takeover bid?"

"Why not?" Vinson asked.

"I suppose it's possible," Oliver replied. His gaze wandered as his mind buzzed with mathematical computations. "The current market price of a share of Yahoo stock is around twenty-five, with outstanding shares of around one point four billion. To take majority interest, we would need to buy up half of that—seven hundred millions shares, give or take—at a premium of say…a buck above market. So, to put it in a ballpark, my guess is we're looking at a price tag of just under twenty billion dollars, including the normal expenses, etc. etc."

"Exactly what I figured," Vinson said. "I'm glad to see the cerebral calculator's still functioning, John. It took a football team of analysts a week to give me the same number you just produced in ten seconds." Vinson's mood was bordering on jovial, a rare occurrence on occasions such as these.

"I have to kick it once in a while, like an old furnace, but let's not go there," Oliver said, his own stoic mood lifting barely an inch off the ground. *Stay focused,* he told himself. *Don't let Louis swing the conversation away from the matter at hand.* It was one of Vinson's oldest tactics to sway or silence the opposing voice with an unexpected compliment. Oliver knew enough to steer clear so as not to get hung up in its wash.

"I think we can raise twenty billion, but the hurdle is going to be amassing enough willing sellers. Forty five percent—nearly half—of Yahoo stock is held by institutions or mutual funds. If I recall my reading correctly, there are over six hundred of them and they're not as easy to entice as your average blue collar investor."

"So, we go after the middle class," Vinson said. "We've done it before. We just appeal to their sense of greed. And if that doesn't do the trick, we'll go to work on their other five senses. It's amazing what grandma will do with a knitting needle in her eye." He erupted once again in laughter, his raucous voice echoing off the ceiling like claps of thunder.

John Oliver knew his former best friend wasn't joking. The awkward looks on the faces of Vinson's minions proclaimed he wasn't the only one.

With his theatrics out of the way, Vinson invited everyone to return to their original seats. There was one minor item he needed to add to the agenda before they adjourned, he told them, adding that it would only take a few minutes. As the last person pulled their chair into the table, Vinson stood up and began to pace around the room.

"Elizabeth," he said, referring to the pretty blond woman sitting next to John Oliver. "I'm curious, as I'm sure everyone here in the room is, as to what soured the folks at iAuctionHouse. Correct me if I'm wrong, but I understand they flatly refused our very generous offer."

"That's correct," Elizabeth replied. "But they gave me no explanation as to why."

Elizabeth Hart had been working at Earth Nexus for nearly six months, starting as an acquisitions analyst within weeks of earning her Harvard MBA. She was in her mid twenties, freshly attractive and worked as hard, if not harder, than any of her male colleagues in a field dominated by testosterone. She dressed conservatively in smart suits with knee length skirts, and had a girlish demeanor that put people at ease, doing her best to downplay the curves God had given her. With what Vinson saw as the perfect combination of brain and body, she had everything she needed to become an empress at Earth Nexus, to catapult to one of the coveted top rungs just beneath his. Everything, that is, but the desire to be beneath Vinson the way *he* wanted her—in the missionary position, not to mention a few others. She had rebuked his advances for the umpteenth time several days ago and ever since had the feeling it would the last, but not for the reason she hoped.

"No explanation?" He asked, quizzically. "That seems unusual."

Elizabeth shifted in her seat. *Did Vinson know the real reason?* She asked herself. *He couldn't possibly*, she reasoned. She had only talked to the representative of the budding challenger to eBay, the online auction house and web-based storefront yesterday morning, and hadn't mentioned it to a soul. *But then, how did he know they turned down our offer?* No, Vinson was just testing her, shooting in the dark. He didn't know that she had interrupted the deal, she decided. *Let him trawl, his cursed net will come up empty.*

"Well, I think they had issue with our refusal to take ownership of their existing contracted inventory." Elizabeth said, fabricating the best explanation she could think of on the spot. "It would cost them a fortune to return it all, not to mention the law suits that would follow."

"That doesn't make any sense," Vinson said. He was standing behind her now, posturing like a good cop that everyone in the room knew was about to turn bad. "I seem to recall that during our preliminary meetings, the owners requested that we allow them to fulfill their existing contracts before we took ownership. Is that the way you remember it, John?"

John nodded solemnly in agreement. He knew what Vinson was up to and he wanted no part of it. In their early days together, Oliver and Vinson would eat their lunch outside, sometimes walking a mile to a park just to escape the sounds of the city for a while. John would always have a turkey sandwich wrapped in aluminum foil that Louis would routinely commandeer on hot, sunny days after their meal was finished. He would place the foil on the ground, allow it to heat and then place a worm, an ant or any other small creature he could find onto it. It never got hot enough to kill the poor thing, but there was no mistaking that it was painful. Now, as John watched Vinson slowly walk around the table, he could see that familiar expression of fascination and satisfaction on his face, the look of pure enjoyment Vinson got from watching another living thing squirm.

"Well, I'd be happy to call them for clarification," Elizabeth said, her voice quivering slightly. Her perfect cheeks were beginning to turn red as she crossed her legs, closing her body to the room that was now watching as captivated, but uncomfortable spectators.

"That might be a good idea," Vinson said. "Why don't you do that now, on the speakerphone?"

Elizabeth steeled a look at Vinson before turning her gaze to the conference phone situated in the middle of the table. *Would the rep at iAuctionHouse be so brazen as to admit that he nixed the deal because I wouldn't sleep with him? Could he be that cold and heartless to say that in front of my boss, who I damn well know would have expected me to do just that? Maybe he'd be out and I could just leave a message to call me back. That* would *buy me some time.* Hesitantly, Elizabeth switched on the speaker and dialed the number. The resulting rings reverberated throughout the otherwise quiet room, obnoxiously startling, and almost loud enough to drown out the thumping beat of her hastened heart. *Please be his answering machine.*

As the fourth ring past and then a fifth and a sixth, Elizabeth felt her pulse calming. *He's not there. Thank God!* She could almost hear the recorded greeting in her head—she had heard it so many times in the past week as she attempted to secure the deal. The man was never in his office, she had concluded. More than likely, he was in a cheap motel somewhere, consummating a tit-for-tat trade with some panty-less, middle management tart.

To achieve vertical mobility, a woman must first accept horizontal accessibility. *That was the secret dictum at Earth Nexus,* Elizabeth thought angrily. The words had never been uttered, never floated to the surface, but the underlying current was there. She could see it in many of the men's eyes—in Louis Vinson's eyes. After her first week on the job, she had vowed never to play their game, but as she sat quietly, praying to God for this one small favor, she felt as though she was being violated at that very moment, forced into humiliating submission. Striped naked of her dignity and her pride, psychologically raped.

"Gary West speaking," the speaker-emitted voice said.

"Mr. West, how are you, sir? Louis Vinson here."

"I'm great, Louis. How about yourself?"

"Never better, although my back has been acting up a bit. Too much golf, I think. I haven't seen you at the club lately, been getting out on the course much?"

"No, unfortunately, work has been keeping me pretty busy this month. But I don't have to tell you about that, nobody works harder than you, Louis."

"Save the compliments for another time, Gary. You're embarrassing me in front of my staff."

You're loving every minute of it, you egotistical bastard, Elizabeth thought. Her palms were sweating, her chest was pounding. Sitting on the edge of her seat, she just wished he would get it over with. Let her leave peacefully with what little respect she had left.

What Elizabeth didn't know, was that Louis Vinson had told Gary West to expect his call and to let it ring awhile before answering. She also didn't know that Vinson had already reassigned the deal to another of his minions—a former MTV video vixen he felt had "huge potential" in the acquisitions field. (Apparently his intuition had been correct for within a day, not only did the young woman convince Mr. West to come back to the table and sign, she also managed to suck another two hundred grand out of him.)

Vinson and West's chummy banter went on for what seemed like hours to Elizabeth and surprisingly, talk of the deal she had thought was lost never came up. Finally, after Vinson hung up, grinning knowingly at her as he did, she realized what John Oliver already knew, that the call had been nothing more than a worm on hot tin foil.

"I think that's enough for this morning," Vinson then said. "Enjoy lunch, everyone."

People stood and stretched, exhaled a few sighs and headed toward the door.

"Oh, just one more thing before you leave," Vinson said. "Elizabeth, you're fired."

14

The Three Knockdown Rule

I now knew who Louis Vinson was. What I didn't know was why he sent his over-muscled ape to snatch my file, along with Felix Ostrander's file, who ever he was. And what was the real reason Vinson himself had come to the shelter, picking me out of the crowd with what I could swear was a hint of pleasure? These were questions without answers, but the three of us we're now irreversibly connected—Vinson, Ostrander and me—and the little voice inside me was chirping, coaxing me into digging deeper. Ever since I had stepped foot into the homeless shelter, beaten down and virtually penniless, I had been struggling for a sense of direction. Unwittingly, my close encounter of the deadly kind had given me one. Being that it was my *only* one, I determinedly decided to follow it.

With my new role as business office accountant and catchall flunky, I had access to every filing cabinet in the building. There were lots of them scattered about the place. A dozen in the business office, another dozen lining two walls of Charles Woodland's office and at least two dozen more crammed into a walk-in storage closet just off the Roosevelt Room. If there was any more information to be found here regarding Felix Ostrander or Louis Vinson, it was going to take a while to find it. As soon as Hillary left to take a cigarette break, I decided to start with the easy ones first, the cabinets standing like soldiers right next to my desk. *Thank God, smoking is prohibited indoors.*

I felt like a cat burglar as I fingered through the manila folders, jammed so tightly into the drawers I tore up every cuticle on my right hand prying them apart to get a glimpse at the labels. The first bunch appeared to be current clients as I recognized many of the names of my bunkmates. Presumably, this is where the ape had come looking for bananas, lifting the two files that were later deposited into my cot by my still unknown rescuer. *No point in looking there.* Moving down a drawer, I was just getting started when I heard the doorknob turn, noticing the name "Raeni" on the first center-label folder out of the corner of my Hillary-alerted eye. It wasn't the treasure I come searching for, but it twinkled just the same. *Why hadn't I thought of this before?*

The door began to open, but then abruptly stopped. Hillary was talking with someone—something about her daughter's car and a flat tire—and she sounded annoyed. All I could see was her hand on the knob. *How much time have I got?* Concluding that I had a few more seconds, I reached for Raeni's file and pulled it free after three exasperating tugs. Then, I quickly returned to my desk, sliding the "borrowed" file beneath the bank papers I had been working on just as Hillary walked in.

"I've got to run out and rescue my daughter," she said. "But I should be back in time to help you sort through that stack of canceled checks."

"No problem," I said. "I'll hold down the fort while you're gone."

"Thanks, Daniel," she replied. After grabbing her purse and taking one final sip of coffee, she hurried out the door.

No sooner had the latch clicked shut than I was eagerly perusing Raeni's file for a phone number and address. Scanning her employment form, I found what Hillary had already told me—there was no phone number listed. But there *was* an address—a very close address—one within the reach of a man with limited resources such as myself.

My urge was to jump in my Camaro and make a beeline to her door. *Would she welcome the sight me?* I was confident she would, after all, we had gotten along very well during the brief time we had spent together. But it had been brief, and she had disappeared right out from under my nose without as much as a goodbye. So, should I stay or should I go? *Debatable. Very debatable.*

Then, Charles Woodland walked in, forcing my internal quarrel into another room like bothersome siblings.

"Daniel," he said, standing in front of my desk. "I need you to go down the street and pickup a COD at the post office. It's an envelope with event notice proofs for next month's fundraiser. I'd go myself but I'm up to my eyeballs in board members and they really want to take a look at those flyers before we give the printer the go ahead. You wouldn't mind, would you?"

Well, I am wrestling with something rather important at the moment—how to approach the only friend I've got, I thought.

"It's a beautiful day for a walk," Charles said, enticingly.

"Ok," I said. *The fresh air will do you good.*

"I can't tell you how much I appreciate it." He reached into his pocket. "Here, take this debit card to pay for the package. It shouldn't be any more than five or six dollars. The clerk there knows me, his name is Howard. He won't hassle you about the card, but if by some chance he's not there and whoever is gives you trouble, have them give me a call." He then handed me a business card with the shelter phone number on it to go along with the debit card. "When you get back, bring it right into my office. Don't even bother to knock." He turned and left, seemingly relieved that he could now check that chore off his internal, multi-paged list.

As I walked leisurely down the street, the summer sun soaking my skin like a warm bath, I recalled my last experience with plastic money—a scandalous encounter with a sex-starved motel clerk.

After receiving the less-than-cordial police escort out of my apartment building—the one I had *thought* was mine—I decided to hide out in a cheap motel until the heat was off, as they say. I may have been overreacting; I had no reason to think I was being hunted by the authorities, but with all that had happened that day—losing my job, my home, *my very identity*—I had no idea what to think. Disappearing for a few days seemed like a good idea. Play a little rope-a-dope like Mohammad Ali used to while I got my strength *and* my sanity back. It would keep me out of harms way, allow me to duck what I now feared the most—a third knockdown. I was already staggering, nearly out on my feet, and one more shot would surely put me down for the count. *Eight…nine…ten, you're out! The fight's over!*

The rural roads from Boston to Providence were littered with mini-plazas, gas stations, gift and antique shops and small mom-and-pop motels. Every ten miles there was another little maple-lined town, with another fire station and a post office and by mid afternoon, with my stomach protesting the lunch it never got, I spotted a pleasant-looking place with a glowing orange vacancy sign. Noticing it had drive up rooms around back out of sight from the street, I decided it was perfect. If I was going to hide, I decided I had best do it right.

I pulled up in front of the modest red and white building, noticing as I got out that the gas gauge was dipping below half a tank. *I'll fill it up after I secure a room*, I thought. O*n the way to a restaurant,* my stomach chimed in. As I walked to the door, I reached into my pocket and pulled out my available cash, counting it as I walked to the door. One dollar and fifty seven cents. Not even enough for a Happy Meal. Stopping at the door, I scanned up and down the road, searching for a bank that would have a universal ATM. Not seeing one, I sighed over the gas I would have to burn looking for one and went inside. I had only been out of work for a few hours and already I was fretting over money.

"Good afternoon," the woman behind the counter said. She was a big woman, as tall as I was but heavier, with a beehive hairdo that was the first thing to say "hello." She had a wide smile that said "Howdy, stranger," and battleship bust that shouted "Hey, sailor." Upon seeing me, she immediately put down the magazine she was reading, leaned forward on her elbows, exposing a good section of her bow as she welcomed me to the *It'll Do Motel*.

"What can we do you for?" she asked.

"Just a single room, preferably around back, if you've got one available," I said.

"King, queen or double?" she asked.

"It doesn't matter, as long as it's clean and firm."

"Honey," she said with a smile. "All the beds here are firm and clean. Now me, that's another story," She then winked and licked her dry lips provocatively. Mighty Matilda was hitting on me.

I tried to laugh, make her think I was too bashful to pursue any further, but it came out like a choking cough.

"You all right, darling'?"

"Yeah," I replied. Desperate to keep things sterile, I asked again if she had an open room around back. "Where I won't hear the traffic," I added to conceal the real reason that I was "on the lamb."

"I surely do," she said. She slid behind the weathered cash register, a massive metal machine that only partially eclipsed her ample chest, and pressed a series of keys. A few bells rang and some lights flashed on the scratched and cloudy display before she informed me that room sixteen was ready to "rock and roll." I didn't dare ask what she meant by that.

"Cash, debit or credit?" she asked.

Thinking I best reserve my bank account, considering the situation I was in, I handed her my VISA credit card.

She took it from my hand slowly and swiped it through the

card reader, a little more suggestively than I had ever seen at Wal-Mart. She then set it on the counter between us. A few uneasy seconds later—I think she was undressing me with her eyes—the little black box erupted in a volcano of sound. My card had been denied.

"Over your limit on that one, honey?"

I didn't think so. I only had the one and kept the balance at zero by paying it off each month, which happened to have been last week. *It must be an error,* I thought. I hadn't bought anything of any consequence since moving to Boston, nothing that would fill up my five thousand dollar limit. *There had to be a mix up at the credit card company,* I concluded. They put a hold on my card, mistaking it for someone else's. It happens all the time. That's what I was hoping, anyway.

Reluctantly, I handed her my debit card. I had over three thousand dollars in my savings and checking accounts, so one hit for forty-six bucks wouldn't kill me. At least, that's how I tried to console my unemployed self.

Five seconds later, that damn machine went off again. Card Denied!

What the fuck?

Matilda looked at the card and then at me, warily. The lust in her eyes was fading, shifting toward apprehension. "Maybe you better show me some ID," she looked at the card again, "Daniel."

Acting like one of Pavlov's dogs, I reached for my wallet before remembering that the cops had my license—Officer Marty to be exact. And since Bruce—or George, whatever—the security guard at my former place of employment had my only other picture ID, I just stood there gapping at her, wondering how long I could have the room for a buck fifty seven.

"You are Daniel Rayne, aren't you?" she asked.

I have no fucking clue, I thought morosely. The fact was, I *was* beginning to wonder myself. Every human encounter that day enforced the notion that I was nuts, cuckoo, out of my mind insane. People I thought knew me didn't know me. Places I thought I belonged refused me. And now, feeling like I'd just been slugged a third time, the bloodied face in the mirror was poised to jump on the bandwagon with the rest of them. *You sir, are certifiably crazy.*

Then, I noticed that Matilda no longer appeared concerned. In fact, she seemed more smitten than when I had first walked in. She was leaning into the counter again, pressing toward me with her bra-challenging breasts nearly spilling out onto the Formica like gigantic water balloons.

"You didn't like, kill him and steal all his stuff so you could pretend to be him, did you?" she asked eagerly. "As an alias, I mean. So you could hide from the crooked cops while you gather enough evidence to prove they killed your wife and kids."

Wow, this woman had some imagination. As I stared back at her, speechless, I could only imagine her sitting alone in the back office, night after endless night, watching countless reruns of NYPD Blue and 24. It seemed apparent that while she watched, she secretly dreamt of one day living out one of the episodes.

"I live in one of the rooms out back," she said. "You can shack up with me until the coast is clear. There's plenty to eat and I'll make sure you're nice and warm at night. Help you forget about what happened to your poor wife, God rest her soul." She started to come out from the behind the counter, which is when I realized I had to say *something*. I mumbled something incoherent and before I knew it, she was on me, cooing like a mother dove. "I'll protect you baby, you'll be safe with me."

"I'm not a spy or a killer," I said, visibly agitated as I pulled her arms from my waist. "I'm just a guy looking for a quiet room. And I'm certainly not interested in sharing it with you, let alone having sex with you." I *had* found her repulsive, I can't lie, but I could have been—should have been—a little more sensitive to her feelings. But the day had been a nightmare and I was in no mood to follow the guidelines one is taught during sensitivity training.

Looking back, a regretful "no thank you, but I'm flattered," would have done the trick nicely. Then, possibly, her response would have been a bit more...workable.

"Well, *excuse me*, Mr. High and Mighty!" She stormed back behind the counter, snatched up my debit and credit cards and stuffed them so deeply into her bra it would have taken an undersea probe to bring them back to the surface. With a look of grand indignation, she picked up the phone and pressed 911. "I'm sure the real Daniel Rayne will be very happy to have these returned," she said, sneeringly.

For a split second, I considered wrestling my property away for her but that would have only added rape to the Roper's claims of property destruction. The old folks had dropped those charges but there was no way I could expect the same from Matilda. Deciding to cut my losses, I walked quickly but calmly out to my car and drove away, careful not to appear like a thief fleeing the scene of a crime.

I have no idea how long I drove aimlessly around Boston before I found myself parked in front of the Kingston Street Shelter. I can't even remember how I got there. All I really know is that I was out on my feet; down for the count; face first on the canvas dreaming about a sled I once had named Rosebud. The almighty referee was imposing the three knockdown rule and I was damn glad to hear his voice. I had lost my mind, that was the only explanation, and at that moment I decided I would not spend the rest of my life pushing a wobbly shopping cart around the city picking up bottles and cans. No, it's better to burn out than it is to rust, especially when the controls have gone south. If it wasn't for an angel's intervention, I would have been content to die right there in my four-wheeled coffin. Standing in the shelter window, it was Raeni who pulled me from the depths of despair, holding out a bowl of soup and motioning me to come inside.

With no way of proving I was who I claimed to be, it struck me as odd that Charles had handed me the shelter's debit card, seemingly without concern I'd hop a bus to Atlantic City and lose it all playing blackjack. I had already arrived at the post office and was standing in line when I realized that he trusted me because I hadn't given him a reason not to. He didn't know me from Adam, but yet he honestly trusted me. That was something I could build on, something that could help me figure this whole nightmare out. And maybe Charles believed me, too; believed I really was Daniel Rayne. Or maybe he just hadn't taken the time to judge me enough to *not* believe me. Either way, it gave me hope that others might follow his lead. That's when I thought about Raeni again, remembering that I now had her address. *I'll go and see her*, I thought, *when the time is right.*

"Next," the postal clerk said. I moved up one space in line.

Then, I noticed one of the displays detailing the passport application requirements, specifically the proof of U.S. Citizenship. According to the poster, all I needed was a previous passport or an original, certified birth certificate issued by my city, county or state of birth. I shook my head. It may as well have been a trillion dollars because I never had a passport and my birth certificate was in a lost box in an lost apartment, the correct memory of which was apparently stuck somewhere in a dead cell of my brain. Reading further, I discovered that if I had no previous passport or certified birth certificate I could obtain a letter from the State confirming who I was and that I had no birth record. However, to get that it said I would need to present as many proofs of my existence as I could gather such as baptismal, medical, school and family records. As I recalled Charles handing me his card and telling me to call him if I ran into trouble, I exhaled a sigh of hopelessness, knowing that it was the only number I had.

"Next," the postal clerk repeated.

15

Follow the Breadcrumbs

That night, trying to sleep in the Kingston Street Shelter's Roosevelt Room was like trying to sink a four-foot putt in the middle of Time Square at one second past midnight on New Year's Day, ridiculously impossible. For reasons unknown to Charles and his skeleton evening crew, a bus load of homeless men arrived just after dinner had been served, leading to a chaotic scramble by the kitchen staff to produce an encore of corn chowder and biscuits. That feeding frenzy was followed by a sleeping arrangement re-evaluation and reassignment that resulted in a double helping of roomies for yours truly. Doubling the bunkmates doesn't double the pleasure or double the fun. It only doubled the hours I spent staring up at the ceiling. Somehow, I managed to doze a few hours, but by four in the morning, with the snore of the snoozing crowd still in full swing, I was wide-awake and aching for something to occupy my haunted mind.

I couldn't stop thinking about Louis Vinson and his limo driver, the muscle man who had nearly escorted me out of this world. From what I had gathered from the internet, Vinson was a very intelligent man with an insatiable thirst for women and wealth. A middle-aged Harvard Business School graduate with a wife and no children, his name appeared equally as often on the websites of CNN and Forbes as it did on those run by the newsstand tabloids. By all accounts, he was worth billions, had several homes on each coast of the United States, as well as several others scattered about the Caribbean and Europe and, reportedly, relationships of one sort or another with dozens of beautiful actresses and models from around the globe, depending on what you read and where. His true passion however, was cyberspace, "the vastly unexplored domain of man's technological evolution," he had been quoted as saying. So obsessed was Vinson, according to one unofficial biographer who disappeared mysteriously several years ago while vacationing in South America, he kept a personal diary detailing his plans to one day legally own the internet outright. What he might do with it, no one really knew, but many hypothesized that Vinson would become the richest man on the planet if his "outlandish delusion" ever came to fruition.

It appeared to be common knowledge that Vinson had a wife, but of the hundreds of pictures I found of him schmoozing tuxedo-clad executives at lavish fund raisers or cutting ribbons at yet another grand opening of one of his many enterprises, I never saw a woman standing by his side. Aren't those the places you take your wife to share in the success and celebration? If I was to judge only by the photo opportunities, I would have guessed he was a bachelor, and an active one at that, based on the paparazzi shots. But many of the feature articles I found routinely mentioned Claire Vinson, his wife of nearly twenty years, so I had to assume she was no apparition. Though I must say that the lack of visual evidence certainly heightened my skepticism, as I'm sure it did the media's, much like the existence of mermaids.

I had surfed the web for hours that day and lying in my cot in the dark, feeling as though I'd only scratched the surface, I wondered if Louis Vinson knew me as one of his former employees the day he came to the shelter. Had I seen a hint of recognition in his devilish eyes? Or had it just been paranoia, my mind overwhelmed by the events of the prior thirty six hours?

Optimistic I could redirect my thoughts into something more productive, I got up and navigated my way through the maze of cots to the large storage closet located in the back of the room. Inside, there were two dozen filing cabinets full, I assumed, of records that might tell me more about Vinson or Ostrander or even Daniel Rayne. All I needed to start digging was a key, and thanks to Hillary's excessive smoking routine, I had that in my pocket.

The lock was a bit rusty and alarmingly squeaky, but I managed to get in, turn on the light and close the door without stirring up any of my partners in grime. Peering down the length of the closet, I quickly conclude there were a lot more filing cabinets than originally thought.

"Damn," I whispered. "There must be little clerical elves that come in here each night just to keep up with the government paperwork."

Undaunted by the sheer volume, I rifled through drawer after drawer and by the time I heard the telltale sounds of the awakening life outside, I had unearthed a few breadcrumbs that I was confident would lead me somewhere. The first was a three-year-old listing of the fifty or so board members of the shelter, complete with contact information and short profiles detailing their employer and job title. On it was another Earth Nexus executive named John Oliver. The name wasn't familiar to me, but who knows what I might find on the web. The second item of interest was a client listing—some sort of role call sheet, by the looks of it—that included Felix Ostrander's name. The date on the form told me something I hadn't learned from Ostrander's file itself—when he had been here. At first, I had thought he was a current resident, but after reviewing the files in the business office and casually questioning a few staff members, I had learned he wasn't. The dates also clued me that Hillary did not purge her files very often. Now I knew that Felix Ostrander had been here in the spring. It was a start. The next obvious question was; *where is he now?*

I left the closet quietly, joining the others as they dressed for breakfast. With visions of pancakes and spam dancing in their sleepy heads, no one seemed to notice my movement.

In the dining hall, Charles came over and sat beside me, his ever-compassionate face looking tired and harried.

"I wanted to let you know personally, Daniel," he started off before looking down as his shoes. "Because I know you were fond of her." He then straightened back up and looked me in the eye.

Is he referring to Raeni? He appeared way too serious to be telling me she was running late. I don't think I want to hear this.

"Raeni," he said. "Called me yesterday and...resigned."

Ouch. I really didn't need to taste anymore boxing glove leather.

"She asked me to apologize for her for running out on you the other day," he added. "She said she had forgotten all about an appointment with her doctor and didn't have time to explain. I told her that I was sure you would understand."

I nodded as if I did, even though I knew it wasn't true. Something had caught her off guard that day—the arrival of the limo, the appearance of Louis Vinson, or maybe the limo driver himself. Had Raeni seen him pilfering the files on another occasion? And if so, had he seen her?

Charles was surveying the dining hall now, making sure everyone had been served as I poured some genuine imitation maple syrup on my short stack of pancakes. He looked like a sheep dog keeping a wary eye on his sheep, content in his role, if not worn out by it. There must have been a hundred hungry, destitute people in the shelter that morning—twice what I had seen before—every one of them appreciative for the meal while secretly wondering where the next would come from. That was something on my mind, so it only seemed logical that these poor souls might be thinking the same.

Looking around the table, the men reminded me of pieces of

paper crumpled up and thrown away. Time had soiled many of them, weathered most of their edges, but still there were words written on each one, a story of life and its unyielding progression. In time, I would ask, but I wasn't ready yet to look in the mirror.

I'm sure none of them started out this way, in the gutter. They must have had normal lives at one time, just as I had, crisp and clean and full of promise, an open notebook just waiting for the stroke of the hand to fill the pages. So what strange hand of fate banished them to this existence? What cursed calamity placed them in the bowels of society, friendless and freefalling, with nothing more than Charles Woodland's tattered net to catch them? Could it be as simple as one misstep? One wrong turn? The death of that one crucial brain cell that held the key to your own identity? *Hold on, Daniel, that's a straight jacket tailored just for you.*

Something had flocked us all here, or...*someone*. Pushing my half-eaten plate away—the pancakes tasted like wet sheetrock—I tried to reconstruct the arrival of the wolf, Louis Vinson. Here was a billionaire who could travel the world on a whim and he shows up at a patchwork shelter within days of myself, a former employee who just happens to have tripped over more than a few accounting irregularities in his books before being shown the door. A coincidence? And then, his flunky gets caught stealing the personal file of a man who's not really sure he is who he thinks he is, the same man left flailing in the backwash of Earth Nexus. Another coincidence? Now I had a cluster, and it was beginning to take the shape of a plot. *Easy Daniel, that jacket is eager for a fitting.*

After running the scenario through my mind, what didn't make sense is why I was still breathing. I mean, if Vinson knew I suspected his accountants were cooking the books, why didn't he just have me killed? Why not entice me with a business trip to South America with my lusty secretary, Irene Doolittle, where I would then disappear just as the unauthorized biographer had? Dead before I had a chance to do a little something with Irene, no doubt.

The more I replayed it, the more the hypothetical conspiracy unraveled. Why the sudden loss of my home and livelihood? Why the canceled credit cards? What would that accomplish for Vinson? And how could he have manipulated all those government and private records, not to mention the people involved like the security guard and Horace and Doris Forrest? It didn't make a whole lot of sense. Regardless, I could still testify about the manipulative accounting entries I had seen, couldn't I? If someone—a legitimate someone—brought suit against them, that is. As I sat there thinking about it, the clatter of plates and table talk filling the void around me, I realized that perhaps I couldn't.

"For the record, please state your name," the bailiff would say, to which I would answer, Daniel Rayne. Next, the Earth Nexus defense attorney would erupt with objections, insisting that all charges be dropped based on the lack of any credible proof that I was, in fact, Daniel Rayne, the former Acquisitions Controller. "He's a fraud, a charlatan, out to defame my client by any means possible," the attorney would scream. The judge would then turn toward me, order me to produce some identification, only to watch me shrug, embarrassed that I could not comply.

That was the biggest question of all—*Who am I*? Not just in my mind, but in the eyes and physical records of the world. No one knew me. Who would believe I was Daniel Rayne if I first didn't believe it myself?

"Oh, and Hillary called in sick today," Charles said, interrupting the episode of Perry Mason playing in my head. "So you won't be able to work in the office. She should be back tomorrow, she said. Just a twenty-four hour bug, she thought."

"No problem," I said. "I've got something I need to do today anyway."

The first order of business was to bolster my confidence that I hadn't imagined my whole life up until that moment. That it wasn't all just a mirage conjured up by a man bumped in the head one too many times by the hard knocks of life. What I needed was to talk to Raeni, to feel her optimism—her sunshine—warming the cold hallows of my uncertainty. She knew something about Louis Vinson; I could sense it in my gut along with the putrid pancakes. If I had any money, I would have bet it all that she had met Felix Ostrander, the former shelter resident the limo driver found as interesting as I did. She could tell me something about the two people who I was guessing knew something about Daniel Rayne. I was sure of it.

The day she disappeared something had scared her enough to make her run. That was the only explanation that made any sense. Had it been anything else, she would have said something to me—like goodbye. I don't know why I felt so strongly about her—about her honest intentions. I had only known her a day, but there was no denying the feeling.

With Raeni's address in my pocket and her smile in my thoughts, I stepped away from the table and headed to my car, hoping that I had enough gas *and* sanity left to find her.

16

A Flat Tire

I wasn't terribly familiar with the section of Boston where I expected to find Raeni, busily making telemarketing calls from the comfort of what I imagined was a one bedroom flat. Hillary was under the impression Raeni didn't have a phone, but I had concluded that she had only said that to avoid late night calls to come in to work. Daydreaming as I drove, I pictured a quaint little bachelorette pad above a little Italian restaurant with a giant couch filled with fluffy pillows dominating the surrounding assortment of offbeat accessories and near-antiques. A Renaissance woman with her own agenda and a passion for life, I could imagine her creating frescos on her walls in the evening, scribbling poetry on the back of napkins whenever inspiration beckoned and singing like Alanis Morrisette in the shower while her lover—me—listened serenely from the bedroom. It was a scene from a movie I'd seen somewhere, but with no life of my own, it was only natural that I would create a fantastic and completely unbelievable one.

As I turned onto Shawmut Avenue in the middle of Boston's South End and began scanning the row of buildings for her address, I felt a wave of nervousness wash over me. Unquestionably, she would be surprised to see me, but *happily* surprised? *There's only one way to find out.* With the convertible top down, it was easy to spot house numbers but I slowed down just the same so I wouldn't miss her building.

Her neighborhood was just as I imagined it, handsome red-brick structures with cast iron railings and granite trim, classy. Many of the buildings had elegantly bowed middle sections filled with shutter-augmented windows, while a few others were sprinkled with architecturally crafted bump-out windows that reminded me of the knobs of an old oak tree. I cursed good-humoredly as I passed an inviting restaurant with olive green awnings and red umbrella covered tables, disappointed that the number didn't match the one I'd found in Raeni's file. It would have been a great place to pacify the lust-induced hunger I was fantasizing, or at least talk about why she had pulled her Houdini.

She would have questions for me; that would be unavoidable. *Where is your family? Have you called them for help?* Perhaps she might even offer to fill my gas tank so that I could drive to them, back to Rhode Island to put the pieces of my life back together. Raeni was that type of person and though it would be a generous gesture, I would have to refuse. I had no family, no one back in Rhode Island or anywhere else for that matter. There was no one to turn to, no pieces to fit together, only a blank slate that I had hoped to fill as I traversed north a month ago, headed straight into the jaws of the magnificent Boston skyline. How could I have known then that it would chew me up and spit me out like a rotten peach pit?

The opportunity at Earth Nexus *was* my lifeline, my only lifeline. Before they offered me the job—one that literally appeared out of nowhere—I had been unemployed for six months and living in the room of a house recently sold during an estate auction. The new owners were decent enough, giving me a few months to find a new place to live. I think they took pity on me because they sensed that the previous owner, a self-employed accountant whom I had been working for since I was sixteen, meant more to me than just a paycheck. And they were right; the man had been like a father to me. When my mother passed away, he took me in, teaching me about business and how to keep a set of books. He never told me why he did it, never fully explained his relationship with my mother, only that he loved her and that he loved me like a son. I asked him once if I *was* his son and he regretfully replied that I wasn't. "Your father died in a car accident before your first birthday," he told me one night a few months before he passed in his sleep, when a brief resurrection of acknowledgment crept through the barbed wire of the Alzheimer's that had imprisoned an innocent man. "You were almost five when I met your mother. She was much, much younger than I was and beautiful, and funny, and I fell into her spell the moment I saw her. And you, you were a bonus."

The man I knew never returned after that, regressing back into a child until his will to live was no more. The disease took him and everything he knew about my mother and our past. It must have been ravaging his mind for years. This I discovered when his will was read, a document I had never seen before. There was no mention of my mother or me, no reference of our relationship with him. Everything he had, he left to charity. In his closing statement, he regretted never having family of his own and thought the best use for his modest wealth would be to help the underprivileged.

His words hurt, but having watched him slip and slide on that terrible genetic ice for so many years, I realized that they weren't really his. It was the child talking, the one that had slowly taken his place right before my unknowing eyes.

Thinking about him now as I searched for Raeni's place, I wondered if perhaps I was destined to suffer the same fate. Did I have early Alzheimer's? Is that why I can't recall who I really am? But then why Daniel Rayne? Why that name and all the memories that go along with it? That wasn't the disease that claimed the only father I ever knew. Alzheimer's didn't replace old memory with new, false memory; it takes all the memory away. *No, that can't be it.* Feeling a headache coming on, I switched on the radio and concentrated on the passing buildings.

After three blocks, I was familiar enough with the numbering scheme to anticipate the next block was the one. Almost there, I cursed again as a red light caught me, leaving me to peer forward like a theater patron stuck at the back of the line. Oddly, all I could see was a line of trees guarding the outline of a huge park. The parade of three and four storied structures had come to a stop at the same intersection that I had. *Strange.* I double-checked her address. If the sequence I had been monitoring remained steady, her place should have been the first one on my right after I crossed the street. But there were no buildings standing there, only a handful of kids along side their parked bicycles.

As soon as the light turned green, I drove slowly past the park, an eerie pessimism staring back at me in the rear view mirror as my tires crunched over some broken glass. I went a few more blocks, and few more just to be sure. As I feared, Raeni's number fit right in the gap between the stately row houses. The address she had listed on her employment form was a park. Did she live in the park? Was she homeless, too? *No, I don't think so. She made the address up. Now what do I do?*

The clippity-clap of deflated rubber answered that question for me.

17

An Unexpected Treasure Map

"What happened to you?" Charles Woodland asked. I had just arrived back at the shelter and was drudging past his office. I think my dirty smell of street and sweat arrived seconds before I had, alerting him to my presence.

"I got into a nasty wrestling match with a flat tire," I replied. I stepped into his doorway, stopping there as I assessed my hands and clothes, suddenly aware of the grime I was spreading with each step I took.

"I'd say by the looks of you, the tire won," he chuckled.

"Yeah, it's an old car and I don't think the lug nuts have been off in a long time."

"I've been there," he said knowingly. He then stood up and came out from behind his desk. "Listen, I need to talk to you about the possibility of your working for us full time. Hillary told me that you clearly know your accounting and I just got a two-week notice from another one of the office staff. First Raeni, and now my bookkeeper. I know you weren't planning on staying long, but we're in a bit of bind and I was hoping you could help us out." He started to put his hand on my shoulder, but noticing the fresh oil stains, thought better of it. "Why don't you grab a shower and some clean clothes from that pile of donations we got yesterday and come back so we can discuss all the nitty-gritty? You know, like salary and benefits?"

I wasn't sure about the job, but the shower sounded so good I nodded in agreement and walked out. Committing to Charles would mean staying here a while and that was something I had no desire to do. As I headed toward the men's locker room—the shelter at one time had been a high school gymnasium—I quickly recognized that I had no other option but to take the position. If I was ever to escape the chin-deep poverty I found myself in only a few days ago, I needed money—a steady income that I could count on. I could do the work, there was no worry there, but what would happen when Charles submitted my W-4 to Uncle Sam for payroll tax withholding? The government required a social security number and having never memorized mine, I didn't have one to offer. My card was back in my apartment along with everything I *used* to own. Could I get a new one with no way of proving I was Daniel Rayne? Would Uncle Sam have a record of me? No one else did. It presented yet another interesting dilemma to add to the pile.

While the soothing spray of hot water rinsed the day's struggles from my body, I seriously began to consider paying Horace and Doris another visit. If I could prove that I had indeed lived there, uncover a box of my stuff perhaps or a receipt for my cash rental payment, this whole weird hoax—if that's what it was—might begin to reveal itself. *If only I had paid by check.* As I kicked myself for being so foolish, a new thought appeared, glowing like a firefly and quickly overshadowing my desire for vengeance against that conniving old couple. Raeni had worked for the shelter, which meant she received a paycheck, which meant she must have filled out the necessary government forms, which meant she must have provided a social security number, which gave me another potential way of finding her. The only question was; where in Hillary's unique and utterly confusing filing system were those payroll forms? I hadn't seen one in Raeni's main file, though most logical minds would have agreed it should have been there. *Finding Raeni won't help solve your immediate problems, Daniel. Focusing on the job Charles is offering will.*

The voice was right, but I was only half listening. Whether it would help or not, I wanted to talk to Raeni again.

The selection from the mound of donated clothes stacked neatly against a wall of the Roosevelt Room like tidy curbside trash was revoltingly limited. What didn't have holes, had stubborn stains. What didn't have stains, had rips, tears and gashes. *Did people ever donate good clothes?* The only reasonable pants I found were a pair of blue jeans two sizes too big; the only wearable shirt too red to be looked at without sunglasses. I put them on anyway, vowing to avoid mirrors at all costs. After adding a belt to keep the baggy drawers up—white patent leather was all I could find—and some knee high athletic socks, I slid back into my burgundy penny loathers and went looking for Charles. I found him sitting at Hillary's desk in the business office. Dexter was in there with him, feverishly typing away on the computer he had set up for me, mutely oblivious to my arrival.

"You know," Charles said with a wide grin, "that's a good look for you."

"It smells a little better than my stuff," I replied as I sniffed my shirtsleeve. "But that's about it." I'd been wearing the same clothes for days and hadn't noticed the odor, that is, until I put on something cleaner to compare it to.

"Don't worry, we have it all washed before it comes to the shelter. The underwear goes through twice."

I had passed on the jockey shorts, choosing to go commando until I had a chance to wash my own. The jeans *were* a bit scratchy, but that was better than the soiled horror I saw in the donated pile. A double washing or not, the shorts were untouchable.

I sat down on the front of the desk I'd been using—Dexter was in my seat—and told Charles that I'd take the job.

"Don't you want to hear the starting salary first?" he asked.

"I'm sure it's more than I'm making now," I said. "But there is one small problem. I don't know my social security number for payroll withholding and I've lost my card."

"No problem, I've got the form for applying for a replacement," Charles said. "In this business, I've needed to do that a few times. All we need is proof of identity, like a driver's license or passport."

"Well, there's the rub," I said, looking down at my shoes. Vincent had never asked me for ID when I first arrived at the shelter but now the rash of vagrant shame was beginning to itch. I stole a sheepish glance at Dexter, expecting to spot a smirk or grin but his expression remained vacant. *Maybe this guy is deaf?*

Charles didn't act surprised. "I've got a contact at the Social Security Administration. We'll work out something until we can straighten it all out. In the meantime, are you ready to get started?"

"As ready as I'll ever be."

By the way Charles reacted, my accepting the position as bookkeeper had made his day. "I knew you'd help us out," he exclaimed happily. He then explained that Dexter was already in the process of loading the accounting software onto my computer as well as establishing a user profile for the web-based payroll application the shelter contracted through a local payroll-processing vendor. Assuring me that when Dexter finished I would have access to everything I needed to do a "stellar job," he stood up and came over to shake my hand. "It's great to have you on board, Daniel," he said genuinely.

It was well past five o'clock by the time Charles finished outlining my first order of business—assisting Hillary with the preparation of next year's budget. "The shelter's fiscal year ends on September 30th," Charles explained, "which only gives us a few months to establish a new spending plan to present for board approval. The board is made up of volunteers—local business men and women—who like to see it and tweak it before *we* actually start living it. They're funny that way." He was joking, but I suspected a tiny hint of annoyance in his laugh as he said it. Charles struck me as a capable administrator who, I imagined, felt strapped at times by the bureaucracy all nonprofits were expected, if not required, to live under—the well-meaning oversight board. (I had assisted my mentor with many nonprofit clients before his passing and was quite familiar with the donating public's expectations. "Community and local business involvement, that's what keeps the United Way's of the world working," he would always say to me after retuning from one of the meetings I never participated in. I had never met any of his clients—our clients. I'd never received a formal education and in the diploma-heavy world of financial management that was surreptitiously forbidden. I did my share of the work, often covering for his failing memory, but that fact never went beyond the four walls of his office.)

Surprisingly, Louis Vinson's name hadn't been on the board list I'd found in the files during my night raid on the storage room. From what I had learned about him, that fact was probably a well-calculated move on his part. Maybe he wanted his connection to the shelter to be unofficial or perhaps just less apparent to the interested observer. Regardless of why he stayed off the board, I sensed he was a man who exercised his considerable influence in other ways.

With his long workday coming to a close, Charles handed me Hillary's folder and headed for the door. "You should find a few spreadsheets in there projecting next year's payroll costs that I believe Hillary had already started. Take a look at them and check with her tomorrow if you have any questions. I'd like you to complete it if you can so I can get her on another project. But I don't expect you to work all night."

After assuring Charles that I wouldn't, I watched him leave before opening up Hillary's folder. *What a mess!* There were pages and pages of green ledger paper, each heavily decorated like a Christmas tree with yellow sticky notes, none of which I could read due to Hillary's poor penmanship. I sighed and looked over at Dexter. His eyes were locked on the glowing monitor, obsessed with whatever he was doing on my computer. I wanted him to finish so I could log onto the payroll system and find Raeni's data file. I hadn't determined how I might dig for information using her social security number—it's not like the government would hand over everything I wanted to know about the owner of that number—but I wanted to see it for myself nonetheless. With all that had happened to me in the past few days combined with her disappearance, I needed every shred of evidence I could find to keep my sanity from falling off the cliff's edge.

As Dexter's busy fingers clicked away, I returned my wandering focus to the hodgepodge in front of me, thinking it better to keep my mind occupied while I waited for him to finish. I leafed through the first few sheets, wondering if I would ever be able to make any sense of it. I'd seen some gnarled spreadsheets in my travels but Hillary's appeared to be the blue ribbon winner. Then, just as I was about to give it up and go check the dinner menu, I spotted a notebook scrap with Raeni's name on it. It listed a post office box where she wanted her final paycheck sent to. *X marks the spot!* Thankfully, it wasn't written in Hillary's illegible scribble, but she must have absentmindedly placed it in the folder when whoever wrote it brought it into the office. Digging deeper, I found the other half of the unexpected treasure map—Raeni's final paycheck. Hillary hadn't mailed it yet.

Hungry and optimistic, I got up and headed for the dining hall, committed to making sure Raeni got her check, vowing to mail it just as soon I as knew where her post office box was located.

18

Back in the Saddle Again

Raeni knew that this wasn't a very good idea. She had promised herself she would never dance again; remembering how Marko, dying in her arms, had warned it would be the first place Caesar would look for her. *Marko was right!* Her better judgment had screamed an hour ago as she stood before the mirror, assessing the white hot pants, red-striped halter top and six inch spike heels she had chosen for her audition. Somehow, another voice had drowned that caution out, fueled by her ache to escape her troubled past once and for all. *It's the only way*, she kept telling herself over and over during the twenty minute cab ride to the club. *The only way you'll ever get that horse farm.* Once, at a stop light she felt a twinge of fear, an urge to jump out and run back to her apartment. But she didn't.

Standing now in the club manager's office, waiting patiently in front of his desk as he wrapped up a phone call, her intuition was telling her it would be all right. *Caesar will never find you in this out of way hole-in-the-wall*, it was saying. Deep down, Raeni knew it was horse sense of the wrong kind.

The club Raeni had chosen for her quiet return was a small, intimate place, dimly lit with photograph wallpaper commemorating every dancer to ever lace up a bustier. Scarcely clothed blondes, brunettes and red heads of every shape and ethnic color were represented, smiling proudly for the camera as they hugged happy customers enjoying the warm and friendly atmosphere. Raeni liked the vibe she got, especially from the woman bartender who'd given her a sisterly smile when she came in before yelling for "Bobby" to get his butt out to the bar.

"I'm Phyllis, and Bobby, he's my brother," she told Raeni before giving her a wink. "Regardless of what he tells you, we *both* own this dive."

The two women had chatted for a while, comparing notes about the type of men who frequented strip clubs and the best juice to mix with Vodka until Bobby appeared and led her into the back room. That's when the phone rang. Now, after some gruff talk about the quality of his last shipment of wine, he was finally hanging up.

"So, you ever dance before?" Bobby asked. He was an older man, mid-fifties Raeni was guessing, with a full head of greased-back gray hair and a fatherly gaze that instantly set her at ease. A white tee-shirt covered his protruding belly, adorned with silver and black letters promoting the establishment Raeni had found in the yellow pages—*The Rock Hard Café*.

"A few places in Vegas, no place you would have ever heard of," Raeni replied. She stood tall and proud, providing a full view of her slender and taut body, smiling sweetly to encourage him to bypass further questions about her experience.

"Uh huh," Bobby said. He tilted his head as if to say he'd heard that line before as his eyes raced through Raeni's curves. "You've certainly got what the boys are looking for," he said. Staring at her chest, he asked if she was a C-cup.

"You've got a good eye," Raeni said.

"I've been in this business a while. It's second nature now. They look natural. Are they?"

"One hundred percent."

"Good, cause the regulars who come in here like the natural stuff. Not like those balloons you seen in porn movies; firm and perky like yours. Fake titties are on their way out, if you ask me." He was leaning back in his chair now, scratching his chin as he idled slowly over her flesh one final time. "Yeah, I think you'll do all right here. I think the boys are going to like Raeni Knights."

"I've got a last name now?" she asked with a grin.

"Got to babe. Customers expect it. You have to admit, it's got a nice ring to it. I'll get Jason, our DJ, to play some thunderstorm sounds during your entrance. Like that shit in the beginning of the Garth Brooks song *The Thunder Rolls*. The crowd will love it; get their blood flowing and the money flying. You like country music?"

"Not to dance to," Raeni answered honestly.

"You don't pull any punches, do you doll," he said, smiling. "I like you. How about you work a couple of fifteen minute sets tonight and we'll see how it goes."

"Sounds fair to me," Raeni said. She already knew how it would go. The same it always went with men when she stood half naked in front of them—whatever way *she* wanted. Only this time, her dancing would never leave the club. That was the deal her two voices had made.

"My name is Bobby, by the way. But you can call me Uncle Bob, all the girls do."

Uncle Bob then escorted her to the dressing room, explaining the rules of the club along the way. "No sex with the customers, no drugs on the premises and if you get hammered on tequila while you're working I will personally throw you out the front door, no questions asked." His words were frank, his tone deadly serious. They suited Raeni perfectly. "I expect you to be here on time, dressed to kill and ready to wow 'em each and every night you're scheduled. Phyllis takes care of the scheduling, by the way. You have any problems with the other girls or a jealous boyfriend, you come see me and I'll straighten them out. Any questions?"

"No," Raeni said. "I think you've covered it all."

Hearing him say all those things only confirmed Raeni's first impression of the man, that he was someone she could trust, someone like Marko; not an old letch looking to get into her pants, or a cheat aiming to rob half her tips. He was Uncle Bob and she was beginning to believe that returning to the stage hadn't been such a bad idea after all.

Uncle Bob looked at his watch. "It's early yet and Thumper is the only one here so you can go on as soon as she's done; kind of a warm up for later when the place is hopping. I'll tell Jason to pop in and you can tell him what songs you want him to play."

"Does he have any Garth Brooks?" Raeni asked.

Bobby chuckled. "You know, I liked you the second you walked into my office."

It was well past three in the morning before Raeni had a chance to thank Bobby and his sister, Phyllis, for giving her a shot. The evening had gone very well and with over five hundred dollars –mostly singles—stuffed into the tight pockets of her hot pants, she said her goodbyes before catching a ride home with Thumper. Thumper reminded Raeni of Diamond back at The Sin City Lounge, a big sister type who Raeni had a greater appreciation for ever since leaving New York City. There was definitely room for another one now.

She had kept a watchful eye on the entrance all night, wary of the wicked smile she couldn't chase from her mind. But the man she'd seen enjoying her pain only a few months ago—the same man she'd seen step from the limo in front of the shelter—never showed. *That's because he's never going to show up here*, Raeni told herself as she walked with Thumper to her car. *He doesn't know where I am, it's my own paranoia that put me into hiding in the first place. Well, no more.*

Neither of the women talked much as they rolled along the deserted streets. They were both tired and ready for sleep, anxious to remove their bling and glitter, hunker down into the bed covers and dream of quieter nights by a fire cuddling with a movie actor or sports star. They'd talked about men all night, Thumper confessing her desires for Johnny Damon, the former Red Sox turned New York Yankee, while Raeni drooled over Grey's Anatomy star Patrick Dempsey—Dr. McDreamy as he was known in the tabloids.

"You know, I met a man the other day that looks a little like him," Raeni said. She had her shoes off and her feet pressed up against the glove box as she massaged her aching calves. Her head was tilted back, while eyelids drooping lazily.

"Looks like who?" Thumper asked. Her real name was Tracy but she preferred being called by her stage name, even when she wasn't on duty.

"Dr. McDreamy, of course. Who else have I been fawning over all night?"

"Well, you did look pretty cozy with that little guy with the bow tie and the lisp," Thumper said. "He would have married you tonight if you'd asked him."

Raeni laughed, remembering how the man's tongue tied tighter and tighter with each gyration of her hips. "He was cute, but a little too short for me, not to mention obsessed with my cleavage. I need a man who will see me for more than just my boobs."

"Honey, the problem with him was he wasn't tall enough to see past your boobs."

The two then erupted in laughter.

"So, tell me about this McDreamy look-a-like," Thumper said. "Is he good in bed?"

"Thumper!" Raeni exclaimed. She knew she was blushing and she turned toward the window to hide it. "That's none of your business."

"You haven't rolled with him yet, have you?"

Raeni looked back at her sheepishly, "No, I haven't even kissed him."

"What are you waiting for? An invitation? There's not a man on the planet that doesn't have a need for what we got, girl. Next time you see him you grab him by the hair and plant one on his lips so wet it'll make his toes curl. He does have hair, doesn't he?"

"Yes, but who said I wanted to kiss him." She turned again and gazed out the window, wondering silently if she truly did want to kiss the homeless man named Daniel. She wasn't sure, but Thumper was.

"You do," she said. "I can tell by the way you deny it."

"It doesn't matter, anyway," Raeni said. "I doubt I'll ever see him again."

"Why the hell not?"

"It's complicated. We both have some issues to straighten out."

"Let me tell you something girl, if *I* was waiting for Mr. Perfect to walk through my door, I'd still be a virgin on a one way train to old maid town. You hear what I'm sayin'? Everybody's got their problems; it's one of the things that make's life interesting. Take my first husband, Joey. Oh, how that man could fuck." Thumper was smiling now, copulating in her thoughts as she ran a red light. "And a tongue as long as the Mississippi." She then gleefully shook her head in disbelief before illustrating her pleasure by rolling her hips around in the bucket seat. "Talk about a raging river ride."

Raeni giggled, a little embarrassed by her new friend's shameless reenactment.

"But that poor man couldn't hold a job if you duck-taped it to his hands."

"Was he dumb or something?" Raeni asked.

"No, just lazy, except when he crawled into my bed."

"The guy I'm talking about isn't lazy or stupid, just..."

"Just what?" Thumper asked.

"I don't know," Raeni replied. "I haven't figured that out yet. But like I said, it really doesn't matter because we're both headed in different directions."

"Well then," Thumper said. "I'll just have to invite the real Dr.

McDreamy down to the club and introduce you two."

They laughed again, draining the last ounce of energy they could muster.

At long last at home and in bed, Raeni drifted off to sleep wishing that she could see Daniel again, if only to explain why she'd left him standing at the corner that day. Maybe she felt more for him than she was willing to admit, but she was too tired to think about it. Forgotten for the moment was her worry that a man she only knew as Caesar might find her at the club; find her and silence what she knew about him. Tonight, she had made some serious money and put her ten year plan back on track. Now it was time to dream about Pilgrim, the first horse she planned to buy when she awoke to a new life, a thousand mornings from now.

19

Two Dates with Destiny

Louis Vinson loved New York City. It had all the things he wanted to take, all the things he needed to possess and, looking down from his penthouse window at the tiny specks marching like ants on the streets below, all the things he wanted to crush. People, that's really what Louis Vinson loved. He loved to crush people.

By his colleagues, Louis Vinson was referred to simply, and often grimly, as Caesar, the conquering general. He accepted the moniker proudly. A master showman with a flair for the dramatic, he ruled his entrepreneurial kingdom with an iron fist just as the famed Roman Emperor had in the first century B.C. While he governed mightily over his realm, ambition ruled his life. He wanted to own New York City—he wanted to own the world—his unchallenged ego believing nothing was beyond his reach. A virtually impenetrable genius, he suffered dandyism just as his namesake had, fretting excessively at times over his clothes and appearance, and womanizing shamelessly in front of employees and family alike, including his wife. "I see these not as flaws," he once said to John Oliver, the closest thing he had to a real friend. "But more as indulgences to pamper the soul."

The son of a crack-addicted prostitute and her equally drugged-out pimp, Vinson was a classic rag to riches story, the epitome of the American dream. At the age of thirteen, he became a ward of the state after both parents were found dead in the roach-infested apartment he shared with his mother, each the apparent victim of a simultaneous, and suspiciously self-inflicted, overdose. With only the meager savings his mother kept hidden in a hollowed out heel of her five-inch pumps, he took to the streets of New York City, selling anything illegal he could get his hands on—sex, drugs, and bootlegged rock and roll CDs. He was his mother's son and his father's unwitting protégé, an uncontrollable extremist like his parents with a deep lust for the wilder side of life and the money that often accompanied it.

Before he reached the age of eighteen, he had been in and out of almost every juvenile detention center in New York. His confidential files read like a light version of an Al Capone biography—gang related racketeering, petty theft, and assault and battery. But when a sadistic encounter with a homosexual guard nearly cost him his life, Vinson vowed to rewrite his future and never step in front of a black-robed bastard again.

Using money from the clearance sale of the last of his cocaine inventory and a neatly forged high school transcript, he enrolled in City College, majoring in business and finance. An eager learner with an impoverished education, he quickly charmed his way into the panties of an exceptionally bright and comely co-ed who willingly became his relentless tutor and bed slave. Gloria Chaldu was the daughter of a prominent banker with more years of real-world experience than most of the professors who lectured her. The perfect muse for Vinson, she had been interning for her father since she was fourteen, learning what Donald Trump like to call "the art of the deal." Gloria didn't need college to enter the business arena, but her father insisted her resume be complete, consequently her stint at City College. Unknown to the elder Chaldu's at the time, their daughter also had a great curiosity of her own sexuality, a subject they had gone to great lengths to inhibit, if not completely suppress. Vinson had spotted it the moment their eyes met, sensing a caged animal ready to prowl. For four years, he preyed on that weakness relentlessly, indulging her every erotic fantasy with hypnotic potency. Though he had loathed her, Louis Vinson had learned a great deal from his mother in the art of seduction and dependency. It would become one of his greatest strengths.

Hungry for more knowledge after graduation, Vinson parlayed several compromising snapshots of an aspiring local politician into a Harvard Business School acceptance letter. The photos were taken by an associate, a high priced hooker specializing in domination, who Vinson bankrolled in exchange for the occasional crack of her whip. After starting college, he had walked away from the drug trade, but not the sex trade, discovering during his first semester that the college faculty's fetishes could provide him the necessary means to support himself, all while he learned the more formalized lessons of life.

Armed with street smarts, a modest amount of startup capital, a graduate degree from Harvard and an unquenchable thirst to possess whatever caught his eye, Vinson returned to the streets of New York City—albeit the pricier sections of Manhattan this time—and jumped into the capitalist fray, hell-bent on making his first million before he was twenty-five. Surprising even himself, he achieved it before turning twenty-four.

To expand his ever-widening empire, Vinson decided to focus on technology—the internet to be exact—taking a lesson from the pages of history that proved time and time again that superior technology conquered all. For the Romans it had been steel swords and armor; for the Eurasians, firearms and oceangoing ships; for America, the taming of the atom and the creation of the nuclear bomb. For Vinson it would be the World Wide Web, capable of informing and influencing the entire globe with whatever message its master desired. Now in his mid-thirties, Vinson had worked tirelessly for over ten years to dissect and harness its force, amassing a billion dollar, multinational conglomerate of internet service providers that made him one of the richest and most powerful men alive. But he hadn't reached the pinnacle yet—complete and unimpeded control over the internet itself and the content it presented.

Detractors called him crazy, insane even, but never to his face. That could get a man killed, and had, unofficially. Vinson had been questioned a number times regarding the suspicious disappearance of a colleague or a competitor, but not a single shred of evidence was ever found. The authorities couldn't pin a thing on him, not even a parking ticket. He was above reproach and he knew it, always willing to sit down with a visiting detective and taunt them with mock civility.

Over eight million people, Vinson thought as he gazed down from his perch. *With the spellbinding power of the internet, I can command each and every one of them. Fill their minds with whatever I choose; reconstruct their moral beliefs anyway I choose. With unfettered control, they will drink from whatever pool I lead them to, swallowing happily, before asking sweetly for more. Nothing but a helpless flock of sheep, following whichever sheepdog promises to steer them toward the Promised Land.* The Web had the potential to touch everyone on the planet, and as Vinson awaited the arrival of his afternoon appointment, he sat down at his desk and pulled up onto his computer screen the matrix detailing his grand map for dominance.

Utilizing the same electromagnetic microwaves as cell phones, the hub of Vinson's plan was to offer wireless internet access to all consumers—residential and commercial—absolutely free. No hidden charges or fees for additional usage—free, just as television used to be before HBO and MTV. Currently, the majority of the world was held hostage by the telephone and cable companies, paying anywhere from ten dollars a month to thousands a month just for the privilege of boarding the information superhighway. Vinson knew people would gladly dump their existing ISP and the monthly charges that came along with it, provided the free service was dependable and allowed them access to everything on the web. It was human nature—grab as much as you can get for nothing. All he needed was a few dozen modified GPS satellites to get the ball rolling, a relatively simple, but still very expensive business proposition since the signing of the Commercial Satellite Act of 1962 allowing private space operations. Once people cut their ties to the AOLs and Verizons of the world, he could channel them through the Earth Nexus portal, invisibly controlling their cyber travels without them even knowing it.

"Humans are creatures of habit," John Oliver surmised the first time Vinson shared his vision. "They will still want to Google and Yahoo; still want their YouTube the same way our generation wanted our MTV. We won't be able to take all they've grown accustomed to without a rebellion, Louis."

"We're not going to take away any of their little pleasures, John," Vinson had assured him that day. "We will simply steer them away from the morally reprehensible in favor of the more honorable content, which coincidentally, we will own and control. There, we'll persuade them to buy our environmental safe products, vote for our honest politicians, hell, even worship at the churches we recommend."

"There's a revolution going on, John. People are tired of having shit thrown in their face while sitting in the sanctity of their own family room. Even as we speak, middle class families are lining up outside the courthouse with finely tailored lawyers at their sides and multimillion-dollar lawsuits clutched in their calloused hands, awaiting their claim for justice. And do you know who Middle America is going after John? The most influential group in the world is on a witch-hunt for the scum that allow sexual predators into their homes. MySpace, YouTube, Facebook, they're all getting sued because Mr. and Mrs. Brady are sick and tired of worrying about Peter and Marcia chatting with some guy who wants them both to come over and watch Jenna Jameson deep throat some tattooed hillbilly. They want decency,

John. Sound moral decency. And we're going to give it to them while making sure the competition serves up a constant barrage of filth and decadence."

That day, the conversation abruptly ended there, John knowing better than to get into a battle over human psychology when his friend's blood was simmering. He didn't agree with or even like Vinson's underhanded methods, but up to now they had made him a very wealthy man and he enjoyed that far too much to walk away. Instead, he nodded in agreement and left with his newest marching orders—complete an in-depth financial performance analysis of Yahoo over the past five years along with a frontal lobotomy of their current ownership. Vinson wanted to know who the major stockholders were and what, if any, the obstacles might be during a "purely hypothetical" takeover attempt.

Gazing keenly at his skillfully charted plan as it glowed in vibrant colors on his computer screen, Vinson looked like Yankee manager Joe Torre assessing his lineup card for a night game against their arch rival the Boston Red Sox. Like the Bronx Bombers, Vinson had compiled a stacked lineup with speed and power in every slot—no weak hitters, no easy outs. The green markers indicated companies he'd acquired, the red the ones he was still working on. The majority of the list was tagged green. The leadoff hitter was a hatchling world and local news source with state of art visuals and an empty wallet that Vinson had gobbled up for a song. On deck was the number two hitter, a social networking site with youth group themes that parents would instantly akin to dropping little Johnny off at the YMCA. The pivotal three spot was Vinson's YouTube challenger, a user defined online entertainment center with the look and feel of a church recreation center. But the cleanup hitter—Yahoo, arguably the world's most popular search engine and content provider and Vinson's most coveted free agent—was yet unsigned.

"All in due time," Vinson said aloud. Satisfied that the rest of the lineup was in place or on the cusp—an online auction house to rival eBay, a combination encyclopedia and almanac site for reference information, a bulletin board, a bloging site, and an assortment of other online services—he closed the file. He then checked his watch. His three o'clock was due at any moment. He clicked on a desktop shortcut and typed in the password to a file that no other pair of eyes had ever seen. If Vinson had anything to say about it, no one else ever would.

It was a simple spreadsheet and another scorecard of sorts, with no main header and only three titled columns across the top. The first twenty-seven rows were filed with names—"Name" being the title of the first column. To the right of the name were dates, in most cases a series of two. Only toward the bottom did Vinson see several blank cells, no date entered. The twenty-sixth name was Felix Ostrander and the date next to it was March 15, 2006. To the right of that was a box highlighted in red. Noticing it, Vinson's jaw tightened. It was one of only two empty cells, and the only one highlighted in red. *The three o'clock had better have a good explanation*, he thought.

The last name on the list, sitting just below Ostrander, was the name Daniel Rayne. It had a date next to it of July 10, 2006. That row contained a yellow highlighted box just below the red one. Noting that cell, Vinson grinned. He recalled seeing Daniel in the shelter, helpless and hapless, like a worm on hot tin. *A little while longer*, he thought just as a knock at the door protruded into his silent realm. His appointment had arrived.

Anxious to talk with the man at the door, he quickly typed in a date in the yellow square. Next, he scanned his desk for his BlackBerry, wanting to upload the spreadsheet he'd just revised. Not seeing it, he searched the suit coat hung over his desk chair but found nothing but empty pockets. At a loss for where he had left it, he agitatedly closed the file, the crisscrossing lines and symmetrically written words vanishing like a genie into a bottle, along with the two date column headings he enjoyed every time he read them. He would add the new entry to the file copy on the BlackBerry when he found it—Daniel Rayne's expiration date.

20

Glowing Like a Beacon

For the first time since I arrived at the shelter, I got a full night's sleep. The boys were quiet for a change, worn out from a hard day wandering the streets I assumed, too tired even to snore. They didn't look like much, dirty and tattered like the orphan cast from Annie, but they weren't bad guys. Many of them had had normal lives at one time or another, an average Joe existence derailed by bad luck or poor decision-making, often times a combination of both. Listening to their stories I came to the realization that we all were walking a wobbly rope and plank bridge, and that at any moment one rotted board could snap in half and send you head first into a misty chasm. That's all it took, one misstep. It didn't seem real but yet here we all were, living proof that anyone can slip.

Before I'd gone to bed that night, I'd located the branch that held Raeni post box, a small office about ten miles from the shelter. It hadn't been easy, but by pretending over the phone to be an assortment of my bunkmates looking for forgotten mail, I'd managed to zero in on the right one. As I contemplated pitching a tent in front of that building, the smell of frying bacon sifting through the otherwise putrid Roosevelt Room, I felt a lump under my behind. *More files?*

I got up and peeked under the towel. It was cell phone; a *nice* cell; a fucking BlackBerry. I dropped the towel and glanced around to see if anyone else had seen what I had just seen. No one appeared interested, the cook having already seized their limited attentions. Hurriedly, I wrapped it up in the towel, got dressed and decided to skip breakfast, heading instead for the only reliably private spot within earshot—the front seat of my Camaro.

Why the cloak and dagger? I asked myself as I walked briskly to the parking lot. I didn't have an answer, but this pint-sized computer with a dial tone was the second Secret Santa gift I'd gotten in as many days and my gut was telling me it was somehow related to the first. Unless, of course, *everyone* had found a new BlackBerry in their bed that morning? *No, I'll bet this belonged to Felix Ostrander.* Either way, I wanted the chance to explore its memory before someone (Charles) noticed me with it and began asking questions. After all, not many homeless men own working cell phones.

This particular model was one of BlackBerry's finest, touting a surprisingly fat display screen and a full keyboard—a Star Trek communicator compared to the three year old flip phone lost during my apartment fiasco. I turned it on and watched excitedly as the full color menu appeared, an impressive array of cartooned icons set before a spectacular shot of the Colosseum built by the Roman Empire. Without hesitation, my fingers went to work and after a few dead ends, I finally found what I wanted to know first. The cell phone didn't belong to Felix Ostrander; its owner was Louis Vinson.

For the next hour I was Sherlock Holmes at the Bates Motel, scouring every inch of Vinson's microprocessor, hoping to unearth a bloody knife—any reference to me or Felix Ostrander that might clue me in about Vinson's interest in our files. But I found nothing—not a single mention of the two of us anywhere. We weren't listed in his contacts, or in his calendar. A thorough pan of his emails didn't yield any gold either. I could have concluded that Vinson didn't know me or Felix, but I didn't believe that. I was convinced he sent his goon to the shelter that night to fetch what I caught him with. I just didn't know why. I decided that he was just smart and didn't keep any sensitive information on his handheld. Rolling down the window to let some of the early morning heat escape, I decided to keep digging.

Another twenty minutes went by before I began to realize that this was too easy. I was able to access everything on the device without a single request for a password. *Why hadn't Vinson set some security on this thing? A man of his wealth and stature had to know an enemy would love to get their hands on it and strip it of every critical name and number.* Suddenly, it didn't make sense. I paused, attempting to establish a plausible explanation. *Did Vinson want me find this? No, that made no sense either. Had my Secret Santa disabled the security? That was possible.* Concluding that I really didn't care, I pushed on.

What was really cool about this BlackBerry was it had a directory explorer just like a regular computer, allowing me to search the hard drive in a way not available on most cell phones. Unfortunately, there wasn't a single item in the "My Documents" folder. Then, just as I was about to call it quits and hopefully snag some leftover bacon from the kitchen, I spotted a folder called "Rome." It reminded me of the articles I'd seen on the web, referring to Vinson as Caesar. *A code word for his empire building plans, perhaps?* Probing into the subfolders, I came across a very curiously titled spreadsheet. It read "Et tu Brute." It was Shakespeare, I thought, Caesar's last words when he saw Brutus among his murderers. *A list of Vinson's enemies?* This was starting to get interesting; I definitely had to see what was inside. I clicked on it, watched the hourglass materialize before the first password request I'd encountered stopped me dead in my tracks. *Damn!*

First, I typed in Caesar. The thing beeped at me, chirping like a pissed off chickadee before asking if I wanted try again. *Hell yes!*

I tried Brutus and got flipped the melodic bird from the same boisterous chickadee.

Now I was at an impasse. From experience, I knew that many systems lock down after three foiled attempts—three strikes and you're out—and I was down to my last swing. Deciding I needed time and a little fuel to think before I leaped, I stuffed the BlackBerry into my pocket and went looking for breakfast. The password would mean something to Vinson, perhaps his wife's name or an abbreviated address. After a meal I would search for those possibilities and more, surfing the web, the source of all things known to man.

The bacon was long gone by the time I returned to the dining hall. I settled for the last bran muffin—Charles insisted everyone's diet include plenty of fiber—carting it off to the Business Office where I could pick at it from my desk while I Googled for facts about Louis Vinson and Julius Caesar.

After logging onto my computer, I decided to make a copy of one of my own spreadsheets and experiment with the password security before I jumped onto the internet. Using my first name, I assigned it and then counted the number of times the software allowed me to guess incorrectly before telling me to take a hike. It never did. I typed in one word after another—every curse and cuss I could think of—and the password window just kept begging for more. Finally, I typed in my name and sure enough, the file opened like a sail in the wind. *Cool! I had the green light to swing away.*

My first stop along the information highway was the free online encyclopedia, Wikipedia. The site boasted over one and a half million articles, complete with pictures, bookmarks to related sections of the site, as well external links to web sites around the world with additional information. It was a researcher's wet dream, an amateur sleuth's playground and I entered it sensing it held the key to Vinson's password.

Clearly, Louis Vinson had a thing for Julius Caesar and Rome, so I called that up first, typing in the search box the phrase, "Roman Empire." Vinson's nickname *was* Caesar; his BlackBerry screen displayed the Colosseum; and his use of references from the ancient emperor's life to label his files reminded me of how I used to brand my Matchbox cars with star baseball players names to rate their status in my heart. (I had favorite players and favorite cars and being an only child, a little too much alone time on my hands.) If he was like me, he would have drawn a name or an expression from something he loved, something he wouldn't forget when it came time to reopen that file.

As I read page after page about the civilization that succeeded the five hundred year-old Roman Republic, beginning around the time of Jesus Christ, I jotted down the better potentials until I had filled a whole page with names and dates. I'd never studied ancient history, I'd been home schooled by my long deceased mother who stuck to basic reading, writing and arithmetic, but if this slice of ancient Rome was any indicator, there certainly was a lot of it to learn, and more discouragingly, way too many password possibilities.

Undaunted, I tried everything on my list before leaning back in my chair, frustrated when the last one failed. *Maybe it's something simple,* I thought, *like his wife's name or his birthday.* I reached for the mouse and just as I was about to begin a new search, I noticed a bookmarked phrase. *Caeser's cipher.* I clicked on it.

It seems that Caesar was one of the world's first cryptographers, the originator of one of the simplest and widely known encryption techniques ever devised. Aware that any message he sent out from Rome might fall into enemy hands, he used the coding whenever he needed to communicate with his campaigning generals. According to Wikipedia, the Caesar cipher, as it is known, can be found today in children's toys like the caramel-encrusted secret decoder ring found at the bottom of a Cracker Jack's box.

Reading further, I learned that the Caesar cipher was a type of substitution cipher in which each letter in the plaintext is replaced

Erased 139

by a letter some fixed number of positions further down the alphabet. A shift of one would result in the letter A being written as the letter B. The word cat would then be written in code as the meaningless word "dbu." I also discovered that Caesar himself had a preference for a shift of three, using it more and more as loyalties swayed and his suspicions of murderous plots grew.

"Clever," I whispered as I returned to the spreadsheet file and typed in "fdhvdu," the encrypted version of the name Caesar. *Bingo!* I was in.

Perhaps it was the accountant in me, the one who'd tripped over some irregularities in the Earth Nexus books before being shown the door, but I really was expecting to find a wealth of financial data in the spreadsheet, a trove of swindled deals detailing the millions Vinson had pocketed from unsuspecting investors and business partners. Isn't that the kind of information you protect with a well thought out password? I was disappointed. The spreadsheet contained nothing more than a list of names, none of which I recognized until, that is, I scrolled down to the bottom of the page.

"Daniel Rayne," I mumbled, reading it off the screen. *So I do exist.*

And so did Felix Ostrander. His name was right above mine.

I then read the date next to my name. It was the day I got shit-canned from Earth Nexus, the day I lost my apartment and my identity, the day my world stopped turning. I cocked my head as a shiver ran up my spine. I quickly scrolled to the top of the page, lining up the date with its column heading. My jaw dropped.

Then, slowly, my hands noticeably shaking, I rose to my feet, staring unbelievingly at the single six letter word glowing like a beacon in black and white. I wasn't insane. I had been *ERASED*.

21

Catch 22

The discovery of Vinson's BlackBerry and its startling contents completely sidetracked me from finding Raeni. I still had her last paycheck in my pocket but a more pressing issue on the brain. How could Vinson have erased me? How could he have possibly wiped out all record of my existence from the DMV, from my bank, and from the minds of people I'd interacted with again and again since moving to Boston? Computer records could be deleted, paper trails burned, but human memory? That required willing collusion and that's when I realized that the security guard knew me; he'd just been paid to pretend he didn't. In all likelihood, Horace and Doris had been compromised as well. As I stood up from my desk and stretched, stiff from the many hours in front of my computer, I couldn't help wondering, *who else?*

That question triggered the more immediate and distressing concern—how far had Vinson gone? How deeply into my past had he traveled in search of every footprint I'd ever left on this Earth? My fear was that he had dug deep, so deep in fact that I might never find my way back to the surface. Everything I had read about him indicated he was a fanatic, a balls-to-the-wall extremist who never did anything half-assed. If he erased me as the spreadsheet indicated he had—a conclusion fully supported by my experiences of the past days—I was willing to bet my saggy cot at the shelter that he did a damn good job of it.

Asking myself what Raeni would suggest I do if she were standing next to me, I decided it was high time I started to resurrect my life. Vinson couldn't have wiped out everything. If I could just find one valid reference to my existence—one picture, one government document, or one scrap of paper linking me to me—it would most certainly lead me to others. It had to. My lost life depended on it.

Starting a brand new spreadsheet, I began listing everything I could think of that could prove my identity. Remembering the passport application poster on the post office wall, I tried to recall if I'd ever been in the hospital. *Certainly as a baby*, I thought. *They would have record of my birth along with some real footprints.* But then I recalled the story my mother had told me countless times of the harrowing home delivery of her only child. "You were ready to come out," she would say to me, "and you weren't going to take no for an answer." Fortunately, her neighbor—who had six children of her own—had come by that morning for coffee, I remember her saying. "Otherwise, I think I would have been saying goodbye to the world just as you were saying hello." Sixteen years later, she did say goodbye, but at least we had had the first part of my life together.

I'd always considered myself lucky for never having broken a bone or suffered an appendicitis attack. Now I didn't feel lucky, only undocumented.

As I thought about my mother in a way I hadn't for years, a flood of happy memories invaded my consciousness, lifting a heartfelt smile onto my face for the first time in days. Katherine was her name and she was a good mother, kind and compassionate. Instead of money, she rewarded my childhood efforts with generous hugs and words of encouragement. That may have been because we didn't have much money, but I believe it would have been no different had we been rich. The two of us managed alone, uprooting every few years to explore new people and places, the questions about my father going unanswered before finally disappearing, silently, in the rear view mirror of my mother's rusted out Chevy.

We settled down, finally, in Greenville, Rhode Island, a small town just west of Providence. There, my mother worked afternoons and evenings as a hostess at a local steakhouse. During the morning, she was my teacher, choosing my lessons herself instead of busing me off to the local high school. She was smart and pretty, a favorite amongst the local bachelors who often times appeared at our door with flowers and hopeful eyes. And then, one day she was gone. A grease fire exploded out of control one night at the restaurant, trapping my mother and several waitresses in the back with no means of escape. The ensuing funeral was well attended by hundreds of people I didn't know, employees and patrons of the restaurant I was told later by her visibly shaken, former manager.

That same day, as I knelt empty and numb in front of my mother's headstone, a man I never met before put his hand on my shoulder and offered me a ride home. He was an older man— what my grandfather might have looked like had I ever known him—and he said that he had known my mother for a long time. "She was a beautiful soul," he said, his face flushed and streaked with tears like a midwinter windowpane. "I promised her I'd look after you if anything ever happened to her." His name was Joseph Jones and he fulfilled his pledge to my mother, taking me into his modest home like a son and finishing the lessons my mother had started until his death less than a year ago.

Ok, so there are no hospital records to go looking for, I concluded. But I did have a birth certificate which meant my arrival into the world have been recorded somewhere. I kept it in a filing cabinet along with my social security card, twelve months worth of bank statements and an accumulation of bills, letters and misfiled junk. The only pictures I had of me and my mother were there too, a handful of snapshots taken each time we arrived at a new homestead. I had never gotten them framed, putting it off year after year, too weak to confront the stabbing pain I felt every time I looked at them.

Jumping back on the web, I went searching for the government agency responsible for birth registration. I hadn't looked at my own birth certificate in years and had no idea what emblem was stamped at the top. I only knew I'd been born somewhere in New York, on Christmas Eve in 1977. "You were my present that year," my mother had always told me. "The best one I ever got."

Within minutes, I determined that the New York State Department of Health maintained the birth records for all babies born in New York, dating back to 1881. However, for births in one of the five boroughs of New York City (Manhattan, Kings, Queens, the Bronx, and Staten Island), I would need to visit the New York City Department of Health and Mental Hygiene. *Had I been born in New York City?* I honestly didn't know. My mother had never talked about New York City so my initial guess was no, I hadn't been born there. I decided to start off with the state agency first, praying my intuition was right. I didn't get very far.

According to their website, I could request a copy of my birth certificate, but my application needed to be submitted with a least one form of identification—a photo ID such as a driver's license or passport, or two original utility or phone bills addressed to the same person listed on the application. I didn't have either. Horace and Doris Forrest had all of it, or a landfill somewhere. I realized right then that I missed my opportunity to go back to that apartment building and go searching for my irreplaceable belongings. Vinson would have certainly taken care of that loose end by now.

Obtaining another copy of my birth certificate looked to be no easier than getting a passport at the post office. Each agency needed identification, the one thing I didn't have. Completely frustrated, I pushed away from my desk, exhaling a deep sigh as I threw my hands in the air. This whole mess was proving to be one huge catch twenty-two. With no means of *proving* who I was, there was not way for me to *obtain proof* of who I was. *Was this how Jesus had felt when he claimed to be the son of God?* I thought, clinging to what little there was left of my sense of humor. *If only I could walk on water.*

With my own records gone, I needed outside documentation from a trustworthy source, like a school or a police agency. But I'd been home-schooled, so I had no transcripts and I'd never committed a crime in my life. I'd thought about shoplifting a video game console once when we were living in Ohio. All the other kids in the building had them but my mother couldn't afford one. Desperate to fit in, I plotted a strategy to sneak one under my jacket from a local store, only to then bail out at the last minute. I knew I couldn't have faced my mother if caught, it would have crushed her. *If only I had been bolder and less concerned for her feelings,* I thought. There would then be an escape to this nightmare—documented fingerprints.

What else could prove that I'm Daniel Rayne? Think, man, think.

Then, remembering the plot of a cheap, paperback murder mystery I'd read a few months back, I tried to recall the name of the last dentist I'd visited. In the book, the grisly dead woman turns out to be the mayor's wife, her mutilated remains identified only by her gold crowns and bridgework. Not as solid as fingerprints, but unique enough to get my resurrection rolling. The only problem was I hadn't gone to a dentist since my mother died. It had been over thirteen years since my last checkup; something my mother had been a stickler about, escorting me every six months for fresh x-rays and a cleaning. It had paid off; I'd never lost a tooth and had only a few minor cavities. On the other hand, Poppa Joe, as I came to call him, wasn't much for dentists himself so he never required that I go.

Confident that x-rays of my teeth could be my ticket home, I searched my brain for the name of my dentist in Greenville, the last one I ever visited and therefore the likely owner of my medical records. *Doctor...doctor...doctor somebody. Damn it!* Nothing was materializing. What a time for a brain cramp.

Vinson certainly picked the right guy to erase, I lamented. *Jack the Ripper left a clearer trail to follow than I have.* Then, it hit me. Had Vinson known this? That I was an easy mark—a man effectively written in pencil instead of ink? The more I thought about it, the more it made sense. He had done a background check on me before making the job offer—a really deep check. How else would my secretary, Irene Doolittle, have known what I preferred for lunch? I'd only been there a day and hadn't said a word to her about it. And yet, she nailed it, right down to the lettuce but no tomato. A twinge of anxiety rippled through my body as I realized Vinson would have then known about my forged resume, the one I had copied from Poppa Joe's, altering timeframes to fit my age and membership in Generation X. I didn't truthfully have a high school diploma or a college degree as my fill-in-father and mentor had, only the wide breadth of knowledge bestowed upon me by a dear old man with Alzheimer's.

But if Vinson knew that, why would he hire me?

Shaking my head, I logged off my computer and headed toward the dining hall, hungry for some dinner and the answer to a very interesting question.

22

Variety, the Spice of Life

Sammy Johnson was a former everything. You name it—semi-pro football, golden glove boxing, ultimate fighting, second-tier celebrity bodyguard and military man—at one time or another he'd done it. Tattooed on sixty percent of his chiseled body, including one of Winnie the Pooh at the base of his penis, he'd been in and out of prison since he was eighteen—assault charges mostly—but had managed to stay clean for the past year and a half, largely due to the far reaching influences of his current employer, Louis Vinson. Today, he came to Vinson's magnificent penthouse suite for their weekly face-to-face, a grueling hour of question and answer that typically saw Vinson asking all the questions while Johnson scrambled for the right answers.

The past week had not been a particularly memorable one for Sammy. He had botched a burglary and received a whipping from a homeless guy, neither of which he told Vinson about yet. It had been his only assignment and he fucked it up royally. As he sat before Vinson's desk in a plain, uncomfortable wooden chair that seemed out of place in the plush surroundings, he braced himself for the upcoming rake-over-the-coals.

Still pissed off about misplacing his BlackBerry, Vinson was not in a good mood and though he didn't know it yet, Sammy's weekly report was only going to make it worse.

Erased 147

"Have you got those files for me?" Vinson asked. He rarely tiptoed around the issue at hand, except when he wanted to make someone squirm. Sammy wasn't a squirmer though; just a very strong man with a really short fuse, one Vinson knew enough not to light. He got up into Sammy's grill only once, a few days after his hire, and that had proven to be a mistake. Carefully selected words faired better against Sammy Johnson. In those battles, he had few means for defending himself.

"Oh, shit," Sammy said in exaggerated disgust. "I left them back at my place. I apologize, Mr. Vinson. I'll bring them by first thing in the morning, if that's all right with you."

Sammy's boss glared at him. Vinson knew bullshit when he smelt it and Sammy was reeking.

Holding firm, the former Marine washout glared back, his muscles coiling instinctively, preparing to counter if Vinson came charging over the desk. It was a reflex that had gotten him into trouble many times, but Sammy couldn't help it, his temper never strayed far from the surface, lingering like a hungry swamp gator.

"Tomorrow, first thing," Vinson said. He knew Sammy was lying but he had more pressing issues to discuss. The first being Elizabeth Hart, the acquisitions analyst he just sent to the unemployment line for not sharing her considerable charms with an important client. She was a pristine bitch who refused to uncross her legs and now she would have to pay the piper for her prudishness. Had her pedigree been less impressive—and less documented—Vinson would have opted to erase her like so many others, relishing the sight of her wandering the streets like a worthless crack whore. But her rescue net was too big—family, friends and colleagues far too expansive even for Vinson's gang of computer hackers and arm twisters to wipe clean. No, he couldn't get his jollies with pretty young Elizabeth that way. He would have to choose another route, one that would be equally entertaining, while at the same time rock the foundation of Earth Nexus's fiercest competitor—Google.

Vinson handed Sammy a snapshot he'd taken at a recent Earth Nexus team building retreat. It showed a casually dressed Elizabeth Hart walking up the hallway at the conference center, her slender arms full of reading material, her blushing smile full of life. No one else was in the picture.

"Nice," Sammy said, nodding his head in appreciation. "You want me to assist her to the curb?"

"No, Sammy," Vinson replied. "I've got something better in mind for Ms. Hart. Her address is written on the back. Pay her a visit. Take her for a ride. Show her some sights, but make sure you get her to the villa by midnight."

Sammy knew the villa. It was a nondescript house in Brooklyn with a middle class appeal above ground and a state-of-the-art visual recording studio in the basement. It was where Vinson produced much of the content for his pet project, Manhattan Uncut, a candid camera style video sharing website aimed at taking pornography to a new all-time low. Sammy had escorted many unsuspecting strippers and hookers there, watching intently as several other men raped and abused the women in front of the cameras. The resulting videos were then uploaded onto the website for anonymously worldwide viewing pleasure. Observing from only a few yards away, Sammy always hoped that one day he'd be asked to join in on the sadistic action he found very arousing. He knew he could do it better than the chumps Vinson was using. He only needed a chance to prove it.

Perplexed as to why he needed to get the woman there by midnight, Sammy asked, "What, will she turn into a turnip like that Cinderblock chick if I don't?"

Vinson laughed. Sometimes Sammy was priceless. "No, Elizabeth's got a show to do, her internet debut."

Sammy leaned forward as he glanced again at Elizabeth's picture, his carnal interest rising. Vinson had never used someone like her before. "Porn? I could get into that; wear a mask while I bang the daylights out of her. Nobody would recognize me then.

And I'd do her good, Mr. Vinson. You'd see. That bitch would be begging for mercy, just the way you like it."

Right, Vinson thought. No one would even notice the tattoos, especially Winnie the Pooh. "I'm sorry, Sammy, but the script calls for a solo performance. But now that you mention it, I think a good time might be just the thing to help her relax before she takes center stage."

Sammy's disappointment was evident until he realized what Vinson was instructing him to do. "How good a time should I show her?" Sammy asked, grinning. He could feel his blood migrating south, engorging his currently famished appetite for an unwilling partner.

"That's totally up to you, Sammy," Vinson replied. "And don't worry about mussing her hair or makeup. That's the way the character she'll be playing is suppose to look." Vinson paused, thinking. "In fact, make it point to mark her up a bit. It will save us some time in the studio."

"What's her character's name?" Sammy asked, thinking it would be one of those great porn names like Bambi Cumsalot or Cherry Poppins.

"Elizabeth Hart," Vinson replied coolly.

Vinson then handed him a second picture, this one of a handsome young man sitting at a desk. Irene Doolittle had taken the picture weeks ago and emailed it to Vinson.

"I already know where to find this guy," Sammy said, recognizing the face instantly. It was the man he'd been choking in the homeless shelter, the same night his own lights flickered out before he found himself lying in an alley a few blocks away, bruised and bloodied. He didn't know the man's name and he didn't care to.

Sammy then noticed the date on the back of the photo. "You want him at the studio a week from now?" he asked.

"No, that's the day I want him dead," Vinson snarled. Sometimes Sammy was thick as a brick. *People who don't play ball* the way I tell them, Mr. Daniel Rayne, get taken out of the game—permanently!

Sammy liked both assignments. They were completely different and he was one of those guys who liked variety, the spice of life. As he was leaving, his footsteps light and airy as he imagined the amusement that awaited him, Vinson's voice caught him at the door.

"One more thing, Sammy. When you catch up to him, let him feel it for a while before you put him out of his misery."

"Sure thing, boss," was all Sammy said.

23

Partners in Crime

As was her punctual nature, Raeni arrived at the club early that night only to find the owner, Uncle Bob, leaning against his car under the only working light in the parking lot, looking haggard and contrite. Other than his Cadillac, there wasn't another spot taken in the lot. Normally there was a half dozen or so cars by this time, customers eager for a drink and the aromatic smell of young flesh. Noticing there wasn't another soul within sight, the situation suddenly made Raeni uneasy. Had she misjudged Uncle Bob?

Walking up to him slowly, Raeni asked what he was doing outside.

"A temporary shut down," Uncle Bob said. "The Health Department made a surprise visit an hour ago and ordered the doors closes. The guy mumbled something about not being able to assure public safety. I've already called my lawyer. He can weed through all that mumbo-jumbo better than I can."

"So, none of us can work tonight?" she asked, thinking about her horse farm schedule and her need to do at least three hundred dollars a night to keep pace.

"I'm afraid not, doll, and maybe not for another week or so."

"A whole week?" Raeni asked.

"I'm really sorry, Raeni, for you and all the girls. I know you got bills to pay just as I do, but there's nothing I can do right now. I've been through this before and it takes time to fix whatever they want fixed and then a few more days before they'll send somebody out to sign off and let me open up again."

Raeni's shoulders drooped. Just when she thought she was back on track, the horse pulls up lame. Ever the optimist, her distress didn't linger long. *A week isn't that bad*, she thought, *Uncle Bob will let me work a few extra nights when he opens back up to make up the ground I've lost.* As she tried to recall when the next return bus would be coming by, she heard Thumper pulling into the lot in her muffler-challenged Ford Escort.

"What's going on?" Thumper asked as she exited her car. "Are we doing an outdoor show tonight?" As always, she was ready to dance and shake the money tree, as she liked to call the customers. A tall, slender brunette in her mid-twenties, her autobiographical club profile described her as an eye popper with perky breasts, a pleasing plump bottom, and long, smooth legs that stretched from heaven all the way to hell. She was all that and the consummate saleswoman to boot, capable of selling English etiquette lessons to a NASCAR fanatic with the wink of her eye.

"They shut us down," Raeni informed her.

Uncle Bob nodded. "The Health Department, not more than an hour ago. I thought I best wait here and let everybody know."

"That sucks!" Thumper said, disgusted.

"We'll be back on stage in no time," Raeni said. "Consider it a vacation."

"Listen to little Miss Sunshine," Thumper replied sarcastically. She stood glaring at Uncle Bob, one hand on her cocked hip, the other holding an unlit cigarette that she then pointed at her feet. "How am I supposed to pay for this new leather I just bought on credit?" She held out her left leg to show off the white leather thigh-highs that added six inches to her already statuesque frame.

"Nice," Uncle Bob said, enthusiastically. He stepped toward Thumper, admiring how they glowed under the street lamp.

When confronted by a pissed off and scantily dressed employee, Uncle Bob had found that compliments worked almost as good as a round of free Jello shots.

After Thumper chilled, cooled by the breeze of Uncle Bob's infatuation with her boots, she offered Raeni a ride home. "The bus ain't no place for a fine young thing like you this time of the night," she insisted. Raeni readily accepted, relieved to avoid the blitz of catcalls and come-ons from the public transportation crowd. Leaving Uncle Bob coughing in her oil-burning exhaust, Thumper wasted no time making her passenger an offer to help her replace the night's lost income.

"I'm telling you, Raeni," Thumper said. "It might be a month before Bobby gets the place opened up again, maybe longer. What are you going to do in the meantime, pay the rent with blowjobs? Axel, my brother, belongs to this huge gym on the west side of town. It's crawling with guys looking for bachelor party entertainment. If I give him the word, he'll have 'em lined up at our door."

"What kind of entertainment?" Raeni asked warily.

"Relax, little sister, Thumper's got your back. Most nights it would be the same as the club. Warm up the boys with a couple of show-time dances, and then your basic looky-no-touchy bump and grind in a back room for anyone named Benjamin."

"Benjamin?"

"Benjamin Franklin, girl. The old geezer on the hundred dollar bill."

"They'll pay a hundred for a lap dance?"

"Damn right. And why not, we're worth it."

Raeni forced a smile. *I am really worth it?* Sometimes she wondered why men would pay so much just to feel her rubbing against them, why they would pay even more to watch her being raped and strangled. Men were a mystery, a dangerous puzzle that sometimes produced images that made her turn away—her father, who wandered off with her heart when she was three; her stepfather, who almost robed her of her soul; and the demon who nearly took everything as he watched her life draining away into the hands of her executioner. Still, for reasons she couldn't understand she enjoyed the way men looked at her when she was dancing in the club, gazing hypnotically as if she were the only woman in the world. On stage, she was desirable and most importantly, she was the one in control, dog walking her admirers with an invisible leash—the tilt of her head, the wave of her hips, the wanton look in her eyes. In the club, the dancers dictated the rules, not the men who strutted in with fists full of dollars and visions of getting laid in the girl's dressing room. In the club, no one got laid unless the girl said so. The bouncers saw to that, the burly line drawn in the sand that only the foolish and drunken crossed. Inside those protected walls Raeni felt untouchable. Beyond, she was a young woman in a man's world—a puzzling world with many razor-sharp pieces.

"Girl on girl action is where the real money's at," Thumper said, continuing her pitch. "Guys will pay anything for it. One thousand, two thousand, shit, I had one guy offer me five thousand if I'd do his ex-girlfriend with a strap-on in front of his buddies."

"His ex?" Raeni asked, muffling a sudden giggle. Up until this point she'd been fending off Thumper's proposals with wary shakes of her head, remembering Marko's lifeless eyes and the shivers that shook her entire body when she saw his assassin arrive at the shelter. *No more private shows. Never again.* But Thumper persisted; assuring her it was as safe as flying in an airplane. "Axel escorts me everywhere," she said. "And nobody messes with Axel." Thumper made it sound so easy and now, as she described the vengeful ex-boyfriend, amusingly ridiculous.

"Oh yeah," Thumper replied. "I get all kinds coming up to me at the club. It seems this guy was getting married in a few days and his ex was after him for one last kiss, if you get my drift. He had no interest in boffing her again, or so he claimed, but thought it would be funny if he accepted her offer, got her drunk and took her to a hotel room where I would be waiting along with the peanut gallery. He said she was bisexual and would fall into my arms like a lost puppy as soon as she saw me while he and his friends cheered us on."

"That's really strange," Raeni said.

"Not the strangest request I've ever gotten," Thumper said, grinning.

"I don't want to hear about."

"Who said I wanted to tell you about it?"

Raeni laughed. Thumper was working on her defenses and Raeni could feel them softening.

"Anyway," Thumper said. "I never got to break in the new nine inch dildo I bought just for the occasion. Axel caught mono from some bimbo he met at Chunky Cheese and forced me to cancel."

Entertainingly shocked, Raeni stole a glance at Thumper's lap. Thumper noticed. "What are you looking at?" she asked.

"I'm trying to imagine you with a hard on."

"Just because I wasn't born with a hammer, that doesn't mean I don't know how to pound a nail."

Raeni giggled, blushing invisibly in the darkness of the car cabin. For a stripper, she was sexually inexperienced, an irony that she kept to herself. In truth, she was inexperienced for the average twenty-year-old woman regardless of her profession, a choice she made out of uncertainty and fear. It wasn't that she wasn't attracted to the opposite sex. She was. Just not the creeps that never failed to find their way to her door. Her stepfather had been pawing at her since she was fourteen, his friends following his example shortly thereafter. Careful to never get caught alone with any of them, she always shadowed her mother when she could, stayed out of the house when she had to. And sometimes she fought back, accepting that a black eye was better that being raped. On her eighteenth birthday she woke up realizing that she was still a virgin, staring resolutely at the suitcase she'd packed the night before, wondering if she would ever meet a man that would make her feel differently.

Noticing her shyness, Thumper said, "Not your cup of tea, ay girl?"

"I can't say that I ever thought that much about it."

"It ain't no thing, really, just sex. It can be fun, like a pillow fight. You must have had a few pillow fights with your girl friends in high school. Mine always turned into make-out sessions."

Raeni threw her a shocked smile.

"Oh, come on, Raeni, it's the twenty-first century. Don't give that catholic school girl look. I expected enthusiasm from you, not guilt-ridden horror. You see the sunny side of everything, so why should this be any different."

"That used to be my stage name," Raeni said.

"What did?"

"Sunny. That used to be my name when I worked in New York."

Thumper smiled. "Sunny. That suits you, girl. Why'd you change it?"

"Things got a little stormy in New York."

"And so you changed it to Raeni," Thumper said, nodding in appreciation. "That's really cute. To bad some of the other girls aren't so creative. I mean Star, Foxy and Pepper? Those names were already old when you and I were born."

"Don't tell anyone, though," Raeni said, her young face turning suddenly serious. As soon as the words had left her lips, she wished she hadn't said them. But it was too late to take them back now.

"Do I look like a blabber mouth to you, girl?"

Raeni relaxed in her seat and reassured her friend that she trusted her.

"Anyway, most of the time I leave Big Butch home," Thumper said. "That's what I named it, my imitation Johnson, that is. That's what Axel calls my strap-on, *my imitation Johnson*. Says it looks just like his." She turned a corner, snorting a laugh as she wrestled with the wheel. "In his dreams," she said.

"Well, imitation is the best form of flattery," Raeni said.

The two women erupted into laughter.

A few minutes passed before Raeni's curiosity and thoughts of Pilgrim tossed her better judgment out the window like a spent cigarette.

"So, if Butch stays home in the toolbox, what would the two of us be doing to earn our fee?"

As Thumper's sub-compact sputtered its way along the shadowy trail, alone beneath the stars and the sleepy street lamp posts, the willowy brunette promised her new partner that it would be nothing she couldn't handle.

24

Buoyancy

I was truly grateful for all the shelter had provided me in my hour of need—a roof, a bed, a clean shirt—but I couldn't deny the fact that I was growing damn tired of bean soup. The broth was always over salted, the beans dryer than cotton and the accompanying week-old bread donated by a local bakery dotted with enough mold to start my own pharmacy. But as they say, beggars can't be choosy. I'm sure if Charles could have afforded a better variety he would have offered it, perhaps erecting an all-you-can-eat buffet and a salad bar that even the liquid-lunchers would have appreciated. But I knew from looking at the financials, that wasn't possible. The place was flat broke and hanging by a thread, the opposite end of which was held, I feared, by none other than Louis Vinson. It was apparent to me now that he had a grip on one of my strings as well.

Vinson knew I didn't have a formal education when he gave Hank Stallworth the green light to hire me, just as sure as he knew I had no where else to go when I packed my belongings and came to Boston. And my good fortune in meeting Gloria, the real estate wheeler-dealer with the harbor view, dream apartment? In all likelihood, staged, a setup to soften me for what would come later—the recruitment of a creative and mute accountant. The promotion and raise was a nice touch, momentarily turning my head away from the glaring sun of deception baking every page of their ledgers, until its sweltering heat began to singe the hair on the back of my neck.

I should have seen it rising on the horizon, bright orange and yellow, but I chose not to. Instead, I slapped on a pair of sunglasses and willingly ventured down the crooked garden path, skipping gleefully all the way, led by a sexy secretary and fat paycheck.

Had I walked away when I first smelt the fraudulent stench slathered all over my boss' spreadsheets, I might be eating a nice steak right now instead of a bowl of dripping cotton balls. I knew what it was—the game Earth Nexus was playing—but it wasn't until I asked for a timeout that the real rules became clear.

Poppa Joe had introduced me to more than one set of cooked books, alerting me to the telltale signs as well as the legal repercussions should I find myself in a desert without the proper screening lotion. "The CEO will claim accounting ignorance," he warned. "Tell the judge you were the one roasting the numbers. *Had us all fooled,* he'll say." Poppa Joe told me to never get involved in that sort of thing. It wasn't worth the risk. It wasn't until Hank Stallworth approached me that I realized I'd been listening to my mentor.

That Friday, just a few days before my world began to unravel, Hank entered my office and shut the door. He had a thick folder in his hand and a staid look on his face. I'd never seen him so serious, never noticed the way he fussed with his thinning hair, straightening a perfectly straight part again and again with twitchy fingers.

"Daniel, I think it's time you rolled up your sleeves and got your hands in the mud," he had said as he dropped the bundle in front of me. He then pointed at the file that was now oozing papers all over my desk. "Inside you'll find over twenty-five million dollars worth of expenses incurred during our failed attempt to acquire eBay. The board wants a ten percent increase in profits over last quarter, which means this lovely little pile needs to wiggle its way off the income statement and onto the balance sheet. I don't care how you do it as long as you break it down into digestible chunks. Nothing an auditor or overzealous stockholder might choke on, capiche?"

Based on my dismissal the following Monday, my shrouded hesitation at the time appears to have been far less subtle than I thought. Somehow, Hank knew I couldn't, or wouldn't, do the deed and decided to cut his losses by cutting me loose. I can only guess that when news of it got back to Vinson, he didn't take it well—an eye for eye, or in this case, an identity for refusing to be an accessory. *Damn, these people played for keeps!*

Earth Nexus had hired me *because* I was hiding something. They knew I had the skills but also a motivation to remain under the radar, no matter what they asked me to do. *If you don't ask questions, Daniel, we won't ask any either. Live and let live.*

But they'd guessed wrong with me and consequently the rules changed to live and let die. Vinson had done his best to put me down and keep me down, but in a strange way, I felt proud that such a powerful man had been bruised enough by my integrity to enter me into his secret spreadsheet. I'd caused a ripple in his pristine pond and if there was any consolation in this hell, that was it.

Finished with my bland dinner, I pushed my bowl away and scanned the dining hall, searching the drained faces for a sign of hope or optimism or anything I could cling to so I wouldn't feel so alone. Was each one of these men once me? Was I now irreversibly one of them? Refusing to stay down the way Vinson wanted me, I walked back to the office to work on my resurrection list.

Raeni was right, I told myself as I sat down at my desk. I didn't belong here. I was a smooth river stone who had a life not so many days ago, a life I wanted back. Vinson had had his fun; I couldn't go back and change any of that. Like a town leveled by a hurricane, all I could do was rebuild and that started with the first brick—the documented existence of Daniel Rayne.

When I was little, my mother always told me to find a policeman if I ever got lost. "They'll keep you safe until I find you," she would say. "Always know Daniel, that if that should ever happen, I will never stop looking. And I *will* find you." *If only she were still alive.*

That's when the image of a sweating and pissed off Officer Marty jumped into my head. He was waving my license at me, warning me not to cross his path again as if I were some sort of serial counterfeiter. "I'll lock you up so fast it'll make your head swim," he had said. He succeeded in dunking me that day, but now I was back above the surface breathing again. *Had he been a Vinson pawn too? Him and his scrawny partner paid off to make me think my license was bogus?*

If Officer Marty was indeed on the take, the Motor Vehicle Department would still have record of me. They'd have my picture, a record of the speeding ticket I got last year, as well a history of my renewals. That would certainly be enough to reclaim my social security number, obtain a passport and every other form of identification I could get my hands on. After this ordeal, I planned to get my hands on a lot. Maybe even steal a candy bar from the drug store just to get my fingerprints in the system. *Then again, maybe not.*

I called up my spreadsheet and added the DMV to my list. I would need to go back to the state of issuance—Rhode Island— but I needed to go back there anyway to visit my former dentist. While chewing on a particularly tough lima bean at dinner, I'd needled an old filling which in turn triggered the memory of the office I'd gotten it in. The two-story, converted residence sat on the main drag in Greenville and although the dentist's name hadn't come to mind, I was certain I'd recognize it when I saw it.

I pulled the BlackBerry from my pocket and kissed it. "I don't know how you got here, but I glad you made the party," I said. With two possible leads, I felt a buoyancy that I hadn't experienced since the day I took Raeni on a drive around Boston. Her spirit had lifted me on a day when I really needed it and as I contemplated my road trip and the salary advance I would need from Charles for food and gas, the liberating cell phone clutched in my hand, I decided I needed one more thing before I left—Raeni in the seat next to me.

25

Date Night

The weight room at the gym was nearly empty, just the way Sammy Johnson preferred it. Devoted to free weights, he hated that Bowflex shit on television, hyped by some little twerp with white teeth and gay shorts. Pumping solid cast iron barbells was where real muscle came from, not stretching "revolutionary" rubber bands. He was just finishing his three-hour routine, loading a series of plates onto the bar for his favorite exercise—the bench press. Sammy took great pride in his massive chest muscles, taking great time and care to work them properly every other day. Looking around the room, the proper protocol required he use a spotter.

"Hey buddy," he said to a man of equal bulk who was toweling off after completing his own daily regime, "how about spotting me while I pound out a few hundred reps."

"No problem," the man said. He then walked over and introduced himself.

"The name's Axel," he said, extending his hand.

"Sammy," Sammy replied.

The two men shook hands.

Sammy lay down on the bench, lifted the barbell off the hook and began pumping, handling the four hundred pounds of cast iron as easily as a beer lover tilts a bottle to his lips.

"I haven't seen you in here before," Axel said. "Just join?"

"Last week," Sammy said between exaggerated exhales. "Not enough women at the Gold's on State Street."

"I hear ya, brother. We've got some talent in here, though there's not much to look at today. Check out the aerobics schedule by the front desk. That's how I plan my workout times."

"Thanks, man. I'll do that." Sammy said. Finished with his first set, he placed the barbell back on its hooks and sat up, rubbing his pecs affectionately.

"You getting ready for a show?" Axel asked, thinking that the chiseled man was a professional body builder.

"No, I don't do that gay shit," Sammy answered. Then, smiling mischievously, he added, "I got a hot date tonight and I want to look good for the camera."

Axel smiled, knowingly. Paris Hilton had unwittingly helped make videoed sex the in thing and as Axel stood aside his new acquaintance as he finished his routine, he wondered who the lucky girl was.

The sun was just disappearing on the horizon as Sammy rang the doorbell. His flexing muscles still engorged with blood, he stood on the welcome mat eager to begin the evening's festivities, a black camera bag slung over his shoulder. This was the opportunity he had been hoping for, a chance to impress his boss with another of his talents. Until now, Vinson had only used Sammy for chauffeuring and the occasional skull bashing. Sammy could do more—he needed to do more. He feared being pigeonholed as mindless brawn. He had a sensual side, an erotic side, a riveting presence equal to any porn star. Tonight was his chance to prove it. He rang the bell a second time just as Elizabeth Hart was opening her door.

"Yes?" Elizabeth asked quizzically.

"Pooh wants some honey," Sammy said. He then forced

Elizabeth back into her apartment and closed the door behind him.

26

A Six-Letter Word Starting with 'B'

Staking out a post office was easier than I thought it would be. Looking like a needy homeless man certainly helped, giving the apathetic government employees an excuse to ignore me. I also made sure to shower that morning so that the ever-present shelter smog didn't get me shooed away. So far it was working. Sitting Indian style a few yards from the front entrance, I hadn't been approached all morning since handing Raeni's paycheck to the clerk behind the counter. I thought about holding it and giving it to her myself but decided she might think me a thief as well as a stalker. *How did you get this?* No doubt she was expecting it and most certainly would be stopping by here every so often to check. *Would my good luck continue?*

Charles truly was a generous man. He completely understood my need to revisit my hometown, loaning me fifty dollars from his own pocket to fund the voyage. I did lie a teeny bit though, telling him I had a distant cousin there who might be willing to help me get back on my feet. Sitting under a shady maple tree out in front of an official branch of the United States Post Office, I felt guilty about it right up until the moment I spotted Raeni crossing the street and heading straight toward me. Her warm, greeting smile instantly washed away my fears of rejection.

"I've heard of bar flies, but never a post office fly," she said, jokingly.

"I heard they were coming out with a new Elvis stamp," I replied. She looked beautiful, bright and chipper as always, her hair darker than I remembered it. "Did you color your hair?" I asked.

She told me she had, running her hand through it self-consciously.

I told her that I liked it, adding that it made the blue in her eyes leap out. *The blue that always draws me in,* I thought as we both fell into a silent pause. She never took her eyes from mine and as we stood in a dreamlike moment, I felt an urge to kiss her right then and there. Then, just as I was about to throw caution to the wind, she leaned over and kissed *me*. On the cheek, that is.

"I owe you an apology, Daniel," she said. "Disappearing on you like that wasn't the nicest thing I've ever done."

I didn't know what to say. I wasn't mad, if that was her concern, only disappointed that she hadn't come back. I wanted to tell her that, to reassure her, but for some reason I couldn't get the words out. Instead, I just gazed back at her and smiled.

"I hope you're not mad at me," she said.

"Well, maybe just a little," I said, lying through my teeth. The little boy in me had seized control, hoping for another kiss. I got a hug instead, the best one in a long while.

"What are you doing here, anyway?" she asked after I released her.

Another white lie leapt from my tongue before I could wrestle it down. "Hillary asked me to drop off your check. She forgot to mail it and didn't want you to wait another day for it. She thought you might need it for rent or something. My Camaro and I weren't doing anything, so I volunteered."

"How sweet," she said. "Do you have it with you?"

"Its inside," I said. "You know how the post office is about tampering with official mail."

"Oh, well wait right here while I get it and when I come back you can tell me everything that's been going on with you and the gang at the shelter."

"Sounds like a plan," I said. *Exactly the one I woke up with this morning.*

Five minutes later, we were walking to my car, Raeni agreeing with my suggestion to take another drive along Boston Harbor. She said her day was free and being a homeless man, so was mine. I ached to tell her what I learned from Vinson's BlackBerry, to show her the proof of my identity. Explain to her that I'd been setup by a power hungry psycho, erased to essentially render me harmless. But it was more than that. The high tech gadget wedged in my pocket proved that I was an honest man, and most importantly, a viable suitor. Even with all that had happened, attracting Raeni's attention remained in the forefront of my mind. Perhaps it was instinct taking over—perpetuation of the species— or a need to grab hold of something to ride out the storm. I liked to think it was something deeper and as we strolled down the street I felt we had a connection like nothing I'd experience before. I just wasn't sure what to call it.

"Have you got enough gas to make it to the harbor and back?" Raeni asked. She opened the passenger door and slid into the seat next to me.

"A full tank," I said. "Charles forwarded me some cash. I'm working full time for him in the office now, maintaining the books."

"You mean Hillary has to share her files now? I'll bet that didn't go over well."

"She's very nice," I countered. I turned the ignition key, feeling the 350 cubic inch V-8 engine spring to life. My Camaro wasn't a gas miser as I might have liked under the circumstances but at least we would look damn good on the road, even if we couldn't travel very far. As long as it got us to Greenville and back I'd be happy. All I had to do was figure out how to inject that detour into the conversation with Raeni.

I estimated that I had about fifteen minutes of road between us and the expressway ramp that would slingshot us toward Rhode Island—fifteen minutes to explain something I didn't totally understand myself. Pulling the BlackBerry from my pocket as I drove, I decided to start off my half-factual, half-speculative account on a positive note.

I handed the coveted means of cellular communication to Raeni. "I brought you a present," I said.

"Awesome! I've always wanted one of these," she exclaimed, excitedly. She examined it top to bottom, front and back, finally finding the button to turn it on. "Now, if only I could afford the service," she chuckled as the screen burst into a rainbow of colors. Raeni's eyes widened, her smile stretching from ear to ear. "Thank you, Daniel. But you shouldn't have; it's way too expensive."

"Well, before you cover me with kisses, I have to be honest. I found it under my cot at the shelter. Actually, someone put it there and then I found it. I don't know who, but I do know who it used to belong to."

"Who?"

"Louis Vinson, the guy who showed up at the shelter that day. In the limo, remember?"

Raeni's smile faded as her eyes went dead. "Has he been back since then?" she managed to ask.

"Not that I know of," I replied. "Although, I'm fairly certain he sent one of his flunkies to snoop around a few nights ago."

Raeni threw the phone into my lap and turned away, the breeze churning in the convertible blowing the tears down the sides of her cheeks. Confused, I asked her what was wrong?

Raeni didn't answer.

As hard as I was trying to connect with her, somehow I kept putting my foot in my mouth. I'd gotten the cold shoulder upon calling her Sunny the day we met and now I'd brought her to tears. Don Juan I wasn't. Sensing that any moment she might ask me to return her to the post office where she would disappear forever, I decided it was time for the truth, straight up and to the point.

"This guy Vinson, he erased me. Wiped out my life and left me for dead."

Raeni turned, wiped her eyes and asked me what I was talking about.

"He owns Earth Nexus, the company I was working for before I came to the shelter."

"I remember," she said. "You said you believed they were cooking their books to attract investors."

This was some serious shit I was trying to explain but I couldn't stop a smile from blossoming. Raeni had remembered everything I told her. Maybe she felt a connection to me after all. Or maybe I was just seeing what I wanted to see. I didn't stop to debate it.

"Well, it appears now that not only was I fired for not pledging allegiance to their fraud, but also stripped of my identity to prevent me from alerting the authorities. Can you imagine if I showed up at the District Attorney's office looking like this?" I was wearing another sparkling ensemble from the shelter's donated pile of discarded K-Mart fashions. "The first thing he'd say is 'Who the hell are you?' I don't even have a library card to show him. He'd laugh me out of his office."

Raeni just stared at me, uncomprehendingly.

"Do you understand what I'm saying? This guy demolished my life to shut me up. Tied a cement block to my ankle and threw me out into a low tide just so he could sit back and watch the water rise. That's why he sent his goon to the shelter, to see if I'd been able to loosen the knot."

"You think that's why Vinson came to the shelter, looking for you?"

"Not intentionally. I heard him talking with Charles, using his financial support to twist his arm for some client records he wanted. Charles didn't cave and Vinson left pissed. That night I caught his goon in the office with a pair of files. The next morning they mysteriously show up in my cot. One of the files was mine, Raeni."

"Who put them there?"

"I have no clue. All I know is that I have a Secret Santa who I believe is trying to lead me somewhere."

"Toward Vinson?"

"Exactly."

"Whose name was on the other file?" Raeni asked guardedly.

"Some guy named Felix Ostrander. You ever hear of him."

Raeni said she hadn't. She exhaled a deep breath.

"I don't think you should go back to the shelter," she said.

"Why not?"

"It's not safe. Vinson is evil and if he finds you…" She shook her head as her words trailed off, her bright face suddenly painted black.

"If he finds me…what then?"

"Just promise me you won't go back, Daniel. Promise me right now!"

"But Charles gave me a job and I have no where else to go. I can't just walk away. That would be foolish, not to mention virtual suicide. What makes you think I'm in danger there, anyway?"

"Let's just say it's a feeling I have."

"I think your overreacting. He erased me, that's all there is; got off watching me flounder. I'll bet he couldn't care less what happens to me now."

"I think you're wrong," Raeni said. I could see in her eyes that she truly believed it.

"Here," I said, handing her the BlackBerry. "Click on that little green shortcut button and I'll show you what I'm talking about. When the file opens, scroll to the bottom until you find my name."

Raeni did as I asked, reciting the date next to my name when she saw it.

"That's the day I told you about. The day the security guard said he didn't know me; the day my landlord tossed me to the curb. Raeni, that's the day that Vinson had me erased."

With one eye on the road, I watched her scan through the spreadsheet, anticipating her acknowledgement of what I was telling her. When she finally spoke, what she said made me veer toward the curb and slam on the brakes.

"Daniel, did you notice the heading on the next column over?"

I shook my head. In my haste, I hadn't gotten pasted the word ERASED. "No, what does it say."

"*BURIED*," Raeni said.

27

Essentials for Success

Louis Vinson was a very happy man. It wasn't even noon yet and already every 24 hour news station across the country was smitten with his brainchild. CNN, FOX, CSPAN, ABC, NBC, CBS, everyone but ESPN had their top personality covering the shocking story. It was more than Vinson had hoped for and as he sat in his executive office in downtown Manhattan, admiring the aroma of the Partagas Lusitanias cigar he'd lit moments ago, he noticed John Oliver hovering in his doorway.

"Come on in, John," he said with a smile. "Pull up a chair and join me at ringside for the bloody knockout that's just getting started."

Knowing it was an order rather than a request, John entered, taking a seat in front of the huge plasma screen television mounted on the wall. The picture was split, transmitting the faces of four different journalists with one compelling characteristic—a seriously grim demeanor. Only the sound from FOX News could be heard.

"I love this bitch," Vinson said, referring to the staid blonde detailing the events of that morning. "She's a real spitfire. I'd be willing to bet she's got a whip or two in her bedside table."

John didn't respond, tuning his ear into the broadcast.

"As we reported earlier," the woman said. "The shocking

video that first appeared on the popular YouTube.com website sometime around 6 a.m. is not a demented hoax as first thought. The woman has been identified, her family confirming that they have been unable to contact her since being notified by authorities."

"Greta, how were the police able to determine who she was?" a male colleague asked, his face suddenly appearing in a small box in the corner of the screen. "It's certainly difficult to discern considering the horrific condition she's in."

"According to our sources, Bill, the White Plains Police Department received a 911 call early this morning alerting them to the video. A woman's name was mentioned and as it turns out, she had grown up there before moving to Manhattan. In fact, she has a brother on the force there that positively IDed her after viewing the video."

"That must have been difficult for him," Bill said.

"I can't even image, Bill," Greta said. "To see your sister—a wife, a daughter, anyone you love—barely alive and have no idea where she is. I mean, this is one of the most heinous acts I've ever witnessed. And then to broadcast it over the internet, there are no words to describe my disgust right now."

"Mine either," Bill said, hurriedly. "Greta, we've just gotten word that the woman's name has been released. We're going to roll the tape as it was seen on YouTube and if you could walk us through, if you would, what the authorities are doing to find her."

"I'd be happy to, Bill. But first I want warn viewers that this is a very disturbing fifteen second clip. I would strongly recommend that children and any easily offended viewers not watch at this time."

"Excellent point, Greta," Bill said as his image disappeared. It was then replaced by that of a battered and bloody young woman slumped in a chair, her helpless eyes glistening with tears, her pallid face awash with blood, and her dry lips lumped with bruises. Clearly, she was still alive, handcuffed to a nondescript wooden chair that sat in a brightly lit room. She wore only black panties and a tattered white t-shirt emblazed with a simple phrase written in what authorities assumed was her own blood. *Help me!*

John Oliver shifted in his chair, suppressing the vomit threatening to erupt. *Louis has finally gone too far*, he thought. He said nothing.

"The woman has been identified as Elizabeth Hart," Greta said as the tape repeated over and over. "According to her family, she's been working for Earth Nexus, the internet communications mega-conglomerate, in one of its major offices located in Manhattan for about six months. Her parents haven't talk to her for several days, which they said wasn't unusual. Her father, Richard Hart, reportedly told police that Elizabeth was very independent and wasn't always quick to share personal items with her parents. Now, if anyone knows Elizabeth, has spoken to her recently, we urge you to call your local police or the FBI at the number appearing at the bottom of the screen. If the authorities are going to catch the scum that did this, they're going to need your help."

"Do they have any leads, Greta?" Bill asked. "A jilted boyfriend, perhaps? Do we know if Ms. Hart was dating anyone?"

"Nothing yet, Bill, but as I said, the FBI has been brought in..."

Vinson flipped channels, pulling up the CNN coverage more relevant to his interests.

"Already the public is crying foul," the reporter said, a handsome, forty-something man in grey suit and red tie. "Our switchboard has been besieged all morning with calls, our website choked with emails, the overwhelming majority urging the government to intervene and pull the plug on YouTube. The appearance of this video depicting an apparently kidnapped and tortured woman has thrown gasoline on the internet censorship fire that I believe has been smoldering for some time and one that won't be extinguished anytime soon. This reporter fears that the

First Amendment is on the line and an outraged public is vehemently stacking the side against it."

Vinson turned the television sound off. He'd heard enough. Taking a long drag from his cigar, he turned toward his colleague and exhaled a satisfying cloud of smoke.

"Do you hear it, John?" he asked. "That flushing sound? It's YouTube going down the toilet."

"They've removed the clip from the site, I assume," John said. He had no desire to join in Vinson's revelry, only a compulsive urge to resign.

"Yes, and we keep putting it back on. You remember that hacker I bailed out of jail, the one that got busted for breaking into the Pentagon network last year? He's good, damn good. I wish I had ten more just like him. We could do some real damage then, John. Shave three or fours years off our ten year plan." He then turned his attention back to the muted screen where four networks busily flashed clips of Elizabeth Hart in between interviews with criminal psychologists, friends and relatives. Vinson laughed openly and heartily. "Look at them go, John; like Piranha in a goldfish bowl. All we have to do is throw a pretty piece of chum into the water and they'll pick it clean."

"I've got work to do," John said. He stood up abruptly, turned on his heel and headed for the exit.

"Suddenly developing a weak stomach, John?" Vinson said, his challenging eyes burning a hole into the back of Oliver's head.

John stopped in the doorway and slowly turned around. "My stomach is the same as it was when we started this thing, Louis. That's not what's changed."

"Change is necessary," Vinson said. "In fact, it's essential."

"Essential for what? Power? Greed? *Murder*?"

"Success, John. It's essential to our continued success."

"You call it what you want, Louis. It won't change the smell."

Vinson chuckled. "You picked a fine time to throw a morality coin into the fountain. Didn't your mother ever tell you that wishes don't come true, John Boy? Or was she one of those apron wearing Suzie-homemakers who told you she found you under a cabbage leaf? Well, guess what? She sucked your old man's dick just like the whores on Seventh Avenue. Took it up the ass every night so Oliver Sr. would keep coming home with his paycheck."

John's face went cold. "Survival of the fittest, is that your point, Louis? Stab a knife into their back before they stick one in yours?"

"Survival of the smartest, John. Since the dawn of time."

John's head drooped, his eyes searching the Italian granite floor for the path that had led him to this place, to this moment in time. *How have I looked past it all these years?* He asked himself. Without another word, he walked away, wondering what he would do when he got back to his office.

Vinson's phone rang. It was the Earth Nexus head of media relations. Larry King was asking for a live interview with Elizabeth Hart's employer who also happened to have a very large stake in the fast-spreading internet censorship firestorm. "I'll be ready in twenty minutes," Vinson said. "Have the teleconference equipment ready when I arrive."

This is going to be a slam-dunk, Vinson thought as he leafed through the closet of suits he kept in his office, searching for a look that would welcome him into the dens and bedrooms of Middle America. He would begin by expressing his outrage, vowing to apply every resource available to tracking and capturing the cyber terrorists. "Because that's what they are, Larry," he would say. "Terrorists in the worst form imaginable, preying upon the young and the innocent right here on American soil." He would then condemn YouTube and other sites like it for their blatant recklessness, consciously neglecting to protect their underage users from graphic and disturbing images. "It's all about money, Larry," he would say, shaking his head in frustration. "It's not that hard to screen and block inappropriate material. Everybody talks about it but few are doing it. You have to be willing to put your money where your mouth is and at Earth Nexus we've made it our top priority." He would then rattle off a number of their "parent approved" websites, assuring Mr. King that he had a staff of former government agents monitoring activity daily, all with express purpose of making internet use safe. "Our children are our future, Larry. We can't afford to let them down."

Dressed now in a conservative suit and tie, Louis Vinson hurried off to the media room, eager to twist the knife already dripping with blood, resolved to do something about the growing problem that was his former longtime friend, John Oliver.

28

Oppositely Similar

"Let me see that," I said to Raeni. She handed me the BlackBerry and sure enough, the column just to the right of the one that read, "ERASED," read "BURIED". It wasn't that I thought she was making it up, I just couldn't believe I hadn't spotted it myself. Scanning quickly down the list, I established that only two names contained blanks under that heading—Felix Ostrander and me. If this spreadsheet was accurate, every other unrecognizable name on Vinson's to-do list belonged to a dead man that had been erased just as I had been; just as Felix had been. I was still alive, but as I sat in my Camaro by the side of the road, a beautiful young women by my side and the top down, the sun showering the two of us with its life giving warmth, I couldn't help wonder for how much longer .

"There's about a two week span between the first date and the second date on every one of these," Raeni said.

Finishing her thought, I said, "Which means I have about one week to live, if Vinson has his say in the matter."

"Did you know any of those people?" Raeni asked. "Meet any of them when you were working there?"

"Not a one," I said. "And judging by these dates, that's because they were all dead before I got there."

"Do you really think all those people were killed?"

"I don't know," I said truthfully. "The first column came true, that much is certain. But why go through all the trouble of erasing me first, only to then kill me a few weeks later? In the gangster movies they fit you with cement galoshes and toss you into the ocean to shut you up, or run you through a meat grinder. Allowing a potential threat to bob on the surface for two weeks seems a little risky, don't you think."

"Not if that's what gets you off," Raeni said.

I looked into her troubled eyes and sensed there was more to her fears than mere intuition. There was a lot I didn't know about this woman and for the first time since I'd met her, I experienced a twinge of doubt about her. Was *she* really who she claimed to be?

Sticking with my plan to put all the cards on the table, I reached over and softly placed my hand onto Raeni's cheek. Holding her eyes in mine, I leaned toward her, offering my trust the only way I knew how. "Is there something you're not telling me?" I asked.

She gazed back at me, searching for something that my heart told me she'd never seen in another person before. Finally she spoke. With her voice trembling, she told me she had seen Vinson before that day at the shelter. "That face," she said. "I'll never forget that face as long as I live."

I can't say how long we sat by the curb, wrestling with our fears in my Camaro while the rest of the world drove by, oblivious to our troubles. It may have been hours, but by the time I pulled back onto the road headed for Rhode Island, Raeni smiling once again the way she always did, I knew we were soul mates. She'd shared with me the identity she was desperate to hide just as I had shared the identity I was struggling to find. Now, forever connected to another being, I felt like a brand new man. Then, with our laughter over the irony of our oppositely similar situations waning, I told Raeni it was time to fight back.

"How?" she asked.

"I don't know," I said. "But getting my identity back is the first step."

I wasn't sure what lay ahead, but as we merged onto the interstate, the road sign telling us it was fifty miles to Providence, I was confident that just having someone who believed in me was enough to make a difference.

"Can you do one thing for me?" Raeni asked.

"Anything," I said.

"Call me Sunny."

29

Backup Plans

There's nothing quite like driving along an empty highway in a convertible to clear one's mind of troublesome thoughts, the fresh air and the breeze blowing through your hair. It took the entire trip to work its magic, but as we pulled into Greenville, I was feeling upbeat again, optimistic about my chances of unearthing my severed roots.

Sunny hadn't said much since bearing her sole, leaving me alone to grapple with the images of her being choked to death by a deranged madman. Even though I knew the feeling, it was still a difficult picture to get my arms around, bleeding both fear and anger from my veins to the point of exhaustion. *How had she managed to escape without completely breaking down afterward?* Yet, there she was sitting next to me, smiling in a way that fueled my own hope. Rolling past the central town plaza where my mother had done most of her shopping, I recalled something she had said to me the first time I confided about a girl down the street who refused to acknowledge my existence. "Love is a funny thing, Daniel," she said, grinning softly. "It doesn't contain any logic; nor does it present itself when it's convenient, no matter how badly you want it." Feeling her presence all around me, I looked at Sunny and concluded that falling into her gravity made perfect sense at a time when mine own was lost.

Turning onto Greenville's main drag, I suddenly realized I hadn't asked my companion an obvious question. "Is Sunny your real name? Given name, I mean?"

"Believe it or not, it is," she replied. "Sunny Davis, but I changed it to Sunny Dai, unofficially. People were always confusing me with Sammy Davis," she added with a giggle.

"Well, there is a slight resemblance," I said. "Just a little around the eyes."

Sunny cocked her chin to one side and crossed her eyes. "A dead ringer, baby."

I began laughing so hard I drove right past the dental office we'd come looking for. "Shit!" I did a hasty and completely illegal u-turn before pulling up to the curb.

"Is this the one?" Sunny asked.

"It's been a few years, but I'm pretty sure this is it. After I've seen the names in the marquee, I'll be more certain."

We exited the car and jogged across the street, playfully dodging a horn-blaring eighteen wheeler delivering a payload to Wal-Mart. Walking into the building lobby, the walnut wainscoting and olive green wallpaper tugging at my memory, I began to feel like I'd found a link to my past. After checking the names of the practicing dentists, that certainty quickly faded.

Noticing my perplexed scowl, Sunny asked if any of them looked remotely familiar.

"Nothing is ringing any bells," I replied.

"Maybe if you saw him again?" she suggested.

"Maybe."

We went inside and approached the receptionist.

"I know this is going to sound a little odd," I said to the middle-aged woman staring blankly back at me. Her nametag read Phyllis, but she looked more like an Alice to me, like that housekeeper that's always wisecracking on late night reruns. "But do you happen to have a picture of the dentists who practice here?"

The woman tilted her head, assessing my request skeptically as she tugged on her ear.

Sunny intervened, putting her hand on my shoulder. "My friend used to come here as a teenager but can't remember his doctor's name." She smiled, disarmingly. "He has trouble remembering my name, calls me Raeni sometimes, whoever that is."

Warming to Sunny's charm, the woman's hesitation dissolved instantly. "When was your last visit?" Phyllis asked.

"At least a dozen years ago," I said, apologetically. I knew how these people frowned upon lapsed checkups. Understanding that this kind of personal negligence was unforgivable, I grabbed Sunny's hand, bracing myself for an oral hygiene lecture. I got something worse instead.

"I'm sorry," Phyllis said. "But that practice closed a number of years ago. An outbreak of hepatitis and the ensuing lawsuits forced them into bankruptcy. The last I heard the partners had scattered across the country, looking to start over. I've only been here a few years but Dr. Heathrow might recall their names. I believe he was one of the founding members of this practice. He may have met them when he bought this building."

I didn't know what to say. I felt like I'd just been punched in the gut by Mike Tyson, who was now hungrily honing in on my earlobe.

"Did Dr. Heathrow or any of his partners take on the patients that had been coming here at the time?" Sunny asked. "If so, maybe you still have Daniel's records. That's what we've really come looking for."

"I don't believe so," Phyllis said. "I recall Joanne, the office manager, telling me they've been overloaded with clients for as long as she could remember. But let me go ask her, I could be mistaken." She tapped a few keys on her computer keyboard—locking it up to keep snoopers like us out, I assumed—and then stood up. "Wait here and I'll be back in just a minute." She disappeared into the back.

"Just my luck," I said, shaking my head.

Sunny rubbed my shoulder. "Don't give up yet, there's a good chance they've kept the records. Doesn't the law require it?"

"Yeah, but not if you're not their patient," I grumbled. After the way the past week had evolved, I had more than a sneaking suspicion how this act was going to play out—another knockdown scene.

When Phyllis returned, her news wasn't surprising.

"I'm afraid we don't have any files of theirs. According to Joanne, the Health Department officials conducting the investigation subpoenaed every record they had. You'd have to check with them to find out where they are now." She shrugged regretfully.

Before we left, Phyllis jotted down the name of the government agency to contact. I wasn't thrilled with the prospect of chasing that ghost but Sunny insisted that we take the information just in case the visit to the DMV office proved fruitless.

Back in the Camaro, Sunny tried to cheer me up, saying, "At least we know the DMV won't have closed due to a lawsuit."

"True," I said as I pulled back onto the road. "Our only worry there will be dying of old age while waiting in line."

There must have been a professional wrestling event going on somewhere in town because when we entered the Department of Motor Vehicle Office there was only one person waiting for the next available clerk. Normally, when I visit the DMV, there are hordes of people milling about, blue-collar refugees of every shape, size and color who seem to enjoy dragging their preschoolers along for the ride. Now, I was one of them, standing nervously in my shelter garb, considering what excuse I'd use for not having a speck of identification.

"What should I say when they ask me for some ID?" I asked Sunny.

"Tell them the truth. You lost it."

"I know that would seem to be the simplest solution, but..."

"If you make up something more elaborate, it will only backfire on you."

I tried to smile through my anxiety, laugh it away. "Are you sure you're a woman, because you're making logical sense right now?"

"Ha, ha," Sunny said. "Men lose all judgment the moment they open their eyes in the morning."

"That's a pretty extreme attitude," I said, laughing indignantly.

"What's the first thing you do when you wake up?"

"I don't know; check to make sure the family jewels are still there?"

"My point exactly."

I exhaled a disbelieving sigh. *She had a point.*

"Next," the clerk muttered apathetically.

Sunny and I stepped up to the chest high counter.

"I've lost my license," I said, glancing briefly at Sunny. I felt like a seven-year-old playing Tiny Tim in the church play, petrified I would forget my lines. "And...would like to get a new one." *That's it, keep it simple.*

"Replacement of a driver's license requires six points of proof of identity," the clerk said, an overweight, but otherwise, nondescript person of questionable gender. He or she spoke in a lifeless monotone that reminded me of the rusting lawnmower I used to cut Poppa Joe's grass—rhythmic, but yet subtly annoying. "To change your name, you must also provide proof of your new name—a marriage or divorce document, a court-issued name change document or six points of proof of identity that shows your new name."

"He doesn't need to change his name," Sunny said.

Noticing the video camera aimed at us, I shook my head, confirming Sunny's statement.

"Replacement of a driver's license requires six points of proof of identity," he or she repeated. "Acceptable documents include a driver license, a learner permit, or a non-driver photo ID card issued by Rhode Island. The photo document must be valid or expired for less than two years." The clerk paused, gazing at us like a cat waiting to be fed.

"As I said, I lost my license so I don't have that to show you," I said. *Consequently, my need to get a new one. Duh!*

Without blinking, he or she continued, "Form MV-45, the statement of identity, can be used if the applicant is under the age of 21. The form must be signed by a parent or a legal guardian, in front of a DMV representative. Proof of date of birth of applicant and Social Security Card are also required." Again, he or she paused.

"I'm over twenty-one," I said before nudging Sunny. "Right sis?"

"He's pushing thirty," she said.

Acting like a homely Stepford wife, the clerk recited more procedural verbiage, saying, "Form MV-45A, the statement of identity for government represented applicants, can be used as an identity affidavit completed by a state, federal or local government agent representative for a mentally and/or physically challenged applicant. Proof of date of birth of applicant and Social Security Card are also required."

"I'm not handicapped," I said.

"You're not physically or mentally challenged?" The clerk asked.

Do I look like I am? I thought, resentfully. After a poke from Sunny, I told the clerk, "No, I'm not."

"Do you have a United States Passport?" the clerked asked.

"No," I replied.

"A Certificate of Citizenship?"

"No."

"A United States Military Photo ID Card?"

"No."

"A welfare card, a Medicaid card, or a Rhode Island Food Stamp Card with a photo?"

"No, no and no."

The clerk then placed a yellow sheet onto the counter in front of us. "Replacement of a driver's license requires six points of proof of identity," He or she said for the third time. "The point value of each acceptable document listed is recorded in the second column from the left. When you have documents totaling six points or more, return to the window for further processing. Next!"

I took the form, studying it as I walked away from the counter, Sunny right next to me trying to sneak a peak. A few minutes later, I handed her the form before throwing my hands up in frustration.

"I don't have any of those things," I said. "No proof of address, no health card, no nothing. How the fuck am I suppose to get proof of who I am, without proof of who I am?"

"If you had proof, you wouldn't need proof," Sunny said offhandedly. She was still perusing the list, searching for a needle in a haystack, as far as I was concerned.

"Don't waste your time," I said. "I've got a better chance of finding my old dentist."

Sunny handed me the form back and said, "It's time for plan B." She then scanned the interior and after spotting whatever it was she was looking for, headed toward it.

"Plan B?" I asked. "What plan B?"

"Stay here," was all she said.

Fifteen minutes later, she returned with a green form in her hand and a satisfied grin on her face.

"Where did you go?" I asked as she handed me the form.

"To have a little chat with the supervisor," she replied. "Roger's a really nice guy; I think you'd like him."

I looked at the form heading, reading something about an

archival record search as I anxiously awaited Sunny's explanation. When it came apparent that she wasn't going to offer anything freely, I asked, "And?"

"I gave him your name, said you were a local boy," Sunny said. "My brother, in fact, and that you'd bumped your head and were now suffering a terrible, but temporary bout with amnesia. I told him you'd lost all your belongings and asked if there wasn't some way a nice man like him could find you in their system."

I looked at her quizzically. "He bought all that?"

"Why not? I tell a convincing story."

I was skeptical and she knew it.

"Well, I did give him my phone number."

"Sunny, you don't have a phone."

"I know," she shrugged. "Anyway, he checked their database for you and came up empty. *But*...as it turns out, a few years ago all the DMV records were copied to microfiche and placed into storage for safekeeping. It was part of a computer systems upgrade or something, I don't recall exactly what Roger said, but the point is they have every license on file, including pictures, histories—the works."

"So," I said, finishing her thought once again. "Even though Vinson hacked me out of their live system, he may not have cut me out of the backup files."

"Exactly."

"Microfiche," I said contemplatively, as I stared at my name printed on the search request form. "Daniel Rayne may yet rise from the ashes after all."

30

Long Lost Cousins

Every scandal-ridden rag at the newsstand had a shocking photo of Elizabeth Hart gracing the cover, her once innocent and promising spirit luridly sensationalized in bloody red, black and white. Picking up the first one to catch his eye, Sammy Johnson smiled contently, recalling his evening with the former beauty with great satisfaction. "You were one sweet fuck," he mumbled, inaudible to the crowd gathered around, every reader eagerly tearing at the still-breathing carcass like a pack of hungry wolves. He'd had a most memorable time that night, delivering Elizabeth to the studio as ordered, looking exactly as Mr. Vinson had wanted her to—unmistakably mistreated. Happily, he tossed the owner a silver dollar and continued on his way, walking purposely with his purchase tucked under his arm. Three blocks later, he stood in front of the Kingston Street Shelter.

Might this be your lucky day, Sammy? He thought. *Two for the price of one?*

Sammy pulled a white, letter-sized envelope from the breast pocket of his suit coat. In a cheery mood, he had decided to dress up for the occasion—a surveillance mission to locate his newest assignment that he hoped might also lead him to a pending assignment. "Why not look the way I feel," he had said to the mirror that morning. "Like a million bucks."

It had been a wonderfully crisp morning but now, in the early afternoon, he was feeling the heat of the day beginning to rise. He loosened his suffocating tie before extracting two pictures from the envelope. The two four-by-six snapshots each contained a different man sitting at his desk, smiling casually. Studying the pictures, Sammy knew he'd met one of them before, the one called Daniel Rayne. *Almost had you, my friend*, he thought. The other—Felix Ostrander—had not yet held the pleasure of his acquaintance. Gazing through the glass of the shelter's front door, Sammy recalled finding both of their files during his midnight raid on the business office. Today, he hoped he'd find they'd become bunk buddies.

Straightening his tie once again, he went inside.

Sammy Johnson wasn't concerned that someone might recognize him. Sure, he had stood outside guarding Vinson's limo a few days back in the chauffeur costume, but he'd worn sunglasses and gotten a haircut since then. Between that and his stylish new threads, there was no way any of these losers would connect the two dots. As for his botched burglary attempt, well, he'd already decided to put that out of his mind. As long as he avoided the man in charge—Woodland, Vinson had called him—he was convinced he'd be in and out in no time. That was the way Sammy thought, and although his boss might not agree, *if it ain't broke, don't fix it.*

Finding the business office right where he left it that night, Sammy walked in and straight up to Hillary's desk. She was alone, just as Sammy had hoped she would be.

"Hello," he said, smiling. "An awful beautiful day to be cooped up in an office?"

"It sure is," Hillary replied, returning a smile of her own. "Can I help you?"

"I hope so," Sammy said. After clearing his throat, he began to recite the story he'd practiced all morning. "A dear cousin of mine has spent the last four years searching for his two lost brothers.

Now, bedridden with cancer, he's counting on me to continue where he left off." He retrieved the two snapshots and handed them to Hillary. "He'd tracked them as far as Boston only to lose the trail when the doctors gave him the terrible news."

After expressing a woeful look, Hillary briefly studied the pictures, a hint of recognition washing across her face before she turned them over to read the writing on the back. It was exactly the clue that Sammy had come looking for.

"You said they were brothers?" Hillary asked. "They appear to have two different last names."

Realizing he forgot that Vinson had written their names there, Sammy quickly improvised. "Different fathers," he said abruptly before taking the pictures back.

As he expected, Hillary informed him that all client information was confidential, but he was free to check the dining hall if he liked. "The shelter is open to the public. As for the clients, they come and go as they like," Hillary added. "So you may want to check back a few times each day. If you're lucky, you may run into one or both of them."

"That's a good idea," Sammy said as he turned to leave. *That's exactly what I was planning on doing.* With an established reason for hanging around the shelter, Sammy waltzed confidently into the nearly empty dining hall, grabbed a bowl of free soup and plopped himself down at a table in the corner where he could easily see the entrance. No one would bother him now and when his *cousins* returned, he would be there to greet them, even if he had to wait there for a month.

31

There's No Place Like Home

I can't say why Sunny and I ended up in front of Poppa Joe's old house, but there we were, parked at the corner like undercover agents on a sting operation. I was the one behind the wheel so I guess I'm to blame, but when Sunny asked me where I used to live I could have just pointed and said, "A mile or two west of here." But I didn't. I drove there instead, thinking it would be nice to see the place again. After noticing that the new owners had already painted the exterior a different shade of brown and trimmed down most of the existing shrubbery, I sadly decided visiting hadn't been such a good idea after all.

"Things don't stay the same very long, do they," I said.

"No, they don't," she replied.

"Just when you think you've got the world by the tail, it turns around and bites your hand off."

She reached over and slid her hand into mine. "You've still got both hands," she said.

I looked at her and smiled, momentarily drifting onto her cloud.

"And friends," she added. "You must have some friends here. You lived here a long time, didn't you?"

"A good part of my life," I said. "But other than my mother and then Poppa Joe, I didn't have any close friends. I knew the manager at the grocery store a little and few guys down at the local bar, but not enough to say we were buddies. After my mom died, I spent most of my time working for Poppa Joe, keeping his client records organized and cleaning up after his memory spills. He never admitted to himself or anyone else, but he had Alzheimer's and it got worse and worse as the years went by."

"That must have been hard on you," Sunny said.

"It wasn't that bad," I said, hiding the fact that the last year had been a living hell. "I had a place to live and money in the bank. That's a lot more than I have now."

Sunny raised an eyebrow as if to say, *what about me?*

"Materially speaking, of course," I said, squeezing her hand.

"And girlfriends?" she asked. "You must have had a girlfriend or two along the way. I mean, you're almost thirty. You can't still be..."

"A virgin," I said, finishing her sentence. "Would it burst your bubble if I said I was?"

"How about the other way around," she said with a glint in her eye.

"Well, I'm not one of those kiss and tell guys, so I guess you'll just have to live with wondering."

She giggled. "You're no fun."

"What about you?" I asked.

She didn't say a word, running a finger across her closed mouth instead. *My lips are sealed*, she was telling me.

"Fair enough," I chuckled.

"Poppa Joe's clients," she burst out suddenly. "They could vouch for you, couldn't they?"

There it was, another opportunity for me to burst that bubble. I was a fraud, but how do you tell that to the girl you think you might be falling in love with? I never met any of Poppa Joe's clients because I shouldn't have been doing the work to begin with. I didn't have the credentials—no high school diploma, no college degree and certainly no state certification like he had.

Poppa Joe taught me everything I needed to know, but explain that to a client who just got billed two hundred dollars an hour for tax return preparation. I couldn't image Poppa Joe telling a client, "I didn't do the work, Harry, the kid in the back did. So, if the IRS calls about an audit, give Daniel a call." What started out as an honest and sincere way to build my independence, ended up being an unforeseen snare. And then, as the Poppa Joe I knew disappeared behind that debilitating genetic cloak, escape became unthinkable, if not nearly impossible.

"None of his clients really knew me," I said. "I was the guy behind the curtain, like that old white-haired guy in *The Wizard of Oz*, working the levers and knobs while Poppa Joe got the face time. I doubt any of his clients even knew I existed."

"Was his memory that bad?"

"The last year or so it was; only occasional flashes of his old self, which might last the evening. During those times, he'd drive me over to my mother's grave and the two of us would sit for a while, talking to her. The next morning he would be gone again, asking me my name and what day it was. Slowly, all of his clients jumped ship, not that I blame them."

"Leaving you unemployed," Sunny said.

"And eventually, homeless," I added. "Poppa Joe never mentioned me in his will. I know in my heart he always meant to, but he kept forgetting."

"Would you like to go visit your mother now?" Sunny asked.

I shook my head hesitantly. Even though she passed many years ago, my mother was still alive inside me and I couldn't bear the thought of facing her like this—a broken son teetering on the edge of oblivion. I wanted to talk to her, to explain the things that had happened, but only after I'd figured them all out. And that meant getting my identity back, the one my mother had sacrificed so much to give me.

"We should go there," Sunny insisted. "I think it would be good for you."

Gritting my teeth, I started the Camaro. "Not yet," I said purposefully. "I'm not going there until I'm Daniel Rayne again." Squealing the tires, I leapt back onto the road.

"Where are we going?" Sunny asked.

"The DMV," I said. "To see how Roger's doing with that record search."

"He said it would take a few days to complete that," Sunny said. "We'll only be wasting our time."

"What better have we got to do?" I shrugged.

"First, I think you should slow down."

Checking my speedometer, I realized Sunny was right. I was doing nearly sixty in a thirty-five-mile-an-hour zone. I eased off the gas and took a deep breath. This whole nightmare was eating away at me from the inside out, and being home again only seemed to sharpen the teeth. Coming here, I thought I would find some comfort, but instead all I felt was shame. I needed to leave.

"I'm sorry," I said. "We might as well head back to Boston, there's nothing more we can do here."

"I've got Roger's number at the DMV," Sunny said, reassuringly. "I'll call him tomorrow and ask how it's coming along."

"Thanks," I said.

"In the meantime," Sunny said. "You can crash at my place."

She was casually looking out the window as she said it, leaving me to wonder what her intentions were. Was she smiling sinfully or counting the utility poles along the sidewalk? My curiosity aroused, among other things, I decided to tease her a bit.

"How do you know I'm not an axe murderer? Or a serial rapist?"

On the verge of laughter, she turned and looked me right in the eyes. "Are you an axe murderer, Daniel?"

"No," I replied.

"Are you a serial rapist?"

"No."

"I'm glad we got that straightened out," she said. "Now, are you staying with me or not."

Sunny certainly was determined. "Ok," I said. "But we need to stop by the shelter first."

"We're not going back there," she said. She was serious now, the playfulness I had grown to love, gone. "It's not safe."

"You keep saying that," I said, frustrated. I needed to go back and talk to Charles. I needed to keep the job he'd given me to fund my resurrection and I needed Sunny to understand that. In an effort to keep what I feared might be our first argument from boiling over, I attempted to make light of the situation. "What are you afraid of, the bogeyman?"

"No," Sunny said as she returned her suspicious gaze to the passing houses just beyond the car window. "Only someone who looks just like him."

32

The Telemarketing Gig

Once we were back on the interstate, working our way north to Boston, the mood inside my Camaro turned quiet and guarded. Sunny had finally agreed to a quick stop at the shelter, although "grudgingly conceded" was probably a better description. It was the first time I'd really seen her brooding and as the miles flew by, I caught myself wishing the sunny Sunny would come out again.

In an attempt to lift her spirits, I said, "You know, my mother used to tell me that the best way to get over my fears was to confront them. In the case of the bogeyman, maybe we just need to look under the bed, pull him out and dissect the bastard. Find out what makes him tick."

"Humanize him you mean?" Sunny asked.

"Exactly."

"What make you think he's human?"

"Come on, Sunny. Vinson is flesh and bone like everyone else. I'm sure he's just as susceptible to jock itch and hemorrhoids as the next guy."

She couldn't stop herself from laughing—a wonderful ray of sunshine bleeding through the clouds. "I suppose so," she said.

Encouraged, I retrieved Vinson's BlackBerry from the dash and handed it to her, instructing her to turn it on and find the

Contacts icon. "Let's see who made our buddy Vinson's friends and family call list."

Over the next twenty miles, Sunny toggled through Vinson's life, excitedly blurting out the names of celebrities, sports stars and the occasional politician of note. I had to give him credit. The son-of-a-bitch was well connected—a real modern day Caesar, just as his nickname implied. A man hell bent on building his own Roman Empire, a new and improve version of the first century dynasty. Only instead of warrior-filled chariots, his modus operandi would be the mind-altering influence of the internet. I'd worked there long enough to figure that out. On the surface it seemed ludicrous. But then, he'd erased me in the blink of an eye. Could he possibly manipulate information on a much larger scale? *No way!* My stomach did a flip. *Could he? Could anyone?*

"Who's Claire Vinson?" Sunny asked, her head immersed in the BlackBerry. "His wife?"

"That's right, I'd forgotten the fucker was married," I said. "Does it list an address?"

"Let me see." She then tapped the screen a few times. "Yup, one in Florida and one in Oyster Bay."

"A woman of leisure, do you think?"

Sunny nodded. "I'm so jealous."

"Maybe we should pay her a visit," I suggested.

"And say what when she answered the door? Excuse me, Mrs. Vinson, but we came to inform you that your husband is a murderous pervert. We just wanted you to know. Thanks for your time and have a nice day."

"Sounds good to me," I said. I wasn't serious but there was a part of me that ached to do exactly what Sunny had just jokingly rehearsed.

"She would have us arrested," Sunny said. "We've got enough to chew on without adding felony charges to the pile."

"It wouldn't hurt my record any," I said with a grin. "I don't exist."

It was at that very moment that I had a fleeting thought that perhaps somehow I could use my virtual death to our advantage. If I couldn't pick up my own trail, what chance did anyone else have? *Half brother to the invisible man...interesting.* Noticing the road sign alerting us to our arrival in Boston, I set the concept aside to focus on the more immediate issue of what I was going to say to Charles Woodland when we arrived at the shelter.

"Tell him you need some time off," Sunny offered.

"I just started. Now I'm going to request a leave of absence?"

She didn't say anything, glaring at me instead.

"You're really adamant about this, aren't you?"

"I don't want you anywhere near that place. In a few days, you'll have your driver's license back and then you can find a new job."

"Provided Roger does his job and Vinson didn't think to destroy the backup microfiche," I reminded her.

Her eyes were spitting bullets now.

"Obviously," I said pointing at the BlackBerry, "getting to know Vinson a little better hasn't changed your opinion of him any."

"No, as far as I'm concerned he's still inhuman. And if the bogeyman truly exists, he's it."

I chuckled, but abruptly stopped when it was obvious she wasn't kidding. As much as I needed the money the job at the shelter offered, I needed Sunny more. Facing my situation alone was a very unappealing prospect. Growing up, I always had my mother and then Poppa Joe after she died. I wasn't built to go it alone, I'd learn that all too well over the past week. Sunny gave me strength; a boldness that inexplicable wavered when she wasn't around. Exiting the interstate, I finally agreed to tell Charles that I needed some time off—a few days—before asking her how long her telemarketing gig could support us both.

"Telemarketing?" she asked, looking puzzled. "Oh yeah, I guess I need to explain about that."

I nearly ran off the road when Sunny told me how she was making ends meet.

33

A Secret

The summerhouse in Oyster Bay was everything Claire Vinson had dreamed it would be, with the exception of one thing. It was very lonely living there by herself. An old sea captain's home along the northern shores of Long Island, the Vinson property was Claire's getaway cottage, a place to escape the reminders of what her life had become since marrying her husband, Louis. Whether tending to the lush gardens or walking along the beach, her mind could wander far, far away from his obsessive business dealings and habitual womanizing. She had no television there, and no internet access— no means of accidentally tripping over images of her husband and his notorious female companions. This was her sanctuary and though it didn't fill her every need, she had resolved many years ago that it was as close as she might ever come.

The daughter of Henry and Claudia Hannegan, an affluent Irish-American family with deep East Coast roots, Claire was approaching forty and although her statuesque figure, long brown hair and warm, hazel eyes could still turn heads, she rarely left the house in search of companionship. She was content, determined to "make lemonade out of lemons" as her mother used to tell her when she was growing up. Besides, she had one special friend that helped make her life worth living. She didn't need anything more.

It had rained steadily that morning, a misty drizzle that began just after breakfast, forcing Claire to retreat inside, away from her prized roses and into the cupboards and closets in search of a neglected victim of her selective procrastination. Spring had come and gone already and she had done none of the compulsory cleaning. After finding an antique oak cabinet in her reading room that upon opening, vomited old paperbacks and photograph albums all over her bare feet, she sat down on the floor and set about organizing.

The mindless, beach-read novels she placed in one pile—tagged as a library donation—the rest in a second pile for further consideration. It was a good time-filler for a wet summer day and it was going along swimmingly until she came across an old family album. As soon as she opened it, her eyes puddled with tears. She almost forgot how beautiful her older sister was, how happy they both had been when they were young.

It had been nearly twenty-seven years since she last spoke to Katherine—the elder of the two siblings by three years—but the thought of the day she watched her sister's empty face pull away in the back seat of a taxicab still made her heart ache. How could their father have evicted her from their home that day? She was only sixteen and three months pregnant. She still couldn't understand how he could have done something so cruel. In the years that followed, Claire understood her father's shame, but that didn't make her hate him any less. She understood it, but she didn't accept it. She would never accept it.

The first letter appeared in her dorm mailbox while Claire was a freshman in college. Katherine told her that she'd had a boy and that his name was Daniel. She asked her not to worry, that she was doing well and hoped her little sister was in good spirits. "Now that you're out of that man's house," Katherine wrote, "We can write to each other whenever we want. But don't try to find me, Claire. I can't bear the thought of you ever having to go through what I went through." The return address on the envelope was a post office box somewhere in New York City.

Then, thirteen years ago, the letters stopped coming and Claire's worst fear was realized. Her only sister was dead before they ever had a chance to reunite. By that time she was married to Louis and with the help of his best friend at the time, John Oliver, she managed to locate Katherine's obituary in a Rhode Island newspaper. It hadn't proved easy—Katherine had changed her last name—but when all was said and done, Claire got a reunion, albeit not the one she'd always wanted. For the first time since her father had banished Katherine from the family, Claire stood next to her sister, laying an armful of roses on her grave a month after she died.

Thank God I found Daniel, she thought as she ran her fingers over the weathered photo of her and Katherine making goofy faces for the camera.

The first time she saw Daniel she couldn't believe how much he resembled his mother. Standing across the street from where she found him living, she didn't approach him. Instead, she observed invisibly from afar, feeling as though she was rekindling the sisterly love taken from her so many years ago. And ever since then she would return to Greenville, loitering about until Daniel emerged on his way to lunch or to complete an errand. So many times she wanted to run up to him and hug him, tell him who she was. But she couldn't. Louis was exactly like her father; condemning Katherine's "promiscuous and disgraceful behavior" anytime her name was mentioned. Like the house she now lived in, she accepted that her hidden relationship with Daniel was the best it could ever be. Until, that is, she saw the For Sale sign in front of the house he was living in. Concerned for his future, she once again turned to John Oliver, the man who'd helped her find Katherine. Never married, John had been Louis's best man and, unbeknownst to the groom, had secretly fallen in love with Claire the moment they'd met. When Claire told him the story of her older sister, he didn't hesitate, seizing the opportunity to spend time with her. As the years went by, it turned out to be time well spent.

After some digging, John learned that the now deceased Joseph Jones had had a sketchy relationship with Katherine. Also, that he had voluntarily taken Daniel in after Katherine's death. "There must have been something more to their relationship than people knew about," John told Claire after his first trip to Greenville. "Something quite meaningful."

Over dinner that evening, John explained that Jones had left his estate to charity and that Daniel would, in all likelihood, be forced to move once the house was sold. He also told her that Daniel's only employment had been with Jones, an accountant with a private practice. "From what I could gather from several of Jones's close friends, Daniel was doing the bulk of the work the past few years due to Jones's ill health. Unfortunately, for Daniel, none of Jones's clients knew that. Now he's between a rock and hard place. None of the clients will stick with him. He doesn't have the required accountant's credentials to attest to their financials."

That very same night, as Claire lay naked in John's arms, she asked him to do something for her; something he could never tell Louis about, or anyone else for fear it would get back to her husband.

"I'm laying here with you, aren't I," he replied with a faint grin. "Doesn't that prove I can keep a secret?"

Claire returned the smile before asking her lover to please find Daniel a job at Earth Nexus. John promised he would.

Setting the photo album aside, Claire stood and went to the kitchen. She filled a teakettle with water and set in on the stove, turning the knob on high. A cup of hot tea would help sooth the hurt she felt over the loss of her sister, a dull ache that had started many years ago and never completely faded. The cause of her pain—their father—had died a few years back and she was glad for that, relieved to never again adorn the disguise she wore in his presence—a mask of daughterly love.

Then, the doorbell rang. She hurriedly set down her tea and rushed to the door, eager to greet her visitor.

John Oliver wasted no time pulling Claire into a tight embrace, kissing her deeply as soon as he closed the door behind him. A dam overflowing, his lips washed over her neck, moving in a torrent to her earlobe. "I've missed you," he whispered.

"And I missed you," she replied. Her moist lips accepted his, devouring his probing tongue as she pulled at his shirt. It had been several weeks since she last saw him and her body was screaming, demanding to be nourished. She tugged loose his belt, yanking at his pants feverishly before slipping her hand in to feel his arousal. There was no denying how badly she wanted him; ached for him. Feeling the fire enveloping her, she became dizzy, lost in the passion that had overwhelmed her the very first time John had made love to her. Years later, the flame was as bright as ever.

"Not here," she whispered. She then took his hand and led him into her bedroom.

Hours later, exhausted, they lay in each other's arms and volleyed dinner ideas as the sun set just outside Claire's bedroom window. John was in the mood for Mexican, while Claire had an overpowering urge for Sushi.

"Maybe you're pregnant," John chuckled.

"Don't even joke about it," Claire replied, alarmed at the mere thought of explaining to her vacant husband how she managed it without his participation.

John kept the tease alive, adding, "Just tell Louis it was an immaculate conception. God heard your prayers and since Louis wasn't going to step up to the plate, he took the matter into his own hands."

Claire slapped John's bare belly. "Stop! You know damn well what would happen if I became pregnant. Louis would castrate every man on Long Island until the culprit was found."

"Yeah, your right, he would." John said with a half grin. He would never tell Claire this, but a part of him wished that Louis knew of their affair; knew that Claire loved him and not her deplorable husband. It would be a sweet revenge for all that he had endured through the years; all that he had stomached from a man that was once his best friend—the man that he now despised from the depths of his very soul. If, one day, Louis learned the truth and came after him, at least he would die with a smile on his face. Knowing that he might never have Claire all to himself, John Oliver had concluded long ago that he could live—and die—with such an ending.

"Executive decision time," Claire said playfully. "We get Mexican tonight and then tomorrow night we go out for Sushi. There's a great new place outside of town that no one knows about yet. We can have a quiet meal and no one will be the wiser."

"You're getting bold in your old age," John said. "What happened to that girl who said we could never be seen in public together?"

"She's getting tired of hiding in the shadows," Claire replied.

John was growing weary of the secret as well. He knew it was only a matter of time before Louis discovered them. Maybe if he told Louis the truth—man to man—he might not erupt as they feared. *Maybe.* Appreciating Claire's determined will, John agreed to go along with her edict. "As long as I get to choose the entrees," he added.

Claire promised that he could before remembering she wanted to ask him about something they hadn't discussed in a while. "How's Daniel doing? Is Hank happy with his work?"

John's mouth began to open, but closed abruptly without uttering a sound. He then looked up at the ceiling, shut his eyes, and began to search for the right words to tell her what her husband had done to her nephew.

34

Loose Lips

"When a woman makes up her mind, you best just saddle up the horse and ride along behind her," Poppa Joe used to tell me. His advice came to mind as I was walking from the shelter's employee parking lot, headed to Charles's office to give him the bad news about needing some time off. Sunny was still in the Camaro, acting like a stubborn two-year-old, unwilling to budge. She was terrified of Vinson showing up again and spotting her. I tried reassuring her, estimating that his reappearance was a million-to-one shot; reminding her that Vinson was a busy man who was probably off erasing people in Europe or Australia. "That's not funny, Daniel," was all she said.

As I entered the backdoor of the Kinston Street Shelter, a new question arose. If Sunny was so fearful of Vinson's need to silence her, why had she returned to the stripper world in the first place? His arrival at the same shelter Sunny was working at had been a fluke; no one could have foreseen and prevented that. But if he was truly searching for her, wouldn't strip clubs be the first place he'd look? *Yes*. It made no sense for her to remain a dancer; it only increased her chances of being discovered. I walked through the kitchen and into the dining hall feeling a dire need to have a frank talk with Sunny.

Charles Woodland spotted me before I saw him.

"Daniel," he shouted, waving me over to his table. He was sitting with Dexter, the scruffily bearded computer ace and Hillary. I walked over and sat down next to Charles.

"Where have you been?" Hillary asked. Her tone didn't sound accusatory, merely curious.

"I needed to go home and take care of few things," I said. "My hometown that is, where I used to live before I moved to Boston."

"Get everything squared away?" Charles asked. As always, he appeared upbeat and I hated the thought of bringing him down. He'd been very generous to me from the moment I set foot in his shelter and knowing how much he needed accounting support, I felt guilty for what I was about to tell him.

"Almost," I replied, addressing Charles directly. "But there's still a loose end that needs my attention, which means I'm going to need more time before I can come back to work." I knew I was lying when I said it, that when I got my license reinstated I would probably not be coming back, but there was a tiny piece of me that wanted to believe I would return. It was a good place to work; Charles was a good man to work for. Maybe that's why my improvisation came out the way it did, awkward.

"Take whatever time you need, Daniel," Charles said. I could see in his eyes that he truly meant it, but still, there was a hint of disappointment on his face that I couldn't overlook.

"It shouldn't be more than a week," I blurted out. I then turned to Hillary. "You can handle things solo until then, can't you?"

"Hell, I've been doing it for years," Hillary chuckled. She then pulled a pack of cigarettes from her purse and excused herself from the table.

"It's not a problem, Daniel," Charles said, reassuringly. "Where will you be staying, with family?"

"With Sun…Raeni," I answered. As soon as her name left my lips I knew I'd made a mistake. Sunny had asked me not to mention her name—her paranoia acting out—and here I was divulging secrets like Deep Throat. "She has a spare room," I quickly added. "And as long as I do all the cooking and cleaning, she said I could crash for a while."

"Sounds better than the Roosevelt Room," Dexter grumbled.

Charles chuckled. "I have to admit, it does."

I hadn't really taken a very close look at Dexter before. Of course, he hadn't said more than two words since I'd been there, so his jealous remark about my new digs was quite an outburst, for him. It made me stop and take inventory. Studying him now, he was a contradiction. On the surface he appeared to be your average vagrant—unshaven for months, his hair an overused mop head, yellowing fingernails, and clothes that should have been burned years ago. Everything about him screamed, "Stay away, I'm a homeless man!" He was a little on the short side, stocky like most of the guys there, but unlike the rest of the shelter population, he always smelled clean. I never caught him talking to himself or urinating behind the building. He kept his cot tidy—again, unlike myself and the other hundred in attendance—and knew his computers like Freud knew psychosis. He looked the part of the lost soul, but it was almost as if it was just a disguise. He reminded me of someone. Dexter reminded me of...*me*.

He must have noticed me eyeballing him and decided he didn't like it, because just that quickly, he stood up and left.

"Would you like some dinner while you're here?" Charles asked. "It should be ready shortly."

"I can't, Sun...Raeni's waiting for me outside." Once again, my loose lips betrayed me.

"She is? Why didn't she come in and say hello? Everyone here misses her terribly. She was such a sweet girl and so good with the clients."

"She isn't feeling well," I lied. I stood up. I didn't what to have to explain and dig the hole any deeper. "And I promised to drive her home."

Charles stood up and extended his hand. "Well, good luck,

Daniel. And don't worry about that money I loaned you. Consider it an investment in your future."

I shook his hand, realizing that Charles knew I wouldn't be back. He understood it was the nature of the business, that people came and went like the seasons. The shelter was just a rest stop where folks like me could catch their breath. The only thing that remained constant was the human need for compassion. As I left the Kinston Street Shelter, perhaps for the last time, it was clear that constant was Charles Woodland.

When I got back to the car, Sunny asked me how it went. "Was Charles upset?" she asked.

"He understood," I replied.

"That's good," she said. "And you didn't mention my name, right?"

Well, technically, I didn't. I referenced Raeni, but since she wasn't Raeni anymore I was being truthful when I told her I hadn't mentioned her name. Granted, it was a minor detail, but remembering another bit of wisdom passed on to me by Poppa Joe, I decided to keep it to myself. "Hell hath no fury like a woman scorned," he warned me more than once. Besides, there was no one at the shelter who cared where I was staying, so what difference did it make.

After assuring her a second time that I was the master of my mouth, I started the car. "Now, how do we get to your place?"

35

Two Birds in One Cage

This bean soup isn't half bad, Sammy Johnson thought as he finished his second bowl full, the ring of his spoon hitting the porcelain bottom and echoing through the shelter's dining hall like a reverberating doorbell. He sat back in his chair, wiped his chin with a napkin and focused his eyes on the man just walking in. "Speak of the devil," he whispered to himself. He then pulled a wired earpiece from his coat pocket and screwed it gently into his ear, turning his body so that the wall was the only one who might notice it. Reaching into the same pocket a second time, he partially extracted a black, penciled sized microphone. *All the better to hear you with*, he thought.

He didn't need the listening device to hear Charles Woodland shout Daniel's name, only a strong sense of anonymity preservation to keep from reaching for the .45 caliber Glock resting comfortably in his other coat pocket. It was more firepower than Sammy needed, but then he always was a child of overkill.

Thanks for the confirmation, he thought as he watched Daniel sit down. Listening intently to the mundane conversation crackling in his ear, he studied the two pictures his boss had given him, glancing up occasionally to compare his target with the photograph. There was no question that he'd found his match for Daniel Rayne, but the other guy—Felix the Cat, as Sammy was calling him—was still an illusive phantom, that is, until Sammy decided to scribble a scruffy beard and mustache onto the picture of the clean cut man in glasses. With his amateurish artwork completed, Sammy smiled. *It appears to be your lucky day after all,* he thought. *Two birds in one cage.*

Ten minutes later, Sammy had a plan. With his surveillance proving beneficial, Sammy concluded that Felix the Cat could wait. Dexter, as people were calling him, wasn't going anywhere, which meant Sammy could come back anytime to put him out of his misery. Daniel Rayne, however, required his more immediate consideration. Danny Boy was leaving and by the sound of it, not coming back. Sammy had heard him say that he'd promised to drive someone named Raeni home—his girlfriend, Sammy assumed—reasoning that Daniel had a car waiting somewhere outside. After placing the earpiece back in his pocket, Sammy quietly got up and headed for the exit, monitoring Daniel from the corner of his eye, placing him squarely in the sights of an imaginary gun. He then wondered if Danny Boy's girlfriend might enjoy meeting Pooh.

Back outside, Sammy hustled to his car, drove it to within a half block of the back entrance to the shelter, and parked along the curb. Daniel had come in that way, so reason dictated he would leave through the same door. Sammy's logic proved correct, for no sooner had he begun to relax in the leather bucket seat when Daniel emerged. Invisibly, he watched Daniel cross the street before sliding into a magazine quality, hot rod convertible, complete with its own pinup girl.

This is going to be too much fun was the last thing Sammy Johnson thought before pulling onto the road, an inconspicuous forty yards behind the sky blue Camaro.

36

The Runt

Loosening their ties and unbuttoning their suit coats, Louis Vinson's executive staff shuffled slowly out of the conference room, exhausted after a ten hour briefing session interrupted only by a fifteen minute catered lunch and one, ninety-second bathroom break. ("Who can take a piss in a minute and a half?" one of the women had grumbled as she scurried into the ladies room, her Prada slacks already unfastened and falling to her ankles.) Vinson's detailed plan for acquiring Yahoo had been unveiled, complete with marching orders for those in attendance. Conspicuously, John Oliver's customary chair next to Vinson was empty and as the room cleared, more than one exiting executive left thankful they were not in John's shoes.

Back in his adjoining office, Vinson picked up the phone and summoned to his office his favorite guard from the Earth Nexus Security Department. Vinson had a job for him.

Jeremy Limpkin could have been entered into the Guinness Book of World Records as the smallest security officer on the planet. At five feet and one inch tall, and one hundred and twenty five pounds soaking wet, Limpkin intimidated no one. He patrolled the grounds in plain clothes, virtually invisible to visitors and staff alike, ever watchful for anything aversive to his boss. His nickname was "The Runt," a moniker he actually enjoyed. It told him that no one took him seriously, that in a moment of supreme confrontation, they would underestimate him, providing him the only advantage he would need. Vinson hired him for that exact reason, using him for the more delicate assignments that often arose. Another reason was the fact that Limpkin knew one hundred and one ways to kill a man without getting caught. Those two qualities endeared him to Vinson, a man always in need of another unsolvable murder.

After entering Vinson's office, Limpkin sat down in the chair in front of Vinson's desk, his short legs dangling off the floor like an eight-year-old at the dinner table. Pushing his oversized glasses higher up his button nose, his demeanor was anything but childlike.

"Is it John's time?" he asked calmly.

"Long over due," Vinson replied. "I think he's been fucking my wife long enough, don't you?"

Limpkin nodded, faintly.

Vinson continued, saying, "But you know, I could live with that a while longer if he hadn't turned into such a moralistic pussy. John has lost his nerve. I don't know when it happened or why, but he doesn't have the stomach for this anymore and it's going to cost me if I don't do something about it first."

Again, Limpkin simply nodded.

Vinson's face grew dark. "This one must be perfect," he said. "Absolutely no loose ends. In fact, I don't think anyone should ever even see John Oliver again, alive *or* dead."

37

Hidden

The first thing I noticed about Sunny's apartment was how small it was. A one-room efficiency where the refrigerator appeared to double as her bed's headboard, I walked in thinking there was no way we could share the meager space without killing each other before week's end. We would be on top of each other morning, noon and night and although a few benefits to that arrangement dashed across my mind, I knew in reality the coziness would wear thin quickly. Noticing that the bathroom had its own door, I headed toward it, thanking God I could at least do one thing privately.

"Don't forget to put the seat down when you're finished," Sunny said, thirty seconds into my Mickey Bliss, as Poppa Joe used to say.

"Yes mother," I replied jokingly.

After flushing *and* returning the seat to its previously feminine position, I stepped back into the matchbox apartment to find Sunny leaning against the counter with two opened beers, one in each hand. She handed one to me and took a long draw from the other.

"Isn't the legal drinking age twenty one?" I asked just before taking a pull from my own.

"Probably," she shrugged. She then tipped the bottle to her

lips a second time.

I returned the shrug, downed a second splash and stood completely thoughtless as the day's tension rippled away like the waves created by a pond diving pebble. I'd felt bad—and a little guilty—ever since leaving the shelter, knowing it was unlikely that I would ever return. As I canvassed Sunny's apartment, feeling an odd sense of belonging, I knew in my heart it had been the right decision. The only question now was what to do next.

"This tastes good," I said, jutting the bottle out in front of me. "Really hits the spot."

"It sure does," Sunny replied. "And to think I'd never had a drink until a few months ago."

"Really? What made you start?"

Raising an eyebrow, Sunny stared back at me.

"Stupid question," I said. "Speaking of the devil, any thoughts on what we should do about Mr. Vinson?"

"You tell me," Sunny said. "You're the one he erased."

"Yeah," I countered, "but he wants to put both our bodies six feet under. Mine officially and yours, well, I think it's safe to assume your name is on a list somewhere, if only on the one in his twisted mind."

"Don't remind me," Sunny said. She took another long swallow of beer. She then wiped her mouth and gazed at the bottle label. "I should have started years ago."

I said, "As much as I wish it could, it won't make Vinson go away."

Sunny smiled and offered her bottle up for a toast, "It will tonight," she said.

We both chugged what was left of our beers and then stood quietly in her kitchen, staring at each other. Half-smiling at me, I had no way of knowing what she was thinking. Did she want me to kiss her? Did she want me to sweep her up and ravage her? The alcohol in my otherwise empty stomach was making it difficult enough to sort my own thoughts out let alone deduce hers, and so instead of making a complete fool of myself in a ventured guess, I just stood there with a silly grin on my face.

"The only problem is," Sunny finally said, giggling. "These were the last two I had." Knowing that it wasn't the best of times to get toasted on beer anyway, I suggested that we order a pizza and think about our next move. Sunny agreed, adding that there was a Domino's just a few blocks away.

"Have you got a phone book? I'll give them a call."

"Sure," she replied. She opened a drawer in one of the kitchen cabinets and handed me a thick yellow book. "Look for the one on West Street."

Digging through the mass of pages, I found the number and then turned to Sunny before scanning the counter and walls for her phone. Her giggling told me what I had forgotten. Sunny didn't have a phone. I couldn't stop the smile spreading across my face. "Wise guy," I chuckled.

After hoofing it down to the pizza joint and back, we sat down with our, by then, lukewarm pepperoni and sausage pizza, and didn't say another word to each other until it was gone. At the restaurant, we had opted for Cokes instead of more beer, thinking that the caffeine would aid our reasoning, if only by keeping us awake longer. Downing the last few drops, my stomach full of bread dough and cheese, I knew it would be a few days before Roger at the Rhode Island DMV might uncover something. I also knew I couldn't just sit around and wait in the meantime. Vinson's *Daniel-Rayne-is-dead* clock was ticking and as I watched Sunny fold the empty pizza box and stuff it into the trash, I could almost here the chimes clanging in the background.

"Maybe we should go to the police," I said as Sunny was sitting back down. "The two I ran into at my apartment were obviously on the take. Vinson can't have paid off every cop in Boston."

"I'm not going to the police," Sunny said, her mood turning

harshly serious. "Marko warned me not to go to the police. It was one of the last things he said before he died."

"But why? What was he afraid of?"

"I don't know. He died before he could tell me."

"Well," I said, thinking it through. "I suppose we should assume he knew something we don't know. And besides, I have no idea where I would begin the story. Ah, Officer, I believe I've been erased and I want Louis Vinson, the billionaire business man, arrested. No doubt they would put me in a padded cell and schedule me for a psychological evaluation."

A hint of a smile returned to Sunny face. "You are a little crazy," she said.

"Crazy about you," I blurted out. The words just jumped out of my mouth like one of those spring loaded snakes in a fake can of nuts. A bolt of anxiety quickly followed. *Did I just cross the invisible line? Move to fast?* With no way of taking it back, I looked at her, at little more bashfully than I would have liked to admit, and waited for a response. *If she starts laughing, I'm sunk.*

Leaning across the table, Sunny placed upon my lips the softest kiss I'd ever felt in my life. How long it lasted, I couldn't say, but when the rest of my senses returned, Sunny was once again sitting across the table from me, smiling as sweetly as the first time I saw her.

"I guess that proves it," she said.

"What?"

"That you're a little crazy."

I nodded.

"As much as I wish it could, it won't make Vinson go away," she said in a voice good-humoredly mocking my own.

"You're not going to let me wander too far from the matter at hand, are you?"

"Not if you want to earn your keep here."

Teasingly, she was reminding me that I was a guest in her home. It brought to mind my own apartment, lost nearly a week ago during a large scale, slight of hand magician's trick. I'd thought about it a lot since then and still carried a fleeting urge to revisit that building and search for my stuff. Deep down, I knew that finding anything now was a long shot. Had I had a chance to pillage the entire complex as I had the mysteriously converted Horace and Doris love nest, I might have foiled Vinson's plot right then and there. *If only I had known then what I know now.*

As if she were reading my thoughts, Sunny asked if it might be a good idea to go back to my old apartment and snoop around.

"If I had a nickel for every time I've thought about that," I said. "I'd be a rich man who could buy a new identity. But I think you and I both know that would be a waste of time. Everything I had is long gone, burned or buried somewhere along with Jimmy Hoffa."

"You're probably right," Sunny said, sympathetically.

"And we don't want to take the chance of hitting Vinson's radar again," I said. "That's why we nixed the shelter, remember? I have no doubt my former landlord would recognize me if he saw me again, especially after demolishing his wife's kitchen that day. He'd be on the phone to Vinson faster than the paparazzi onto a streaking Paris Hilton."

"Did you really trash the place?"

"A bull in a china shop."

Sunny giggled at the thought of it. "Are you sure you wouldn't like to do it again."

"It's not a question of what I'd like to do, more a question of getting arrested."

Sunny nodded in agreement and said, "No, you're right. Now that we're hidden, the best thing we can do is stay out of sight until it's time to go back to Rhode Island."

"And pickup my license," I added. Even though I'd never met the man, I was feeling optimistic about Roger's abilities. Confident, because if I were in his eager-to-impress-a-gorgeous-young-woman shoes, I know I'd be applying some serious elbow grease to the search for her "brother's" records. In a way, I felt bad for him, knowing that he would be disappointed when Sunny wasn't as grateful as he most certainly was fantasizing she would be.

"In the meantime," she said to me coyly. "How about some dessert?"

Before I could answer, Sunny's doorbell rang.

38

Picasso

"Were you expecting anyone this evening?" John Oliver asked Claire. The two were still snuggled up in bed, playfully arguing over what Mexican dishes to order for dinner, when they'd heard a knock at the door. His obnoxiously loud, grumbling stomach had momentary distracted Claire from her inquiry into her nephew's status at Earth Nexus, giving John a little more time to construct a measured explanation. Hearing the visitor at the door, he thanked God for the extended reprieve.

Claire, already out of bed and scurrying toward the trail of clothes tossed about the floor, replied, "No one." She busily gathered up her panties, bra, slacks and blouse, all the while muttering something about how wrinkled they'd become.

"Maybe it's the takeout delivery man?" John suggested.

"I think you have call first, not just wish it," Claire said with a grin. She was standing at the foot of bed now, tickled by her lover's humor while she hastily reassembled the outfit he'd stripped off her several hours ago. "Have you seen my shoes," she said, scanning the floor.

John cleared his throated.

Claire looked up and saw her lover, still nestled under the sheets, holding her high heels in his hand.

"You really are a pervert," she giggled. She then went to

answer the knock in her bare feet.

From the bedroom, John heard the faint sound of the front door opening and then a muffled voice saying something he couldn't discern. Uneasy, he got up, pulled on his shorts and followed Claire's footsteps, his suspicious ear honed into what was happening in the front hallway. His first and only thought— Louis had found them out.

"You must have the wrong address," Claire said to the diminutive young man standing on her doorstep, his bright red shirt and matching cap broadcasting he was in the employ of Antonio's Pizzeria. In one of his small hands, he held a comparatively large square box adorned with the likeness of a steaming pizza, in the other, a slip of paper that was noticeably shaking.

"Is this 2103 Maple Drive?" his pubescent voice squeaked.

"No," Claire replied.

"It's not," the boy said. He was clearly upset, his eyes beginning to tear behind the oversized glasses resting on his tiny, button nose.

Instantly, Claire realized the boy was lost and seeing how very distraught he was over his error, she searched her memory for the whereabouts of Maple Drive. She'd lived in town for quite a few years and knew it well, but nothing was coming to mind. Wishing she could steer the poor thing in the right direction, she was just about to send him back to the restaurant when she felt John step up behind her.

"Pizza!" John exclaimed. "What's on it?"

Fighting back a sniffle, the boy told him peppers and onions.

John was overjoyed. "You're kidding, that's my favorite. How much do you want for it?"

"Twenty bucks?" the boy replied tentatively.

"Sold!" John said. "I'll be right back."

Claire threw the boy a half smile and waited with him at the door until John returned with his wallet.

"Here you go, son," John said as he took the box from the boy before handing him three ten dollar bills. "And there's a little something for your trouble. You just saved my life."

"Gee, thanks mister," the elated boy said. He then turned and hurried down the walkway, skipping all the way back to his car.

"Sweet kid," John said as he opened the box and took a long whiff of its contents.

Glaring at him as she closed the door, Claire said, "You know I absolutely detest pizza. *Everyone* knows how much I hate pizza. What am *I* suppose to eat for dinner."

"Don't worry; we'll still put in an order to that Mexican place you like. This is just an appetizer to tide me over until then. My blood sugar is dangerously low." He closed the lid and headed toward the kitchen, eager to dig into his snack. Claire was right behind him, shaking her head over his rampant appetite while admiring his barely covered behind and wondering how it stayed so nicely trim and tight.

No more than five minutes later, Claire was dialing the phone. She wasn't placing a takeout order for enchiladas and she wasn't calling Antonio's to complain about the skimpy toppings. Claire was frantically calling 911.

Outside, Jeremy Limpkin was still sitting in his car, the red shirt and cap he just exchanged for a t-shirt and a Red Sox hat, resting on the seat next to him. Through a lit window of the house he just visited, he could see the image of a harried woman with a phone to her ear. It brought a smile to his youthful face. He hadn't tried a poisoned pizza before but he was confident it had worked. Pulling away from the curb, he felt a wave of satisfaction wash over his small frame, another masterpiece completed. It wasn't exactly what Vinson had ordered only hours ago—Vinson wanted Oliver to disappear without a trace—but Jeremy was an artist. As such, he had to remain true to himself, to interpret life *and death* as he felt it. No one told Picasso how to paint. No one ordered Beethoven what music to create. Assimilating himself with the greats of history, Jeremy Limpkin left Oyster Bay that night anxiously awaiting the world's response to *his* latest work.

39

Highlight of the Evening

The Democratic National Committee's lavish fundraising event at Manhattan's famed Jumeirah Essex House was in full swing by the time Louis Vinson arrived. Pulling up in his customary white limousine, he stepped out slowly, took a few steps toward the entrance and stopped. Clad in a black tuxedo, his gaze lifting skyward, he recalled his driver—a seemingly well read young man with a tattoo of a scorpion on the back of his neck—telling him that Angelina Jolie owned the penthouse apartment at the top. He wondered silently if she might be home tonight and be interested in joining him for drink. A passing thought, he knew he didn't have time for the famous actress tonight, he already had another young woman waiting with bated breath. Moving toward the Hotel's elegant, art-deco entrance, Vinson walked deliberately, his mind already counting down the minutes until his date with Elizabeth Hart.

With a glass of champagne in hand, Vinson strolled through the crowd, nodding to acquaintances, smiling at the deserving women, making a point of being seen by as many interested eyes as possible. Tonight's affair had drawn an impressive crowd, the rich and the powerful all vying for alliance with the Democrat's latest Presidential hopeful, a fair-haired Senator from New York. Vinson wasn't much for swimming with the world's politicians.

The water was too murky. But there were advantages to rubbing elbows occasionally, the modest price a handsome donation and few hours of his time. The press coverage was of more interest to Vinson on this particular evening, bolstering his "concerned and engaged citizen" image while providing a convenient alibi for the next conversation with his wife, Claire.

"Where's your lovely wife, Louis?" a voiced asked.

Vinson turned to his right and immediately extended his hand to an older, identically attired gentleman. "Benjamin, my friend, how are you?" Vinson asked with a broad smile. The two men shook hands, appearing genuinely pleased to greet one another to the curious swarm surrounding them.

"Splendid," Benjamin replied. "Simply splendid. And it's Benny, old man. Benjamin was my father."

Benjamin Beaufort was a London textile manufacturer who could never get enough of the charity night life. Born into an obscenely wealthy family with estates in every corner of England, Benny, as he preferred to be called, was a self-proclaimed "groupee" of the American fundraising circuit, attending several hundred a year. A tall, heavyset man, with a full grey beard and impish eyes, he had a reputation for being quite generous, along with habitually arriving early and staying well past the event's official conclusion. Vinson had run into him several times at charity gatherings, their initial meeting during a rare occasion when Claire had accompanied her husband. Like many first impressions, Benny had never forgotten.

"So, where is the beautiful and delightful, Claire?" Benny asked again. "She hasn't graced our stage since I can't recall when? She isn't ill I trust?"

She may be by now, Vinson thought, fighting off a grin. "No, no, she's fine," he said. "Camped out at our place in Oyster Bay and preparing her prize roses for an upcoming show in Boston. She enters every year. I'm lucky to see her at all during the summer."

"Brilliant," Benny replied. "Nothing like a good roll in the garden to keep one's blood pumping. Good for the heart, you know. I do a spot of tillage myself from time to time. What about you Louis, do you enjoy the muck as well?"

Not as much as I'm enjoying this conversation, Vinson thought, mockingly. He didn't like Benjamin Beaufort but he knew the blowhard would tell everyone he met that night about running into the handsome young billionaire. And, if Benny followed past practice, embellish their ten minutes together into an all night, two-man carousing bender.

"I'm all thumbs when it comes to plants," Vinson replied. "Neither one of them are green."

Just then, a shapely waitress sauntered up to them with a tray of bubbling champagne. She smiled flirtatiously at Vinson, who in turned smiled back upon accepting a fresh glass. Beaufort took two, toasting with Vinson as the two men watched the tight-skirted temptation slowly slide away.

Inebriated and aroused, Beaufort passed Vinson a wink before heading off after the girl, exclaiming, "Tally ho! Let the hunt begin."

Vinson knew the old man expected him to follow, but he didn't. He got what he needed from Benny so it was time to move on. For the next two hours he would mingle, liberally spreading himself around so that if anyone asked any of the guests later—Claire or a naïve detective perhaps—his attendance at the event would appear far more involved than it actually was. And, if he could swing it, he'd grant some starving reporter an interview, where he could once again express his disgust over the recent YouTube transgression along with his ideas for making the internet more family friendly. Vinson knew it was a small precaution—not completely necessary—but one of those minor details that he prided himself on executing.

Two hours later, his bow tie sitting in his unbuttoned coat pocket, Vinson climbed behind the wheel of a nondescript, black sedan parked several blocks from the hotel on a dark street adjacent to the south end of Central Park. Successful in establishing his presence at the gala, the evening so far had also been a complete bore, but as he started the engine, his excitement grew. The highlight of the night was now in sight and pulling out onto Fifth Avenue, the sparkling glimmer of New York City accelerating his already rising pulse, Vinson drove toward his little hideaway in Brooklyn, thinking there was no better way to cap an evening than to spend it watching a tormented worm wiggle on hot tin.

40

Knock, Knock, Who's There?

I had exceeded the three knockdown rule several days and countless punches ago, praying each time for the sight of a white towel being thrown into the ring, signifying the merciful end to my nightmare. For a week, my ears have yearned for the sound of the bell, a ringing savior that might lift me to a rehabilitating, if only momentary, rest. Neither had come, the closest being in the form of Sunny. Thankfully, she was in my corner now—the only one in my corner—and it gave me hope that the fight was not yet lost. But when her doorbell rang, interrupting our about-to-be-defining moment together, I was suddenly a spectator in the top row, gazing down helplessly at my own image as it lay dazed on the ring canvas floor, *slain* by the bell.

Reacting to the sound with a quizzical look, Sunny stood up and went to the door.

"Don't open it!" I said. "You don't know who it might be."

She stopped a step from the door and turned back toward me. "Well, if I don't open it, I can't see who it is."

Examining the door, I could see that it had no peephole. "Hold on." I left the table and walked up behind her. "Ok, you can open it now."

"If you're so worried, you open it." She then pulled me forward before giving me a gentle nudge toward the door.

"Fine," I said reluctantly. I'm not sure who I thought might be on the other side, but based on the way my heart was racing, something inside me was convinced it was one of Vinson's bogeymen. Slowly, I reached for the knob.

"Boo!" Sunny blurt out while pinching my behind at the exact same moment.

I nearly jumped out of my shoes.

Turning my head back at her, I laughed nervously. "You little…" A second knock aimed me forward again. I hesitated.

"Oh, just open it," Sunny insisted. "No one knows where I live."

I turned the knob, saying, "Famous last words."

Standing on the other side of the threshold was absolutely the last person I expected to see. It wasn't the bogeyman, but I was still rendered speechless.

Peering out from behind me, Sunny greeted our visitor. "Dexter, what are you doing here?" she asked.

The man who rarely poked his head out of his own shell, remaining quietly in the shadows of the Kinston Street Shelter, emerging only to tinker with the computers, now stood before us with a grave look on his face. It wasn't much, but it was the most emotion I'd ever seen him muster and my first thought was something had happened to Charles. My second thought; *how did he find us?*

"It's Felix, actually," he said, never changing his expression. "Felix Ostrander. Can I come in?"

"Sure," I mumbled, still reeling from the sight of him. He walked right in, never noticing the puzzled shrugs Sunny and I exchanged as I closed the door.

"Did you just say that *you're* Felix Ostrander?" I asked.

"That's right," he replied.

"Did you use to work at Earth Nexus?"

"I did."

"The same Felix Ostrander that Louis Vinson erased?"

"Erased?"

"Wiped out every footprint you ever left on the planet. Made you think you were crazy by turning everything you ever knew into a mind-blowing mirage."

Finally, the acknowledgment I had been searching for was standing right in front of me. Felix nodded as he said, "He destroyed my life, if that's what you mean."

I felt the weight of the world lift off my shoulders. "Mine too," I said. I think we would have remained there for hours, captivated like two dodo birds—the last of their species—if Sunny hadn't suggested we sit down at the kitchen table.

"I'd offer you some pizza," Sunny said. "But Daniel ate the last slice."

"I resemble that remark," I said, grinning.

"I'm fine," Felix said. "I had some soup at the shelter before I hopped a bus over here."

"How is everything there?" I asked. "Is Charles all right?"

"Everything is fine," Felix replied. His eyes shifted away, jumpy. I could see he was struggling with whatever it was he wanted to say and that's when it finally hit me. Felix Ostrander—aka Dexter—was my Secret Santa.

"You put those things in my cot, didn't you?" I said. "The files and then the BlackBerry."

He nodded.

"So you must have been the one to pull that steroid-popper off me that night in the office."

"I hit him in the head with an old laptop computer," Felix replied, proudly. "I could never get the thing to work anyway."

This stranger who, looking more like a shabby vagrant than a viable rescuer, had apparently been shadowing my every move and, for some unknown reason, passing along the clues necessary to untangle my predicament. I asked him the burning question. "Why?"

His eyes stumbled over to Sunny and then back to me. He

said, "I was hoping that you might take Vinson on; fight back. Something I couldn't muster the courage to do. But first you needed to know what he'd done to you. That he was behind the madness. That you weren't going insane. It took me weeks to figure it out."

"How did you?" I said, remembering the absolute sense of despair I felt those first few days, clinging to the last thread of my sanity.

"Dumb luck," Felix said. "I'd been at the shelter for a week and half and was out back having a smoke, no clue where else to go, when this bruiser comes along. There'd been some drug traffic taking place at the time and not recognizing the guy as an employee, I hunkered behind the dumpster before he caught sight of me. Well, he stopped short of the door and made a call on his cell phone. Wouldn't you know it, he was looking for me and it wasn't to ask if I wanted to buy some weed. He was a hired gun, Daniel. Vinson sent him there to kill me."

"I remember you now," Sunny said. "You were at the shelter the week I started working there; the cleanest guy in the place. You always smelled like Ivory Soap."

"Still does," I injected. I noticed the distinctively flowery scent the moment he walked in.

Sunny continued. "Left your belongings under your cot and just disappeared one day. Where did you go?"

Felix said, "As soon as Vinson's thug left, I did the same; lived on the streets on the other side of town for a few months until I couldn't take it anymore."

"You took a big chance coming back to the shelter," I said.

"I was a mess by then, wasn't thinking straight. But I did remember Charles. He had offered to give me a job maintaining the computers before I tucked tail and ran. Coming back was the only hope I had of rebuilding my life. The day I began the long walk across town to see if his offer was still good, I noticed my reflection in a shop window. It wasn't me. The guy in the reflection was a dirty, scruffy, homeless man. It may have been the hopelessness talking, but I convinced myself that no one would recognize me; that I could return to the shelter incognito."

"So you became Dexter," Sunny said.

Felix shrugged. "It was a shoe store, where I saw the stranger staring back at me."

"Did that thug ever come back looking for you?" I asked. I was thinking about myself now, pondering the notion that Sunny had been right about the shelter being a dangerous place for me to hide. *Maybe that's why Vinson finances it*, I thought. Besides providing him with good press and a tax write-off, it was an obvious sanctuary for those he'd erased. It was almost like strapping a homing beacon around our necks to determine our whereabouts. Like a dumb animal, I had walked right into it.

"Several times, actually," Felix answered. "But he looked right past me, like I was a piece of shit that he didn't want to step in."

Sunny threw me an "I told you so" look.

"That's why I left," I said. "Sunny and I reasoned that Vinson would come looking for me sooner or later." I pulled the BlackBerry from my pocket and placed it on the table. "There's a spreadsheet in there with a schedule on it; a hit list detailing the timely demise of the two dozen folks he'd apparently dismantled just like you and me before having them killed. He refers to it as being *erased*. I take it you hadn't seen much of the contents before you passed it along to me."

"No," Felix said, looking somewhat ashamed. "I didn't spend any time poking around inside it before I put it in your cot. I was afraid of what I might find."

"How did you get it?" Sunny asked.

"Do your remember Ralphie?" Felix asked Sunny. "A big guy with a long scar on the left side of his face?"

"Not really," Sunny replied.

"He wandered in and out sporadically, but that doesn't matter. He lifted it off Vinson the day he came to the shelter—

caught the fucker with the old bump and grab. You were there Daniel. It was your first or second day, I think."

I said, "Yeah, I remember. Vinson collided with him on the way out. Ruffled his feathers good. But how did you end up with it?"

"Ralphie didn't have any need for a cell phone, only the cash he could get for it. After he told me where he'd gotten it, I bought it off him for ten bucks. I saw it as an investment in our futures. Mine and yours, Daniel."

"I owe you one, Felix," I said, sincerely. And I truly did. His money had been well spent. Without that BlackBerry, there was no way I would know that Vinson had initiated the removal of my identity from the face of the earth. Or that he was circling overhead, eager to amputate my lingering existence as well. I would still be floundering, a sitting duck unwittingly waiting for a bullet to the brain.

"How did you know Daniel was with me?" Sunny asked.

"And how did you know where she lived?" I added.

Felix looked down at his feet, a sheepish grin forming as he told us that some time ago he'd hacked into the Post Office computer system where "Raeni" had purchased a mailbox. "Your data file listed this address," Felix said. "I had a crush on you but never summoned the nerve to pay you a visit. When I heard Daniel tell Charles earlier that he would be staying with you, I dug out the address and, well, you know the rest."

"You told Charles you were staying with me?" Sunny asked in an accusatorial tone. "After I asked you not to?"

"I'm sorry. It just…slipped out," I said. "Completely and irrevocably, my bad."

Felix quickly came to my rescue. "Don't worry, Charles won't tell a soul."

"It's not Charles I'm worried about," Sunny said. "If you overheard Daniel saying it, then someone else could have as well."

"There were only three of us sitting there," I said. "Hillary had gone to have a cigarette shortly after I sat down. She's the one with the loose lips, so I think we're ok."

"*Hillary* is the one with loose lips?" Sunny asked, raising an eyebrow.

She had me cold, but I sidestepped the insinuation by turning to our visitor. "Let's back up a minute. Felix, you said you hacked into the Post Office computer system. Is that what you did at Earth Nexus, hack for Vinson, I mean?"

"No, hacking is just a hobby. I'm not that good at it, actually. Not anywhere near as expert as some of the guys at Earth Nexus. I was just one of several network administrators keeping the computers up and running. A self-taught, red-blooded computer geek."

"No college education?" I asked.

"None, I'm sorry to say. But I knew the systems inside and out. I just didn't have the diploma to back it up."

"I'm not questioning your ability," I replied. "Only taking stock of your erasability. I didn't have a formal education either. And no family to fall back on after Vinson worked his black magic. My guess is that you don't have family somewhere?"

"An orphan since birth," Felix said, regretfully. "Bounced around from one foster home to the next until I realized I was better off on my own. At fifteen, I packed what I had and split. Worked my way to New York City where I got an off-the-books job for a network systems consulting firm that turned out to be more computer scam than computer support. The place finally got busted but not before I learned everything I needed to know. Somehow I slipped away under the radar, landing the job at Earth Nexus a few months later."

"How long did you work there?" Sunny asked.

"Over three years," Felix replied. "Long enough to see some things that I wasn't suppose to see."

"The bogus financial reports?" I asked.

"I didn't have access to any of the financial software. I heard a lot of rumors about that kind of thing, though. Fabricated entries and grossly exaggerated profits. No, the stuff I tripped over one day was a little more shocking than fraudulent accounting."

"You saw the videos, didn't you," Sunny said. Her face had gone pale and her hands were quivering. "The rapes and the strangulations."

Felix didn't say anything, but I knew he understood what Sunny was really telling him. Finally, he looked at her and asked, "You?"

I answered the question for her. "Almost."

Sunny's tiny apartment suddenly fell silent, the three of us gazing pensively at the BlackBerry sitting forebodingly in the center of the table. In one way or another, Vinson had basically raped us all and at that moment there didn't appear to be a whole lot we could do about it. I, for one, wasn't inclined to wait around until he came calling to finish what he'd started.

"What if we took his BlackBerry to the police," I offered. "Show them the spreadsheet and the names listed. Surely after they investigated a few the resulting suspicions would prompt them into further action."

Felix said, "Every one of those people was probably just like us, Daniel. No trail for the police to follow, no scent for their dogs to track. Vinson took care of all that. They'd be chasing ghosts."

Sunny said, "The police aren't going to believe us, Daniel. We'd be foolish to think differently."

Felix readily agreed.

Frustrated, I pushed away from the table, and went to the window. It was dark outside now, the amber glow from a lone street lamp the only source of light for as far as I could see. "There has to be something we can do to put a crack in his armor," I said.

Felix said, "He's obsessively careful, Daniel, a master at calculating out even the smallest detail. They call him Caesar, did you know that. *Emperor* of the new digital world."

"Yeah, I know," I said. "I just wish my name was Brutus."

Felix continued, telling Sunny and I that before his life went topsy-turvy, he'd been digging for dirt on Vinson, attempting to establish an insurance policy in case he found himself unemployed. "But I couldn't find a damn thing. Not a single spec of evidence." He was shaking his head now, dejected. "It's just as well, though; I don't know what I would have done with it anyway. I'm not cut out for this *Goodfellas* kind of shit." He turned to Sunny, apologetic in his tone, and said, "It's just that after I stumbled upon those sick videos files, I felt the urge to do *something.*"

I may not look like Brutus, but maybe someone at Earth Nexus does, I thought. I turned and looked back at the two of them still sitting at the table. "Is there anyone on the inside who might be willing to help us? Someone who's been working at Earth Nexus long enough to be acquainted with a few of the skeletons in Vinson's closet?"

Felix said, "I don't know, Daniel. The turnover rate was pretty high when I was there. If the twenty-hour workdays didn't get you, a pink slip did. I can't recall a single day when someone didn't quit or was fired. Personally, I didn't know anyone who'd been there for more than a year. The fact that I had lasted over three made me the odd man out. Maybe that's why he finally cut me loose. Erased me, as you say."

As I stood there scraping together every memory I could recall of my brief stint at Earth Nexus, my eyes locked onto Sunny's, that funny feeling you get when you know the answer is right on the tip of your tongue. I remembered hearing a name mentioned once, an executive who'd been with Vinson from the beginning. My boss, Hank, had referred to him several times while we were preparing the quarterly statements. "So and so is waiting on these, Daniel," Hank had said, anxious to complete the work on time. But instead of so and so, he had said…"John. Is there a high ranking guy named John working there?" I asked Felix.

"John Oliver?" Felix suggested.

I walked back to the table and stood behind my chair, leaning against it like a crutch as I ran that name through my memory. "Yeah, that's the guy I'm thinking of. He's been there a long time, I'm sure of it."

"Now that I think about it, you right," Felix said. "I remember a few whispers being exchanged about John. He's the only guy that Vinson rarely challenged, at least according to the water cooler talk. There has to be a reason for that. He might be our Brutus, Daniel."

"Is that why you came here, Felix," Sunny said suddenly, her eyes burning a hole into the man's forehead. "To enlist Daniel in some crazy attempt at revenge against that madman?"

"Yes!" He said. "I mean…no, not originally." He then turned to me. "When I heard you tell Charles you needed time off, I had a sinking feeling you'd never be coming back. I'd already convinced myself that you were my return ticket to my life and when you walked out of the shelter, I panicked. So, to answer your question, Raeni, I didn't really have a plan when I jumped on the bus over here. Only a desperate need to tell you who I was and what had happened to me."

Sunny reached out and gave Felix's hand a squeeze, her anger evaporating as quickly as it had appeared. "It's Sunny, actually. Raeni was *my* hiding place."

"Sunny's right about one thing," I said. "Vinson is a madman. Trying to take him on would be suicide. But maybe this guy Oliver is worth a shot. If I was to approach him in a public place, explain my circumstances and gage his reaction, we'd have a better idea if he was a possible ally or not."

"Or he'd tell his buddy Vinson and bang, you're dead," Felix said.

"Not if I suddenly appear while he's having lunch at Subway. I've been erased, remember? While he's wiping his mouth with his napkin, I'll be disappearing back into the woodwork."

Felix was grinning now, in sync with my thinking. Knowingly, he said, "It's hard to find someone who doesn't exist."

"You're playing with fire," Sunny said. She didn't appear angry again, only concerned.

"We have to do something, Sunny," I said.

"Waiting is something," she replied. "In a few days, you'll have your driver's license back and with it, you're old life. Then we have a better chance of getting someone to believe all this."

"Provided your friend Roger comes through," I said.

"I wouldn't count on that," Felix said. "I came up empty after a half dozen tries at the DMV, and Charles the same through his contact at the Social Security Department. If nothing else, Vinson was thorough."

Sunny looked at me, her fearful eyes pleading her case.

"Well, it's going to take a few days to scope out this guy Oliver," I said, succumbing to her silent appeal. "Where he lives, where he works, where he likes to eat and all that." I reached over and picked up the BlackBerry. "There's probably an address for him in here, but I don't even know what he looks like. I'd feel a lot better if I knew I was stalking the right guy."

Felix said, "I can search the web when I get back to the shelter. There's got to be at least one picture of him with Vinson somewhere, the two of them at a charity event or something."

"When you find one, let me know," I said.

The relief on Sunny's face was priceless. I knew she was banking on the resurrected driver's license and its ability to steer me away from my plan to solicit John Oliver, but the truth was, I was going pursue the Earth Nexus executive whether the Rhode Island DMV guy came through or not. Not wanting her encouraged smile to fade, I kept quiet about my intentions.

Then, there was second knock at the door. We had another visitor.

41

Rules of the Hunt

From a block away, Sammy Johnson watched wantonly as the sexy young woman extracted herself from the car he'd been following. He had traveled only about ten miles, trailing invisibly behind the eye-catching Camaro, but in that short span his interest had diverted itself from the targeted male driver to the attractive female passenger. Shifting in his seat to ease the mounting pressure in his denim-encapsulated crotch, he sped forward, snatching an eyeful of the woman as she led the man into the building lobby. *You look even tastier up close*, he thought as he drove by. *Like a sweet pot of honey.* It was at that moment that Sammy decided he deserved a little r and r—rape and ruin, he liked to call it—after attending to his current assignment, the burial of Daniel Rayne. *That stupid fuck doesn't deserve a sweet piece like her*, Sammy reasoned as he swung around and parked along the curb of the next block. *But I certainly do.*

Sammy shut off the engine and got out. Casually, he surveyed up and down the street, searching for a curious eye. He saw no one. After a quick check of the buck knife perched in his pocket, he headed up the street. Like a child's security blanket, this particular knife was his favorite, given to him by his uncle as he stood over the lifeless body of his first white deer. He was only twelve at the time, skinny and shy, but subject to the rules of the hunt nonetheless. "You killed it, so you clean it," his uncle reminded him as he handed him the celebratory gift. Sammy found that he enjoyed the feel of the gelatinous guts in his hands, still warm from the life he just extinguished. He especially relished the taste of blood as he bit into the animal's heart, another ritual introduced to him that day. From that moment forward, Sammy never stopped hunting, even when business kept him in the concrete forest.

Nearing the entrance that had swallowed Rayne and his hot girlfriend, Sammy stopped in his tracks and pulled out his cell phone, pretending he'd just gotten a call. There was a man running toward him from the opposite end of the street. It was dark but Sammy immediately recognized the bearded form drawing ever closer. It was Felix the Cat.

"Hey Joe, what's going on," Sammy said, speaking loudly so that the approaching man could hear. He wanted Felix to think he was just a local resident on his way out for the night and not the lurking killer that he was. Evidently, it worked. Felix paid him no mind and hurried into the same building Sammy had been aiming for.

With an annoyed snap, Sammy closed his cell phone and pondered his next move. Felix had come looking for Danny Boy, he was sure of that, making the odds a little uneven for a bull rush. He knew he could handle the two men easily, but the extra effort required might allow the real prize of the evening—the girl—to slip away in the process. *You may have just spoiled my evening, you lowlife son-of-a-bitch*, Sammy thought. With the vision of the nameless girl's tight little ass and silky legs still dancing in his head, Sammy wrestled with the thought of returning the next day. He didn't want to, but he also didn't want a breathing witness. *I could use the Glock instead*, he thought. *Two quick shots and I'd be knee deep in honey for the rest of the night.* But Sammy was in the mood for some slice and dice, not bang, bang, you're dead. Angry over the turn of events, he stared up at the only lit window in the building, cursing out the inopportune visitor, warning him to keep it brief. "You got twenty minutes, and then I'm coming up," he said. Resigned to what he decided would be a short wait, Sammy then returned to his car, extracting the knife from his pocket as he walked, imagining the best way to skin Felix the Cat.

42

A Seed

Claire could feel him slipping away. Cradling John's head in her lap, she sat on the floor exactly where her lover had collapsed, sobbing uncontrollably as she wiped the blood leaking from his nose with the sleeve of her blouse. Her only reason for living was dying and nothing she did could stop the bleeding. *Oh God, where is that ambulance!* Staring disbelievingly into his vacant eyes, Claire struggled to comprehend the blood-coated words sputtering from his mouth.

"I'm sorry, my darling," John said. His reached out to caress her face; his short breathes becoming more erratic as he willed his arm upward. "I should have known he knew."

"Louis?" she replied. "You think Louis did this?"

John nodded, wincing in pain.

"But how?" Claire asked.

"The boy," John mumbled.

Barely comprehending the meaning of his words, she glanced at the half eaten slice of pizza lying on the floor, an upended calamity of tomato sauce and cheese. Next to it was John's wallet, dropping from where he had stuffed it into his waistband as he fell to the floor.

"Poison?" She was asking God as much as she was asking John.

John started to answer but a coughing fit suddenly seized him and it took every ounce of Claire's strength to carry him through it.

"Don't try to talk," she whispered softly. He needed her calm now, a warm breeze on the cold journey beyond. But John wouldn't hear it.

"I need to tell you something," he said. "I need to tell you about Daniel."

As the poison leeched into John's organs, invading healthy cells and causing them to burst, he parted his parched lips perhaps for the last time and told Claire what he had allowed to happen to her nephew. He said that he was sorry for not having the strength to stand up to Louis; to knowingly aid his quest for ultimate power while turning a blind eye to the truth. "To walk away would have meant to walk away from you, Claire," he said. A surge of blood from his mouth halted further explanation, but Claire understood. The poison was tearing his insides apart, but his love for her remained.

With the faint wail of an ambulance emerging from the silence, John mustered one last assault on his conscience. "You can find him at the Kingston Street Shelter in Boston," he said. "He's ok, but Louis must never find him." His eyes were pleading now, desperate for forgiveness. "Do you understand? Louis must never find him."

Claire watched helplessly as her tears fell, mixing with the blood on John's face as his body began to retreat into her arms like an ocean wave returning to the sea. Louis Vinson had exacted his revenge against the man who had coveted his wife's body and secretly staked claim to her love, but not before his rival had placed the seed to the billionaire's demise into the hands of his wife. Summoning Claire to retrieve a small, folded piece of paper from his wallet, John's barely audible words implored Claire to give the note to the police. "They'll know what to do with it," he whispered. He then squeezed her hand tightly and told her how much he loved her. He smiled, his red lips closed, and he was gone.

The next hour passed slowly for Claire Vinson. The paramedics had arrived too late, entering the house to investigate when no one answered the door. Gently, they untangled her from the lifeless body they found in her lap before helping her to a chair in the kitchen. She was in shock, clinging to a thread while the two men in white attended to the man she didn't want to live without, clutching the note John had given her. A policeman asked if she'd like a glass of water. She shook her head no. Nothing seemed real—the sight of John being wheeled out on a stretcher, his face already turning ghostly pale; the officer hovering over her, inquiring about the pizza delivery man; her eyes suddenly reading an unfamiliar name written in John's unmistakable handwriting.

Then, as if she'd fallen asleep briefly, she was alone in her house, trembling at the sight of the blood still soaking its way into the hardwood floor. The ambulance was gone and the policeman was gone but she couldn't remember them leaving. Still in her hand, the puzzling note. *Why didn't I give it to the officer?*

Unable to remain in the house, she left, driving her car to the nearest diner. It was late and thankfully, the place was empty. After her second cup of coffee, the outside world began to reappear. But so then did her memory. John was dead, the policeman inconclusive about the cause of death. The officer told her that it had been a busy night; that they were shorthanded; that someone would be back in the morning to continue the investigation. He seemed a kind man, offering to call someone to come and stay with her before he left. Regretfully, she told him there was no one anymore.

Noticing a newspaper on the counter, her body shuddered at the thought of a picture of John's dead body plastered on the front page. *Louis will savor it,* she thought. *Place it in his scrapbook along side all the other lives he's destroyed.* Instantly, she hated herself for thinking about Louis at that moment. After controlling her for so many years, it was a hard habit to break. More than anything, she wanted John back—alive and holding her in his arms—but even more, she wanted to be free of Louis Vinson. Claire Vinson wanted her husband dead.

In that brief second of time, as if delivered by a messenger, Claire noticed that the name in the headline of the newspaper was the same name on the note John had passed to her as he lay dying in her arms. Sensing that it was more than mere coincidence, she pulled it over and read the scandalous story. She then unfolded the note for the second time and read the Brooklyn address listed below the woman's name.

After hurriedly paying the counter waitress, Claire Vinson left the diner, concluding that a merciful court appearance and a short jail sentence were far more than her husband, Louis, deserved.

43

The Same Old Knot

For the second time that night, I followed Sunny to the door, an unnerving sense of doom prickling at the back of my neck. Surely, it was one of Vinson's goons this time, having tailed an unsuspecting Felix to our hideaway. I voiced the same concern as I had the first time, only to find myself in the familiar lead position, Sunny urging me forward from the safety of my shadow. Why I opened it, I don't know—morbid curiosity or blind courage, perhaps? Whatever it was controlling my hand as it turned the knob, it didn't vacillate, pulling the door opened so abruptly it startled the person on the other side.

"Holy shit!" the tall brunette woman exclaimed. "You scared the Be Jesus out of me."

She really didn't look that scared to me, more like royally pissed off. Staring back with one hand on her cocked hip, clad provocatively in a mini-skirt, exceptionally high heels and a tube top so tight I could almost read the inscription on her nipple rings, the woman explained impatiently that she was looking for Raeni. No sooner had she said it then she noticed Sunny peeking over my shoulder.

"Girl, don't be telling me you forgot about our gig tonight," the woman said. Then, noticing a second man inside the apartment, a knowing grin spread across her painted face. "Did I come at a bad time?"

As it turns out, Sunny *had* forgotten about the bachelor party Thumper had booked. "Slipped my mind," she claimed. Against my advice, she agreed to perform, feeling compelled, I assumed, to honor her commitment. The only catch was they had to be in Manhattan by two o'clock to pull it off.

"It's a really sweet deal, money wise," Thumper explained to Felix and me while Sunny was getting into costume. "Four grand split three ways. My brother, Axel is driving us there and he gets a cut. He'll hang while we strut; keep the boys on their best behavior."

"But why so late?" I asked. "By the time you get there, won't the party be over?

Thumper went on to explain that a lot of gigs worked that way, arranged to commence after a long night of revelry. "Kind of an exclamation point as the night comes to a close," she said. "To tell you the truth, I like it late. They don't have much energy left by then. Makes my job a hellava lot easier, if you know what I mean."

"What about the guys you'll be dancing for, do you know any of them?" I asked. I was remembering Sunny's last experience in New York City, wishing that she wasn't so stubborn and hoping I could talk her out of the trip when she came out of the bathroom.

Thumper sensed my concerned. "The groom is some rich young doctor from Philly. I'm pretty sure the rest of them are doctors as well," she said. "I've danced for several of them before—perfect gentlemen, totally harmless. And with Axel there, it'll be a walk in the park."

I had never met Thumper before, but listening to her describe the gig, as she called it, I felt an odd sense of déjà vu.

Fifteen minutes after Thumper had arrived, Sunny exited the bathroom, appearing far sexier than I was prepared for knowing that in a few hours she'd be dancing in front of a crowd of drunken gynecologists. She wore a red plaid, pleated skirt and a simple white top with a column of underutilized buttons running down the middle. Beneath the shirt she wore a red lace bra announcing her cleavage. In that short period of time, Sunny had transformed herself from girl-next-door to promiscuous jailbait. I knew it was just a tease—all part of the evening's mirage—but the sight of her dressed like that clamped down on my heart so hard it felt as if every vein in my body was being choked. I was jealous, but also fearful.

I tried in vain to talk her out of it, appealing to her more sensible side, but she turned a deaf ear to my protests, assuring me that we would talk about it when she got back before pecking me on the cheek and disappearing out the door. Thumper then followed her out, telling Felix and me not to wait up for them.

"I hope this guy Axel is a tough son-of-a-bitch," I mumbled moments later.

"And smarter than his sister," Felix added.

I sat sulking for a while, angry that she'd left me behind. It was the same old knot I tied myself into as a boy when my mother would leave the house on a date. I didn't want her to go. I didn't want her spending time with any other man but me. Older now, I came to realize that my mother had her own needs, separate from mine. Sitting there with Felix, wondering if I should ask him to stay, I told myself that Sunny had to live her own life as well.

"You can hang here tonight, if you like," I offered. "I can give you a ride back to the shelter in the morning. Or you can catch a bus, if you'd rather."

Felix surveyed the tiny apartment. His response was less than enthusiastic. "There's another bus in an hour, I'll head back then."

"Granted, it's not the Kingston Street Shelter but it looks comfortable," I said. In all honesty, I was glad he turned down the offer. I really didn't want to share the lone bed with him, Ivory soap smell or not.

"In the meantime, I could sure use something to eat," Felix said. "Is that place you got the pizza nearby? I haven't had pizza in months. Charles never puts it on the shelter menu."

"It's only a few blocks," I replied. "But it may be closed by now. I remember passing a mini-grocery, though. We could try there. It might be open late."

"Do you mind? I don't want to eat Raeni—I mean—Sunny's food."

"If she had anything, she wouldn't mind," I said. "But her fridge is empty. So let's see what we can find down the street."

As we headed for the door, I suddenly realized that I didn't have a key for the lock. Was this a safe neighborhood? Did people leave their doors unlocked when they weren't home? Leaving my home unsecured wasn't my habit, but what could happen in ten minutes, right? And besides, Sunny's place wasn't exactly a burglar's dream. Maybe it was the nights in the shelter that had softened my precautionary judgment—sleeping unprotected amidst a crowd of strangers—but when I closed the apartment door behind me I really wasn't worried we would return to find it vandalized. Nor could I have imagined at that moment that I might never return at all.

44

The Tagalong

Sunny stepped out into the night feeling a quiet calm settling over her. Contrary to the way it had appeared upstairs, she had heard Daniel, his warnings of drunken, testosterone-juiced rowdies eager to add her innocence to their souvenir collection. She listened to every zealous word, and she loved him for that. But her intuition was telling her not to worry. *You'll be fine*, her inner voice was saying. *Thumper's got your back and her brother is covering both our asses. So, go, make some money.* It felt good knowing that she wasn't going in alone, comforting that there was also someone waiting for her when she got home. Courage feeds off companionship, and no one was feeling it more that night than Sunny.

Right on her young friend's heels as they exited the building, Thumper chattered away about how excited she was to get back to New York City. "It's been way too long since I've been to The Big Apple, girl. I miss the lights, the sounds of the people rushing off to here and there, and the food. God, I've got a craving for a hot dog with everything on it! We'll stop on the way back; grab a few extra for the long drive. Axel will eat four or five all by himself. The street vendors are everywhere, so we won't have any trouble finding one. You've been to New York, right? Used to live there?"

Smiling at her friend's animation, Sunny nodded, cautiously

keeping her eyes on the sidewalk ahead. The last thing she needed was a busted heel and a twisted ankle. Had she been looking further ahead, she would have noticed the beefy, rock of a man standing along side Thumper's brother, Axel. The two men were waiting for the women at the curb, proudly guarding a dark BMW sedan.

"Ooh," Thumper squealed as she nuzzled up to the man who was not her brother. "Nice wheels. Are they yours, handsome?"

"As a matter of fact, they are," the man replied. "And, as I was just telling Axel, available for a midnight run to Manhattan."

"Well, isn't that a coincidence," Thumper said as she slipped her arm into the BMW owner's. "It just so happens we need to be in Manhattan tonight."

"You can turn it off, sis," Axel said, chuckling. "I've already set it up. We'll cruise on down in the Beemer and leave my Chrysler here. Don't get too upset now."

Quietly observing from the background, Sunny's stomach flinched. The man didn't *look* at all familiar but he *seemed* familiar. Knowing how little sense that made she shrugged it off to the shyness she sometimes felt when meeting someone unexpectedly. She got into the back seat with Axel, amazed at how quickly Thumper was cozying up to Axel's friend.

"So, how do you two know each other?" Thumper asked. They were flying down Route 95 by this time, the moon and star-filled sky illuminating the countryside like a thousand tiny nightlights.

"We work out together sometimes," the man said. He took one hand off the wheel and flexed his arm, encouraging Thumper to feel his bicep muscle. She did, winking at Sunny at the same time. "I just happened to be in the neighborhood visiting a friend when I spotted Axel sitting on the hood of that old jalopy of his. He told me what you all had going tonight and asked if I wanted to come along for the ride. Little did I know I'd *be* the ride." He was smiling as he said it, playing the amiable tagalong.

"I owe you one, man," Axel said, leaning forward from the back seat. "I wasn't too sure the Chrysler would have made it to New York and back."

"Now he tells us," Thumper said. She turned her attention back to the stranger behind the wheel. "So, Mr. BMW-to-the-rescue, you got a name? My absentminded brother never introduced us."

"Sammy," the man replied. "Sammy Johnson."

45

Tracing the Past

I never would have believed it if I hadn't seen it with my own eyes. The pizza joint that Sunny had introduced me too earlier that evening was closed, but after walking a few more blocks, Felix and I found an open deli. There was a huge glass case as we walked in, displaying every sandwich meat you could imagine, along with pasta salads, roasted potatoes and macaroni and cheese. Even though I'd just feasted on a large pizza, the sight of the smorgasbord made my mouth water. Too weak to say no, I ordered a half-sized Cajun Turkey sandwich and a Coke, while Felix studiously examined the menu on the wall behind the counter. A few minutes later, my sandwich two bites gone, I watched in amazement as Felix sat down next to me with a large bowl of bean soup.

"You've got to be kidding," I said. "I don't think I'll ever be able to stomach another bowl of that shit."

"Actually, it kind of grows on you after a while," Felix replied. He lifted a spoonful toward his mouth, blew off the steam and slid it past his eager lips. "It's good," he then mumbled.

Shaking my head, I took another bite of my meal and gave the place the once over. It was your basic deli, unremarkable, my mind in no mood to assess the decor. There was, however, a crumpled newspaper sitting on the chair next to me, a thoughtful gift left by a previous patron. I picked it up, noticing a small headline that instantly spiked my interest. It was a review of a new book about genealogy, more specifically, as I read further, a guideline for using DNA to answer the puzzles of one's past. I put my sandwich down.

"Listen to this," I said to Felix. "This is an excellent book, blah, blah, blah, explores the many uses of genetic testing for tracing your family tree. It teaches you how the DNA tests work, where to get them, as well as how to further expand your results by joining an established research project, or starting your own family study."

Felix had stopped eating, his soup-filled spoon frozen in mid-slurp.

"We can use DNA to prove who we are," I said excitedly. "We get ourselves tested and then match it up to a relative and bingo—we're an official member of society again."

"There are a number of websites that offer assistance in tracing your family tree," Felix said. His brain was churning now, tabulating the value of the buried treasure I'd just discovered. "We could use one of those to help us identify a relative."

"Yeah," I said, somewhat distractedly. I was doing my own thinking, traveling back to Greenville and Poppa Joe's house. *Why hadn't I though of this before?* Poppa Joe had an attic full of old boxes, several of which I had rummaged through when I first went to live there with him. That first month I must have explored every inch of the place, searching for a private nook to burn off the ache for my departed mother. The attic had been the best I could find until Poppa Joe discovered me one day and put a lock on the door. He claimed the room had nothing but old business records. "Nothing of interest to a young man such as yourself, Daniel," he'd said. Before he'd banished me, I'd unearthed a few photos of him and my mother. *Could there be more hidden in those old boxes? A deeper trail to my mother's past?* Whoever had handled Poppa Joe's estate would likely still have them, *or*, perhaps those boxes were still in the attic of his old house. It was possible no one knew they were up there, not even the new owners. Either way, it gave me a hope with a far better probability than Roger at the Rhode Island DMV. Regardless of what Sunny believed, I knew he just wanted to get into her pants.

"I might be able to dig up something at one of my old foster homes," Felix said. "It's been a long time, but I remember a few of the towns at least. It's a start."

It was. It felt like a good start, briefly pushing aside my worry about Sunny and the gig she'd run off to with Thumper and her brother. A second, much larger headline brought it all back, smothering my thoughts like a murderous pillow.

"Does that name sound familiar to you?" I said, pushing the front page in front of Felix. Covering the top half was a full color photo of a barely clothed young woman, bloodied and beaten to within an inch of her life. In bold, red letters the headline read, "Help Me!"

Without emotion, Felix glanced at the picture, reading the caption silently as he wiped his mouth with a napkin. Then, thoughtfully, he said, "Elizabeth Hart...Elizabeth Hart. You know, that name does ring a bell." He pointed at her picture, the recognition spreading over his face. "An acquisitions analyst and a real looker," he said. "Started a few months before I was let go."

"It's the same woman all right," I said. "My boss pointed her out to me every time he saw her in the employee lunch room. He had a thing for her, along with every other guy in the place. My guess is Vinson put her there."

"You think Vinson is behind this?" Felix asked.

"He tried to do a similar thing to Sunny," I said. "Hired a guy to rape and strangle her while he watched and video taped the whole thing. She was lucky to escape alive."

Felix began to nod in agreement. Staring at the picture, he said, "You know, this is right in line with that nasty shit I saw stored on a remote computer connected to the Earth Nexus network—gang rapes, guys choking girls during sex. Somebody at Earth Nexus videotaped some really fucked up stuff, Daniel."

"Vinson," I said, convinced it was undeniably him. "Where was that computer located? Did you try to track it down after you saw the video clips stored on it?"

"Yeah, but I only got as far as Brooklyn. Do you know how many people live in Brooklyn?"

I couldn't help but smile. I thought of something Felix hadn't—a way to narrow down the search for the suspect computer. Pulling Vinson's BlackBerry from my pocket, I turned it on and went straight to his contacts list, sorting it by city. Low and behold, there was one, and only one, Brooklyn address. I showed the glowing screen to Felix, who smiled, knowingly, in return.

"What now?" he asked.

"We go rescue a damsel in distress," I said.

"What about Vinson?"

"Et tu Brute?" was all I said.

46

Rosa Parks

The little house appeared quiet and dark as Vinson pulled up into the short driveway. In fact, the whole neighborhood was asleep; the endless row of ranches built during the baby boom of the 1950s lost in dreamland, serenely oblivious to the piercing headlights of the black sedan cutting through the calm. Vinson didn't know any of the people who lived along the street, nor they him. He paid one of his employees to maintain the yard and another very discreet Earth Nexus lifer to clean the inside—above ground floor only. He made sure the taxes were paid on time, the holiday lights always in season and the security cameras well hidden. On Halloween, there was even a grandmotherly-looking woman at the door to hand out candy to the trick-or-treaters. To the casual observer walking his dog down the sidewalk, this was a middle-class home to a middle-class family, albeit a nearly invisible, private one.

After punching in his security code, Vinson entered the house and headed straight toward the kitchen, switching on lights as he went. For the nosy insomniac peering out from behind her shaded window, he was the dedicated husband coming home late from work, hungry for a snack before bed. Ever since he was a small boy, Vinson had been obsessed with the fine details of his every move. Everything had to be carefully planned, perfectly executed.

In Vinson's world, there was no room for error, and like his namesake, Caesar, no tolerance for failure.

After taking a bottle of champagne from the refrigerator, he pulled two long stemmed glasses from the cupboard and walked deliberately to the back of the structure, aiming for the door to the basement. With the bottle and the glasses dangling from one hand, he entered the security code into the keypad with the other, opened the door and headed down the stairs. This was where Vinson kept his valuables; this was also where he kept his unwilling, but reconsidering, former employee. Flipping on the lights as he stepped into the room he referred to as "The Stage," Vinson was not happy with what he found.

Still handcuffed to the chair she'd been placed in many painful hours ago, Elizabeth Hart sat lifeless like a child's rag doll. Her face was a mask of dried sweat and blood, her lips cracked and purple. Vinson was certain she was dead and that was not his plan, not yet anyway. Sammy was supposed to have attended to her, keep her in shape for the second act, the purpose of Vinson's visit tonight. Obviously, he'd failed. As Vinson resolved to sever ties with Mr. Sammy Johnson, he noticed Elizabeth flinch, suddenly. Apparently, she wasn't dead after all, the sudden brightness of the fluorescent lighting tripping her back to consciousness. Vinson smiled, opened the champagne and poured two glasses.

"I'm glad to see you're still with us, my dear," Vinson said. "I do so hate drinking alone."

Elizabeth was glaring at him now, struggling to focus the bloodshot eyes that hadn't seen restful sleep in over thirty hours. "Why?" she managed to whisper.

"Because I like to," Vinson said. He then placed a full glass of champagne on the floor at her feet before taking a long pull from the second glass. He swallowed, exhaling a throaty moan of pleasure.

"Actually, Elizabeth, I won't lie to you, it's more than that.

This little three act play—of which you are the star—is teaching America and the world a very important lesson about freedom; that without rules, freedom is just a nicer word for anarchy. And we can't have anarchy in our streets, can we Elizabeth? Everyone running around doing whatever they please to whomever they please; gangs of young men raping young women and leaving them to die in a basement just like this? If you could, you would do something about that, wouldn't you Elizabeth?"

Elizabeth didn't answer. She was staring at the glass of champagne, her mind dizzy with the need for something to drink. She knew Vinson was watching her, relishing her suffering, but she couldn't help herself. She was dying and no one knew that better than the most downloaded woman in America, Elizabeth Hart.

"Well," Vinson continued. "You should be proud of yourself, Elizabeth, because you *are* doing something about it. Right now, you're the poster child for internet censorship. All across the country, mom and dad are unplugging junior's computer, promising to return it as soon as the White House puts a leash on the Web. And the President will do it too, thanks to you, Elizabeth. This is a great moment in history, do you realize that? A turning point in the evolution of our society. You're another Rosa Parks, Elizabeth." He raised his glass, offering a toast to his captive. "Here's to you, Elizabeth. A pioneer, whose name will one day be synonymous with the taming of the World Wide Web." Vinson then emptied his glass and added, "One small step for civilization, one giant leap for Earth Nexus."

For a long moment, Vinson stood there, admiring his accomplishment. His dream of controlling the internet was becoming a reality. All he needed to do now was to keep applying the pressure.

Setting his glass aside, Vinson said, "Enough celebrating. We need to get you ready for the second act."

He left the room for a moment, before returning with a clean, white t-shirt draped over his shoulder and a menacing box cutter in his hand. The honed steel twinkled under the lights, matching the look in Vinson's eyes as he approached the terrified woman. Without hesitating, he sliced her cheek open, the sharp blade seemingly drawing a red line as it slide across her face. This first cut was meant only for effect, the subsequent gash he carved into the tip of her index finger then used to write on the crisp, white t-shirt.

"We'll need to take these off for a minute," Vinson said as he removed the handcuffs. From her broken body, he then pulled off the stained and blood soaked shirt she'd been seen in around the world, replacing it with the new one. After replacing the handcuffs, he stood back and read the new message aloud.

"*I'M DYING*," he said with a satisfying grin. It was short and sweet, written by Elizabeth herself, in her own blood. "That ought to send a few shivers up America's spine."

Vinson then videotaped his prisoner, just as he had before, in living and soon-to-be-dying color. Minutes later, he was logged on to the computer he kept in another room in the basement, attaching the video file to the email he would send to the computer hacker he'd rescued from a long stint in prison. How the man got the clip on to YouTube, Vinson didn't know. And frankly, he didn't care, as long as the well-compensated man got the job done. If all went smoothly, by the time the East Coast was sipping their morning coffee, Elizabeth Hart would be extending her fifteen minutes of fame.

No sooner had he clicked the send button, than Vinson noticed movement on one of the security monitors mounted on the wall. There was a man approaching the front door, his murky image illuminated only by amber-colored, automobile fog lights. Unable to distinguish the visitor, Vinson logged off the computer, opened a side drawer to the desk he was sitting at and extracted a Walther PPK revolver. He pressed the magazine release, dropping the rectangular sleeve of bullets into his other hand. Confirming it was full, he popped it back in and loaded the first shell into the firing chamber. It had been a spontaneous, just-because-I-love-you present from his wife, Claire, one of the few gifts he ever kept. They had only been married a short time and were living in a crime-riddled section of New York City that his wife feared might one day catch her alone. He called her a frightened little mouse. She responded by buying his and hers revolvers and taking shooting lessons, gifting one of the twins to her husband to soften his reaction to the purchase. It was a nice gun, fitting into his hand perfectly, and as he headed to the stairs he knew that one day he would have to show his wife first hand just how much he enjoyed firing it.

47

Improvisation

From a darkened window, Vinson observed two men. One was at the front door, attempting to decipher the keypad entry code, clearly agitated by repeated rejections. The other was still in the car with his blank face pressed against the glass, seemingly asleep. Vinson didn't recognize either man, and with little light to see in, he remained hidden, motionless, waiting to see if the visitor might somehow crack his code. After several more failed tries, the man's agitation was quickly turning to anger. He pounded his fist against the solid-metal box in frustration, cursing wildly as if his obscenities might magically lure the door open. To Vinson's amusement, the fool even offered the phrase "open sesame" to gain entrance. Not surprisingly, it didn't work. Finally recognizing the figure, Vinson decided to have a little fun, reaching into his pocket and pulling out a wireless remote. Then, after waiting for just the right moment—when the man began pleading to be let in—he de-activated the lock, springing the front door open. By the time the two men stood face-to-face, Vinson's jovial mood had already evaporated.

"You Neanderthal fuck!" Vinson growled. "You were supposed to be here this afternoon to walk and water that dog downstairs. Now we'll be lucky if she lasts the night. Where the hell have you been?"

Instinctively, Sammy Johnson's fingers curled into a tight fist. He had just driven over two hundred and fifty miles, dodging caffeine-juiced truckers and slipping radar traps all the way from Boston. What he needed now was a good stiff drink, not his fucknut boss ripping him a new hole. *Maybe it's time the two of us shared a dance*, Sammy thought, his taut muscles coiling like a cornered rattlesnake.

"I'd think twice about that, Sammy," Vinson said, easing the revolver forward into clear view. He had noticed the purposeful look on the man's face, perhaps even before Sammy had felt it. "Now, explain to me what you're doing here."

Yielding reluctantly, Sammy proceeded to provide his boss with the down-and-dirty version of his impromptu road trip. He explained how he'd been stalking Rayne; how Ostrander had showed up unexpectedly and created a two-on-one mismatched he wasn't prepared for. "I know where those two jokers are hiding now, Mr. Vinson," Sammy said. "It'll all be cleaned up tomorrow."

The second part of his story was a little more ticklish, at least for Sammy. Except for Elizabeth, he had hoped to find the house empty; counting on an old password Vinson had given him months ago to gain access. He had his own ideas for a Manhattan Uncut premiere video, and after seeing Sunny and Thumper, he knew he had finally found his leading ladies. His plan was to keep the whole thing a secret; make his movie and then roll the three-passengers-full BMW into the Hudson River as the closing credits rolled across the screen. It seemed like a good idea at the time, at least before Vinson showed up with a Walther in his hand. Sammy now figured his plan was toast, except maybe the river part.

Anticipating that his boss might erupt into a rage at any moment, Sammy described running into a friend from the gym and the events that followed. He made a quick pit stop, he explained, insisting on running into the mini-mart himself. Then, before returning to the car, he placed a few drops of Chloral Hydrate into each soda bottle—enough, he claimed, to keep the two women out another hour and their bodyguard a few more than that. He concluded by reassuring Vinson that the two women lying in the back seat of his car were absolute knockouts. "If you'll pardon the pun, boss," he said, cracking an uneasy grin.

Much to Sammy's surprise, Vinson was actually smiling.

"You just saved your own ass, Sammy," Vinson said. "There's no way that worthless bitch in the basement is going to make it to act three, so we'll have to use an understudy, which you have so opportunistically provided. Improvisation, Sammy, is the key to a man's success." Vinson then stuffed the gun into his belt and told Sammy to go downstairs and put Elizabeth into the storage closet. "And then get the equipment ready," he said. "We've got a show to do."

48

Don't Haves

"How much farther do you think it is?" Felix asked. During the whole trip he'd been acting like a bored child, inquiring about our arrival status every ten minutes. *Are we there yet?*

"Maybe another hour, hour and a half, provided we don't hit any traffic or road construction." I replied. Speeding down the interstate, we'd already driven through Rhode Island and were now deep into Connecticut, just over halfway to New York.

"At this time of night?" Felix snorted.

"We're going to New York," I reminded him. "The city that never sleeps."

Felix said, "Speaking of which, why aren't we doing this rescue thing in the morning, after we've had a chance to get some shuteye."

"That girl could be dead by morning," I said. I knew there was a good chance she was already dead, but didn't want to openly acknowledge it. Weaving through the slower traffic, I needed to believe she was still alive, clinging to the hope that someone like us would pull her from her prison. Time was on Vinson's side, I'd learned that well enough after he had erased me, waiting far too long to consider returning to my apartment in search of my belongings, the priceless lifeline I would never recover. Sleep or no sleep, I wasn't waiting any longer then I had to this time.

"We don't even know if she's at this address," Felix said. He had held the BlackBerry in his hand ever since we'd left Boston, suggesting that we first visit a few of the closer addresses in Vinson's listings.

"Brooklyn is the one," I said. "It only makes sense that he'd store the video files on a computer located where he did his filming."

"I suppose."

"I suppose nothing! That bastard wiped out our lives and now we've got a chance to fight back. If we find that woman there—hopefully alive—along with videos of all the others Vinson had raped and murdered, we can nail him and get our own lives back in the process. A three to four hour drive in the middle of the night is a small price to pay for that."

"I suppose," Felix repeated.

It was becoming very obvious why the man sitting in the passenger seat of my Camaro was nearly destined to live the rest of his life in a homeless shelter. Other than an occasional moment of inspired motivation, this seemingly capable being was what my mother often called some of her lackluster dates. Felix Ostrander was "milk toast"—crisp and firm in the beginning, soggy as slush minutes later. My mother couldn't stand a man with a rubbery backbone and as we passed a sign informing us that New York City was eighty miles away, I realized that I didn't have much use for one either.

"Maybe you should have brought your laptop with you," I said, remembering him explaining how he'd brandished it that night in the shelter office, and saved my skin. *Could I count on him again for another flash of courage if I needed one?* My best hope was that I wouldn't need one.

Felix held up the BlackBerry. "Don't worry, I'm armed," he said.

I chuckled. "Yeah, that might split somebody's lip if you

threw it hard enough."

"That'd be enough to send me packing," *So much for that flash of courage*, I thought.

"Speaking of fat lips, don't you think you should slow down?" Felix asked. "I have no desire to become intimate with the windshield."

"Relax, this is just a stroll compared to what this baby can do."

"Well, if you get pulled over and the cop gives you a ticket, don't blame me."

"What's the worst he can do? Take away my license? I don't have a license. Put points on my record? I don't have a record. Schedule me for a court appearance under threat of arrest if I don't show? Good luck, Officer Friendly, you'll need a truck full if you expect to find me. I don't exist!" I was laughing now, scarily so, while a perplexed Felix measured me for a straight jacket.

"I'm glad you think this is funny," he said sarcastically.

"Quite honestly, Felix, I think it's the only way I've been able to stop myself from going mad."

He turned to gaze out the window, scratching his scraggly beard thoughtfully. "I suppose," he muttered.

I noticed that the traffic was beginning to thicken, a sure sign that we were getting ever closer to our destination—New York City. I turned my attention to the road. Even in the wee hours of the morning, the sunrise only a few hundred miles out over the Atlantic Ocean, the landscape was alive with activity. I had been to New York City before, but yet each time I came back, I was still amazed at the overwhelming mass of people. *This is the perfect place for Vinson to conduct his dirty business*, I thought, *lost in an endless sea of faces, an abyss of anonymous desires.*

Passing a sign for Manhattan, I remembered Sunny and just that quickly the knot in my stomach returned. God, how I wished she hadn't gone off with Thumper to that bachelor party. Who knows what they might encounter in this crazy place? She was only twenty years old—much too young to dancing half naked in front of men twice her age. Sunny needed to find a new line of work.

"So, what's our plan, anyway?" Felix asked. "This address could be a fortified castle for all we know, with a twenty foot moat circling the place. And armed guards? What are we going to do if the place is surrounded by armed guards?"

I didn't respond. I didn't have an answer to his questions.

"We do have a plan, don't we Daniel?"

"No, I don't actually have a plan."

"We don't have a plan."

"That's what I said."

"No plan."

"No plan," I replied. Then, taking my eyes off the road, I turned to Felix and explained, without another word, how serious the situation was. The look he returned told me he was beginning to see it my way.

"All right," he said. "But if we come up empty tonight, we focus our efforts on contacting that guy John Oliver. No more heroics; just good, logical information sharing. We tell Oliver everything we know and hope that he has the guts to put the noose around Vinson's neck. The police will believe him. They wouldn't believe us, but they'll believe him."

By the way Felix was presenting his case, it was clear he was struggling to convince himself as much as he was trying to convince me. Originally, it had been my idea to pursue Oliver, but the more I worked it in my mind, the more it crumpled in my hand. Every sign that pointed at Oliver advertised him as Vinson's right hand man. The two had started Earth Nexus; gotten rich together. They were probably drinking buddies, sharing secrets and providing alibis to the other's wife after nights of indiscretion. Christ, they might even be swapping their wives, for all we knew. Maybe that's why I was never able to find much on the internet regarding Claire Vinson. Louis kept her under close wraps. Now, because two homeless men claim your partner is a twisted murderer, you're going to go straight to the police and insist an arrest be made? *Not likely.*

The truth of the situation was we didn't have many other options, none in fact. Reluctantly, I promised Felix to adopt contacting John Oliver as Plan B. "We just better hope he's a reasonable and honest man," I said. "Willing to hear us out. Because once we put our cards on the table in front of him, there's no turning back."

"I suppose," was all Felix could muster in response.

49

Hide and Seek

Slowly, the mechanical door creaked open, revealing only blackness within the small garage. A car pulled forward, the red spark of a taillight winking as the driver braked to a stop. The engine cut. A man exited the vehicle, a large man illuminated briefly by the interior cabin light. He closed the door—the light vanishing—and moved to the one behind it, a dark form working in the shadows. The garage door began to close, metal on metal echoing across the street to where Claire Vinson knelt behind a short arborvitae hedge. It was then that she saw Louis, his unmistakable frame a silhouette in a glowing doorway at the back of the garage, swallowed seconds later as the lowering door fell silent.

Shaking in her hand, Claire held her cell phone. She had punched in 911 already but had stopped short of completing the call. *Make it*, she had been telling herself for the past ten minutes, crouching in the bushes as she had a hundred times during childhood games of hide and seek. As a preteen, she was the indisputable champion of the neighborhood, always finding the best places to hide; always knowing when to make her move to make it safely "home." The world was simple then, decisions easily made. Feeling the weight of the Walther PPK revolver sagging in her windbreaker pocket, the nearly forty year-old wife of the man she was convinced had murdered her lover had no idea what move to make now.

Looking back at the invisible trail she had taken through the backyards, she considered returning to her car, parked on the next block over. *I can still leave*, she thought. *Go back to my house in Oyster Bay; back to my life as it was before John.* Her eyes swelled with tears. John was dead. It didn't seem real to her, a nightmare that now saw her huddled in a stranger's garden, contemplating using the bullets she was too terrified to load into the weapon she had brought with her nonetheless.

You can't go back to that! Her mind screamed. *You can't leave Daniel to die as John had. You can't turn your back on it any longer.*

Rising to her feet, her thoughts suddenly clear, Claire Vinson left her hiding place, determined to do what she knew she had to do. Never in her life had a decision been so clear. Until this moment, she'd only been half living, which is the same as half dying, isn't it?

On a warm, star-filled night, reminiscent of the ones she treasured as a child, Clair Vinson decided it was time to complete the other half.

50

Old Acquaintances

Sunny awoke to a gnawing pain in her wrists. Her mind was groggy and her eyes, blurred. She summoned her hands to her face to wipe the fog away, but they didn't respond. They were frozen, it seemed, behind her back. *No, not frozen*, she quickly surmised, *handcuffed*. With a sudden grunt, she tugged at the bindings with all her strength, but they didn't yield an inch. Instead, a shooting pain rang through her arms and into her shoulders. *Let's not try that again*, she told herself. *And let's not panic, not yet anyway.* She blinked her eyes several times, ironically feeling a sense of relief that the chair she was sitting in was comfortable. *I might be here a while.*

With her vision clearing, she scanned around the room, the video cameras and extensive electronic equipment telling her she was in some sort of television or movie studio. There was a chill in the air, and she began to shiver. Looking down, she saw that her feet were bare. *What happened to my shoes?* As the nerve endings blanketing her entire body began to protest, she realized her shoes were the least of her worries. The skirt and blouse she left her apartment in were gone. All she wore now was a pair of black panties and a white t-shirt—a blood stained t-shirt she would come to understand later.

Just as Sunny was recalling the plush leather interior of the luxurious BMW and the stop it had made at a Mini-mart just outside of Boston, the sibling banter between Thumper and Axel as they argued over who should sit in the front seat, the driver of said car suddenly appeared before her.

Sammy Johnson didn't say a word to his captive. He wasn't interested in a conversation, only a physical exchange in which he chose the subject matter. Tonight, the topic was sex—hard and brutal—followed by a simulated strangulation. Elizabeth Hart was to have been his co-star, but because of her decaying condition, a change in casting was ordered. Sammy had a new leading lady, and after placing a blonde wig onto Sunny's head, he stepped back, peering at her salaciously as he compared her likeness to that of the woman now lying in her own blood in the storage closet.

"I don't think anyone will know the difference, boss," Sammy said. "With the wig, she's a dead ringer." He then laughed, finding humor in his callous pun.

Vinson's voice erupted through a hidden speaker. "Move so I can see her!"

Realizing he was blocking the main camera, Sammy apologized and took a step to one side. "A perfect match, don't you think?" There was no reply. "Boss?"

Before Sammy could finish scratching his head, Louis Vinson was standing next to him, gazing intently at the former, shorthaired brunette now donning the imitation blonde mane.

"We know each other, don't we," Vinson said. "Old acquaintances." The pleasure on his face was unmistakable. He could now kill two birds with one stone.

Sunny glared back at him, her eyes steeled, but acknowledging. *Yes, I know who you are,* she was saying. *And what you are.*

"Do you know who this is, Sammy?" Vinson asked. He didn't wait for an answer. "This is the bitch responsible for your buddy Rico's death. I'd set up a voyeur shoot for him at a hotel in

Manhattan. Blondie here was supposed to spread her legs like a good little girl, but instead, she blew a three-inch hole into his forehead. I saw the whole thing." Vinson then brushed a lock of hair from Sunny's face, stroking her cheek and chin as he pulled his hand away. "A real doll, this one, as long as you don't put a gun in her hand."

"He was trying to kill me," Sunny said. She knew her explanation would mean nothing to Sammy, who was now fuming with anger, but she needed to say it anyway. She knew that she was going to die, but she wasn't about to cower under Vinson's lies. Locking onto Sammy's furious eyes, she then said, "I didn't pull the trigger, Caesar did."

Vinson just laughed. He knew what the little whore meant—that his unquenchable thirst for power had indirectly killed Rico—but to think that Sammy could comprehend it was hilarious. The Neanderthal only knew about two things: stabbing a man with a six-inch steal blade, and stabbing a woman with his cock. Sammy didn't know—couldn't know—that he was just an expendable soldier in Rome's army. And he never would, if Vinson had anything to say about it.

His laughter subsiding, Vinson instructed Sammy to go and get ready. "We've got the final act of this play to film," he said. Then, just as Sammy was disappearing out the door, Vinson stopped him, offering his leading man the added role of director. Looking at Sunny, he said, "Since you were the one to find her, I'll leave it up to you as to how we dispose of her. I'm talking improvisation, Sammy. I think our faithful viewers are ready to step beyond mere simulation, don't you."

Sammy nodded as he grinned knowingly.

"With that being said, I'll leave tonight's script up to you."

51

An Even Buck

All the way from Boston, I kept hoping that the Brooklyn address was a simple, unguarded house in a quiet neighborhood—a place where Felix and I could slip in and out easily and discretely, before transporting Vinson's latest victim, alive and well, to the nearest police station. It was a best case scenario and way more than I should have been counting on, I realized, when we found the address with a million lights on inside. The letdown I felt was immeasurable.

"Fuck!" I cried. I'd driven past the house and parked along the curb at the end of the block, switching the headlights off in frustration, but leaving the engine running. "Why did someone have to be there?"

"Maybe no one is home," Felix said. He was leaning over the front seat, gazing back at the only house in the neighborhood showing any sign of life within. "It could be timers to keep burglars away."

"There's a car in the driveway," I pointed out. "I doubt Elizabeth Hart drove it there."

"If she's even in there," Felix countered.

"The fact that the lights are on only makes me believe all the more that she's in there. No one else is awake for miles around."

"Except us," Felix said. He yawned as if to remind me that he would much prefer to be sleeping. "And that woman standing on the front porch."

"What woman?" I'd been staring at the dashboard, trying to imagine our next move, attentively checking the fuel and oil gauges. (My vintage Camaro looked like a dream rolling down the road, but like any aging idol, it could be a nightmare if it wasn't kept well lubricated.) Turning around, I easily spotted the visitor standing beneath the porch light, who was—and this was my first thought—beating us to the punch. My second—and more logical—conclusion was that this early morning caller was there to attend to the assumed property's occupant, Elizabeth Hart.

"Who do you think she is?" Felix asked. "The cleaning lady?"

"Come to clean the toilets at this hour? I don't think so." I searched the street. "How did she get here? We haven't seen another car since we left the main road."

"Maybe she walked. Maybe she lives around here?"

"I don't know, kind of late for a woman to be out walking alone in the dark, don't you think."

"I suppose," Felix replied.

"She's playing with something near the doorknob," I said. "Vinson probably put in an entry system."

"One of those keypad things?"

"That would be my guess." I watched intently as the woman then entered the house, closing the door behind her. "And it looks like she knows the code."

"Which brings up another interesting question. How were we planning on getting inside?"

"The same way she did," I answered. "Using the password."

I went on to describe to Felix how I had gotten into the BlackBerry; how Vinson had protected his "hit list" file using a Caesar cipher, which, to my surprise, I only had to explain to Felix once; and how we were going to use the same coded word to rescue Elizabeth Hart.

"Do you really think he would use the same password twice?"

Felix asked. "I've been working in the computer field for a long time and the rule is to use different passwords for different things and, more importantly, a combination of letters and numbers that have no correlation to your life. That way, the likelihood of someone guessing correctly is extremely remote. Then, when you factor in how careful this guy is, well, I think your setting yourself up for a disappointment, Daniel."

Felix's logic made sense for the average man, but I was certain that Vinson's gigantic ego wouldn't allow him to use a nondescript password for something as important as this house. "I'll bet you ten bucks that the code for that door is the same as the one I used on Vinson's BlackBerry."

"You don't have ten bucks, Daniel. I had to give you money for gas, remember?"

I reached into my pocket and pulled out the last dollar I had. "Ok, make it an even buck."

Felix snorted, "I suppose."

Walking along the blackened street, Felix asked me what I was planning to do once we got inside. "If we get inside," he quickly added.

"I don't know," I said. "But I'm counting on one of us thinking of something."

52

Pick a Hand

Inside, the house was quiet. The entrance hall was illuminated, as was the kitchen, a trail of lights that led Claire to her first stop. Cautiously, she entered, scanning the countertops, searching for any small clue that might provide some semblance of a reason for her husband's inconspicuous presence. She saw nothing irregular. A dirty glass, several stacked dishes, an errant towel. It looked like any kitchen would at three in the morning. *What is Louis doing here?* She'd been trying to reason it out ever since she'd opened John's note. This house involved something serious, something to do with the poor woman plastered all over the front page of the diner newspaper. John wouldn't have given her the address on his death bed if it were merely Louis's discreet hideaway, the place he brought his bed partners. There had to more to it than that.

She stood motionless for what felt like hours, listening carefully to the tiny creaks of shifting wood, the faint drip of the leaky kitchen faucet. *This is where he's keeping her,* she reasoned. Then, the muffled hum of voices began leaching up from under her feet. Cautiously, Claire went looking for the basement door.

Sometimes it seems to take forever to get somewhere, especially when you don't know how to get there. Like a trip to a new vacation spot or tiptoeing through a dark house when you're not sure you'll like what you find around the next corner. Claire eased her way through the dining room, past a half bath, and was moving gingerly down a dim, slender hallway when she noticed a glow upon her feet. Squinting to funnel what little light there was she made out the outline of a door just ahead, the rays beaming out from the gap just above the floor. *That's the one*, she thought. *Am I really going down there?* Frozen with uncertainty, she confirmed the cell phone resting in her jacket pocket, wrapping her shaking fingers around it like a life preserver. Then, with her other hand, she checked the other pocket. The revolver was still there, right where she put it upon leaving her house, offering her a different option. *Enough already, pick a hand,* she chided herself. Still unloaded, she abruptly pulled her hand away from the gun, sensing which script she could ultimately live with. She took out the cell phone, hesitated for a half second and then, as if thrown by a mirror image of herself, her free hand flew up to cover her suddenly shrieking mouth, choking out the sound she had promised herself only minutes ago she wouldn't make. A door was opening, but not the one in front of her startled eyes. Someone was coming in through the front.

Is that Louis? She thought, a wild panic surging through her veins. *Was he outside all this time and not in the basement?* Her mind was scrabbling for an answer, her eyes darting for a place to hide. She put the phone back into her pocket and scurried along the hallway as quietly as she could, slipping into the first opening she could find. It was the half bath she had passed coming in, a sink and a toilet that offered little in the form of concealment. It was dark, though, and with no other option, she shimmied her way between the toilet and the wall, praying that whoever was now heading down the hallway didn't have to use the john.

This was a very bad idea, Clair told herself. Her legs were already beginning to cramp, her shoulders crying out in pain by the time she realized the person she heard coming into the house was not her husband. *A man for certain, but definitely not Louis's voice.* There was a second unfamiliar male voice as well, whispering in the darkness just beyond her sight. *God, please don't let them come in here.*

Whoever it was, they didn't appear to be in any hurry, huddled together, Claire imagined, somewhere along the hallway. *Go into the basement, please!* Unable to endure her discomfort any longer, she ever so carefully twisted herself into a more comfortable pretzel, somehow finding relief but dropping her cell phone with a dull thud onto the linoleum floor in the process.

"Did you hear that?" Claire heard one of the men whisper. Then, she listen anxiously as the other man replied, "It came from the basement. I'll bet that's where the woman went."

What woman? Claire thought. She had seen Louis and another man but no one else. *Had there been a woman in the car that I watched pull into the garage?*

The two new arrivals were moving away now, toward the basement door, Claire concluded. Their whispers were fading, and with it, her concern over getting caught. When she heard the telltale sounds of descending footsteps, she extracted herself from her crypt and started digging around in the darkness for her cell phone. *Where are you, you little…*

Sounding like a hundred swarming honeybees, the fluorescent fixture above the sink suddenly buzzed on, blinding Claire just as her fingers were inching their way around her cell phone. Startled, she dropped it before bumping her head against the toilet tank.

"Misplace your wedding ring, dear?" Louis Vinson said.

53

One Man's Folly

I won my bet with Felix, opening the front door to the mystery house on my first try. As I expected, Vinson was using his ciphered nickname, Caesar, just as he had for the BlackBerry file. To me, it was a sure thing and one I felt guilty about as Felix handed me a waded single. God knows how badly I needed the dollar, but sitting now in the basement of said house, the barrel of a gun staring me in the face, I was angry that I'd been right about Vinson; wishing that I'd lost the bet.

"Isn't this a pleasant surprise," Louis Vinson said. He was standing before me with a modest black revolver cradled in his hand. He appeared very pleased with himself. "All my favorite people all gathered together. So very convenient, I must say."

To my left sat Felix, fidgeting nervously in a plain wooden chair unlike my own. To my right, a woman I'd never seen before. None of us were bound in anyway, unless, of course, you count Vinson's gun and the much larger pistol brandished by the very large man who had greeted Felix and me at the bottom of the basement steps. This second man was dressed in a black leather outfit, some sort of perverse riding getup. Under different circumstances, I might have laughed upon seeing him, but the stoic look on his face, coupled with the way his finger twitched against the trigger, quickly silenced my funny bone.

Amused by our confusion, Vinson offered up introductions.

"I am Louis Vinson," he said. "But then, I think every one here knows that already. Am I right? I think so." He nodded, agreeing with himself. He then moved toward the woman, placing his free hand onto her cheek, caressing it softly as he said, "This lovely lady here is my wife, Claire; Aunt Claire to you, Mr. Daniel Rayne."

He looked at me as the words spilt from his mouth, words that seemed to jumble as they entered my unbelieving ears. *My Aunt? That would make her...my...mother's sister?* As the disturbing comprehension appeared in my eyes, Vinson was quick to tighten the knot.

"That's right, Daniel," he said. "You're mother, Katherine, was Claire's older sister. She didn't think I knew about her, or you, for that matter. But I've always known." He was looking at his wife again, relishing the small, but no less enjoyable act of deception he'd been conducting for years. "Poor little Katherine, banished from the family at sixteen when she got pregnant with you, Daniel, and rightfully so. She was a tramp, a slut, spreading her legs for every man who smiled at her; a humiliation to her parents, a disgrace to the whole family."

"She was no such thing!" Claire cried out. "Don't believe a word of it, Daniel. Katherine was warm and caring, a wonderful sister and a devoted mother." She was pleading with me to believe her, her eyes swelling with tears. "You know it in your heart. Don't let the words of a murderer take that away from you."

Vinson was chuckling now, strangely entertained by his wife's impassioned outburst. "You never fail to amaze me, Claire, defending that pitiful whore to the last. Now you call me a murderer? What is this sad-looking man supposed to think of his uncle if you insist on slandering me so viciously?"

"I don't need her to tell me what you are," I said. "I already know all about how you erased me and how you plan to bury me. How you've erased and killed dozens of people." My mind was racing, attempting to sort through a hundred different scenarios of what to say next. How far could I push the man standing before me with a loaded gun in his hand? When was it time to bluff; when would it be time to fold? Before I could utter another word, Felix placed an ill-advised bet for me.

"We found everything we needed to know in your BlackBerry," Felix said. He was evidently experiencing one of his sudden bursts of courage, ready to wrestle a lion or maybe a guy in a black leather suit. "Every name of every person you ever erased and killed. And dates too."

With growing fear, I watched Vinson's jovial expression change to concern. He knew what he had stored on his state-of-the-art cell phone and the consequences of it falling into the wrong hands. His empire would crumble; his own life, cut short. He motioned to the big man standing behind us to search our pockets.

"You don't think we would be stupid enough to bring it with us, do you?" I asked rhetorically. Fortunately, we hadn't been, leaving it under the driver's seat of my Camaro. Hearing that, the big man stopped and looked at Vinson for direction.

Before Vinson could speak, Felix said something that I have no doubt seriously altered the events that might have otherwise unfolded

"We gave it to your boy, Oliver, just before coming over here," Felix blurted out. "He's showing it to the police as we speak."

Vinson erupted into laughter.

Right at that moment, as Vinson's baritone echoed off the walls, I realized that John Oliver had never truly been a viable option. His assistance had just been a product of wishful thinking by two desperate men, grabbing at any straw they thought might help them regain their lost lives. Was Vinson laughing so hard now because Oliver was in on everything with him? Or tickled by the notion of his partner ever lifting a finger against him? It didn't matter, the opportunity was clearly gone.

"I don't think John is much of a threat, do you Claire?" Vinson said. "Not anymore."

Claire didn't say a word, but I sensed by the hatred shooting from her eyes, that Vinson was saying more than I knew.

"Now, what's say Sammy here was to go out and check inside that nice hot rod of yours?" Vinson asked. "Do you think he might have better luck than searching your pockets?"

My dejected look provided him the answer. The BlackBerry could have been an ace up our sleeve—our trump card—but no more. I wasn't angry with Felix, only frustrated that his bold bluff hadn't worked. Before the sunrise, Vinson would have it back and along with it, any hope I had of taking him down.

"You want me to go out there now, boss?" Sammy asked.

"No, the car's not going anywhere," Vinson replied. "We've got more immediate business to attend to."

Vinson went to a desk in the corner that I hadn't even noticed until now. He set his revolver down and then flipped a few switches on a series of electronic components. Above him, a wall of television monitors flick on, the first screen to catch my eye displaying a panoramic view of the front entryway. Another showed a wide-angle view of the street, including a shadowy shape that I knew was my car parked down the block. *He knew we were here the whole time, watched us walk right into his lap. How stupid could we be not to imagine he had cameras everywhere?* There must have been a dozen or more on the wall, monitoring every part of the house, inside and out. The last screen, a bit bigger than the rest, showed what people around the world had been buzzing about for days. The last monitor to draw my eye framed a slumping Elizabeth Hart.

"Wakie, wakie," Vinson said into a microphone.

Slowly, Elizabeth responded, tilting her head up until her sad eyes were staring directly into the camera.

My jaw dropped, the knot in my head squeezing the very life out of me. The bloodied woman I saw on the screen wasn't Elizabeth Hart at all. It was Sunny. I started to stand up, but the thug behind me quickly pushed me back down into my chair.

"Look familiar, Daniel?" Vinson said.

"How…" was all I could get out of my mouth?

"You can thank Sammy for bringing your girlfriend to the party," Vinson said. "As far as her taking Elizabeth's place, well, that was a last minute thing. Unfortunately for Ms. Hart, she couldn't stay alive long enough to finish the third act. But you know what they say; one man's folly is another man's fortune, or in this case, a woman's."

I was dumbstruck. *How had she gotten here? She was with Thumper and her brother when she left the apartment. Where were those two?*

"Where's the other girl?" Felix asked. His brain was obviously functioning better than mine, asking the question stuck on the tip of my tongue.

"I believe they're still waiting in the car in the garage, aren't they Sammy," Vinson said with a grin.

"They are, boss," Sammy replied. "And you know what? I just remembered that I left the engine running."

"Oops," Vinson chuckled.

"My God, Louis," Claire said. "What have you become?" She was shaking her head in disbelief, sickened by his indifference.

Vinson smiled, knowingly. "Let's just say we've grown apart and leave it at that," he said. Then, looking past us toward Sammy, he quickly changed the subject, saying, "The cameras are rolling and the audience is in their seats. Are you ready to take the stage?"

"I've been waiting for this all night, boss," Sammy replied.

54

Nice Try

Sammy told his boss there was one thing he needed to do before the cameras rolled. Walking up behind Felix, he poked the tip of his gun into the back of the unsuspecting man's head and told him to stand up. "Turn around," he then said. Felix did as he was instructed, albeit very hesitantly.

"You're the guy who whacked me that night in the shelter," Sammy said. "Got the same smell about you; a smell I'll never forget."

Ivory soap, I though. *Ratted out by a desire to stay fresh and clean.*

Felix didn't reply, but he didn't cower either, standing erect and proud like a soldier at attention. A blink of an eye later, he collapsed to the floor as a single shot rang out.

I stared in horror at his quivering body, bile climbing up my throat as dark, red blood oozed across the floor, my shocked brain not registering that Claire was now clutching my arm until seconds later. He'd shot Felix, point blank, killing him instantly, my frenzied thoughts told me. I looked up at Vinson, seeing only satisfaction in his cold eyes.

"Now we can get on with the show," Sammy said.

Suddenly, everything was moving in slow motion. Felix falling to the floor; Sunny looking up into the camera, helpless; Vinson smiling, the devil resurrected. Then, I was unwrapping

Claire's arm from mine, spinning in my chair, leaping to my feet. Thrusting my body forward, I was on top of him in a blink, wrestling with Sammy's gun hand, focused on aiming it anywhere but at myself. We fell and he must have injured himself during our fall—struck his head—because he wasn't nearly as strong as I had anticipated. I was winning the battle and it surprised me; unable to loosen his grip, but matching his effort to lock onto a target with my own to send any future shots into the ceiling.

From the corner of my eye, I noticed Claire's frantic body sprawled face first atop Vinson's desk. She appeared to be protecting something or hiding something, I didn't know which. When you're wrestling with an ox, you don't have much time to reason it out. And Vinson was huddled over her, tugging at her arms, as if he were attempting to pull them from their sockets. *The gun!* Somehow she must have grabbed his gun.

Sensing the tiny sliver of opportunity, I put everything I had into yanking Sammy's gun from his grasp. But he was coming around now, gathering his strength, which indeed was all of what I had imagined, and more. With a gut-wrenching groan he ripped my hands free and knocked me into the wall with a single sweep of his arm. He stood up, glaring at me with a menacing scowl, and aimed the gun straight at my head.

"Nice try, you little puke," he growled. Wiping the knick on his forehead, his body swaying a bit, he started leaning in one direction—still woozy, I concluded—before jerking himself upright again. Staggering, he took a step back, landing his supporting foot squarely into the puddle of Felix's blood. Everything returned to slow motion as Sammy swayed like a stubborn bowling pin and fell. The gun flashed, firing a shot that then pinged off a metal support beam before submerging itself with a dull thud, into its owner's chest. A perfect shot to the heart.

I was back on my feet in an instant, moving in a blind panic toward where I had last seen Claire fending off her husband. If I could muscle him away from her long enough—give her the chance to secure the gun—the two of us would have the upper hand. But as my brain caught up to my eyes, I realized they were no longer wrestling on the desk. Then I saw her, facedown on the floor.

Standing over Claire's motionless body, Vinson was panting heavily and pointing the black revolver at my chest, exactly where Sammy had just received his unlucky farewell. Now, there was just the two of us, and Sunny still slumped in a chair on the monitor. I can't say why I was more concerned for her at that moment, what with a gun poised to split my heart into a million pieces. I only knew that I desperately wanted to free her and take her out of this hell. It's strange where thoughts travel in moments of extreme. Mine were clear. I wasn't leaving alive without Sunny.

55

The Stage Is Set

"That was a gallant effort, Daniel," Vinson said. "One that inspired my foolish wife to act. But don't feel guilty. I knew this day would come regardless; she had too much spirit to be held down forever. When I decided to kill her lover, I knew she would come looking for me. To her credit, I'm impressed she acted so quickly."

"Her lover?" I asked. I already knew the answer, but Vinson seemed anxious to talk. And the longer he talked, the more time I had to think of a way out of this mess.

"Oh, come now, Daniel. Certainly you've figured out by now that John Oliver was fucking my wife?"

I nodded, faintly.

"But I didn't kill him for that. In fact, I was grateful, though I would never admit that openly. He kept Claire occupied, as she did him. The two people who could destroy me were in love with each other. Don't you find that ironic, Daniel?"

My eyes widened. Oliver could have been the Brutus I was hoping for after all. If only I had realized it sooner.

Noticing my reaction, Vinson said, "Oh yes, John would have helped you, Daniel. He reached that point and that's why he had to die. He became a risk I could no longer take. As have you and your pretty little girlfriend."

"Let her go," I demanded. "She doesn't know anything about Earth Nexus or your hit list. She's just an innocent girl I met at the shelter who gave me a place to stay; a girl with a family who'll come looking for her." I knew full well I was trying to bluff a man with no conscience, but sometimes all you can do is play the shitty cards you're dealt. And pray.

"Don't play me for a fool," Vinson snarled. "You and I both know that isn't true. I'm sure she's told you all about our happenstance meeting in Manhattan some months ago; how she was supposed to star in one of my little snuff scenes." He glanced at the monitor—at the young woman helplessly handcuffed in a chair—as a look of resolve washed over his face. "It was a role she was born to play. One I think you can help her fulfill."

"What the hell does that mean?" I asked.

"Improvisation, Daniel. Sammy is clearly in no shape to play the male lead, so guess who's going to take his place?"

"You?"

Vinson chuckled, notoriously. "Ah, you make me laugh. No, nephew, as much as I'd like to, I think my services are better suited behind the camera and, of course, this gun." He then motioned me toward the door. "The stage is set. Let's go."

This was insane. Did this madman really think that I would perform whatever heinous acts were haunting his deranged mind simply because he had a gun to my head? I would just as soon die before harming Sunny. But what if he put the gun to *her* head and ordered me on? As we entered another room, Sunny's tearful eyes reaching out to mine, I prayed to every God who might have been listening, begging them to alter Vinson's thoughts away from that tactic. Before my pounding heart could beat a dozen times, I would know that my plea had fallen upon deaf ears.

Standing in front of Sunny as Vinson released her hands, I whispered words of comfort, telling her everything would be all right. Then, I hugged her as Vinson stepped away, feeling a momentary calm that I knew wasn't going to last. "I'm sorry," I said. "He found you because of me."

"He would have found me anyway," she replied. She was squeezing me as hard as she could, hoping, I imagined, that I would never let go. Vinson had other plans.

"Now," Vinson said, staring me straight in eye. The gun was pointed directly at the back of Sunny's head. She couldn't see it, but I could tell she knew it was there. "You follow my script *exactly* as I say, or I drop her. Right here, right now."

I didn't move a muscle. I couldn't, at least, not until Sunny's grip loosened and she told me to do as Vinson said. "It's all right, Daniel, somehow we'll come out on the other side."

I saw courage in her eyes, and hope where there shouldn't have been any. Hadn't that always been her way? Somehow seeing past an uninvited moment, keeping her heart untouched, her soul, unaltered? I'd seen it the day I met her, and every day since. That's why I'd wanted to call her Sunny, even before she revealed it to be her given name. Sometimes the invisible forces get it right. But still, with a madman holding a gun to our heads, I wondered how this beautiful young woman could possibly believe we might escape the final fate that Vinson most certainly had already written for us.

"I don't think I can do this," I whispered.

She didn't reply, placing her hand on my cheek and kissing me softly instead. It wasn't what Vinson was looking for.

"Do you think I'm interested in a love scene from General fucking Hospital?" he snapped. "Get behind her, Daniel. I want the whole world to see her pretty face as you rape the shit out of her."

I didn't budge. Uncontrollably, my fear was shifting to anger. He was pushing too hard, forcing me into a void I could never enter. My mind raced, searching for an escape. If I rushed him, dove low and aimed at his knees, I might be able to dodge a kill shot and do enough damage in the meantime to wrestle the gun free. But he was smart, keeping his distance, at least three or four paces away, with that dam revolver pointed directly at Sunny. *No, my judgment warned. You'll be two steps short and she'll be two seconds dead.*

"Are you deaf!" Vinson said. "I told you to get behind her. Now, do it!"

At Sunny's urging, I slowly moved behind her, my deadweight arms dangling lifelessly at my sides. *You can't do this,* my thoughts screamed. *Even if it's not really you that's doing it.*

"Rip her panties off," Vinson ordered. "But do it like you mean it; do it like a man."

I shook my head. *No!*

Vinson extended his arm forward, pulling the gun hammer back as he glared at me. "I said, *rip her panties off.*"

The echo of that metal spring sent a shiver up my spine. If I didn't do as he asked he would kill Sunny. And if I did? Sunny's hand suddenly locking into mine prevented me from finishing that unthinkable thought. Before I realized what she was doing, she had moved my hand to her waist, sliding it along the soft skin of her hips before slipping it beneath the black lace. When she finally let go I could feel her whole body trembling. *It's all right, Daniel,* she was telling me again, though I couldn't see her face. *Somehow we'll come out on the other side.*

Watching intently, Vinson said, "That's it, I like a bitch who knows what she wants. See that, Daniel; just like I said. She was born to play this part."

I didn't believe that. I would never believe that. But now the chemicals in my body were shifting again, my anger being replaced by shame. I had fallen in love with Sunny that very first day in the shelter, I knew that now, my desire to caress the soft curves of her body growing with each passing day. As my hand glided over the bow of her bottom, my eyes luring my thoughts toward the unacceptable, I could feel the mounting swell of arousal building inside. How could I want her now? Like this? I was confused, repulsed by my carnal urge, yet aware that my ability to perform might be the only thing to save us. Apparently, Vinson noticed.

"Change of heart, Daniel?" he said, knowingly. A grin was emerging on his face.

I looked away, indignant.

"Oh, come now. Don't be ashamed. You're only feeling what any red-blooded male would feel when a nice piece of ass like that is placed in front of them, no strings attached. And there are no strings, Daniel; except maybe a bullet if you don't. Now, don't make me repeat myself a third time. Three strikes and your girlfriend is out."

As if controlled by another force, my fingers began to wrap around the lace of Sunny's panties, my forearm and bicep flexing, as my mind went numb. The room was suddenly very cold, and silent like the split-second before sleep takes command. *Could I possibly do this to her? Do this horrific act to save her?* I could feel the tears filling my now closed eyes, as my arm began to pull.

"Don't," a voice said. It was a woman's voice—a heavenly voice—but not Sunny's. Opening my eyes, I turned my head and saw Claire Vinson standing in the doorway, a waterfall of blood painted on one side of her face. She appeared steady, firm, and I noticed one hand hidden in her jacket pocket. "You don't have to do anything he says, Daniel," she said. She took two steps into the room and stopped.

Vinson snorted, amused, as he turned his revolver on his wife.

Claire didn't flinch. "Go ahead, shoot," she said, almost tauntingly so.

"You'd like that, wouldn't you," Vinson said. "Put you out of your misery. Now that you're lover's dead." He then turned the gun on me. "But what about you're nephew?"

"Go ahead," Claire replied. "Squeeze the trigger."

Those were not the words I was hoping to hear. Warily, I looked at Vinson, praying that he wouldn't listen to his obviously out-of-her-mind wife. I could only reason that she must have struck her head hard during the scuffle with her husband, and was now on a mad suicide run. *Did she have a gun in her pocket? Was that her plan? He shoots me and she shoots him?* I pulled Sunny behind me, hoping that she might escape unharmed—the lone survivor of the barrage of bullets headed our way.

"Do you think I won't?" Vinson asked.

"I know you will," Claire replied. "I'm counting on it."

Vinson just stood there, his gun aimed at my chest. He was staring at Claire, calculating her objective, I assumed. At the same time, Sunny and I were eyeing him, both of us knowing all to well what *he* was capable of. Then, he eyes returned to mine and I knew he'd decided.

"Have it your way, Claire," Vinson said.

I watched in slow-motion horror as the muscles in his finger clamped down on the trigger, unable to turn away. But instead of a loud bang, all I heard was a short click, like the sound a single raindrop on the hood of my Camaro. Vinson didn't notice it at all, turning the gun quickly to where he wife stood. It was only when he spotted the gun in *her* hand, that his brain processed the fact that his revolver hadn't sent a bullet into my heart. He squeezed the trigger a second time. A second harmless click echoed in the otherwise, silent room.

"I wanted to load it," Claire said. "God knows how badly I wanted to load it and shoot you the moment I saw you. For what you did to John. But somehow, I couldn't bring myself to do it."

Vinson looked at the gun in his hand, the wave of disbelief making his face look timid and small.

Claire continued, emotionless, but resolute. "I switched them on you, Louis. The one you're holding isn't loaded. But this one is. You'll never harm anyone again. Goodbye, Louis."

A single shot erupted, piercing the eerie tension filling the room. Louis Vinson fell to the ground, a crisp, black hole glistening in the center of his forehead.

56

Where Are We Going?

With the sun peeking over the horizon, my left hand on the wheel, my right hand caressing Sunny's head as she nested on my chest, I drove north onto the Brooklyn Bridge, uncertain as to which way I'd turn when I got across. Heading east would lead us back to Rhode Island and the driver's license that could resurrect my life. And if we continue from there, Boston and Sunny's apartment and the tiny sprout of a life she was offering to share with me. She hadn't come right out and said it, but I knew. It was just that she deserved more than Daniel Rayne; more than an erased man. A new man had a chance to be more for her and that was out west somewhere, away from what had been and what would always be if we returned to it.

Standing over her husband's dead body, appearing calmer than I could have ever imagined possible, Claire Vinson—my Aunt Claire—had told me that it wasn't over. "There are many powerful men at Earth Nexus, Daniel," she had said. "With a lot at stake; much more than the insignificant price of our lives. That's why you must go, leave before the police arrive." I told her I wouldn't, pleaded with her to let me stay and face the consequences with her. But she would hear none of it, digging in her heels the same way her sister always had whenever she had her mind made up. She was just like my mother, and strangely, I felt compelled to honor her request. Even with three dead bodies scattered in the basement of that fateful house and two more in the garage.

"But the BlackBerry will prove our story," I had argued.

"Circumstantial," she argued back, assuring me that the Earth Nexus team of lawyers would tear that piece of evidence to shreds. "They'll do anything to protect Louis's name and reputation. As the founder and face of Earth Nexus, the future of the company will depend on it. That's why I'm going to tell the police there was burglar; that Louis and Felix were killed in a gun fight."

"That's crazy," I had said. "They'll never believe that."

"After the heirs to Louis's throne have had a chance to straighten things up here a bit, they'll believe it."

Less than an hour ago I stood hugging for the very first time the aunt I never knew I had. In my arms, I held the one living thread connecting me to my life, the link to my past, the key to Daniel Rayne's future. Feeling very tiny as the Manhattan skyline engulfed Sunny and me, I realized that I might never see her again.

"In life, we can never be more that what we imagine ourselves to be. After death, we are only what the living remembers." Those were the last words my mother said to me before she died. I'll never forget them. I only wish that I could find the hidden meaning that might help me now. Maybe in time, I will.

"Where are we going?" Sunny asked.

"Somewhere," I replied. "If nothing else, we'll always be going somewhere."